A shuffle overhead had the hair on the back of Jilly's neck tingling

Someone was up there.

Picking up a good-sized stick, Jilly headed upstairs. Standing in the hallway, she considered her actions. What was she thinking to come up here with a stick in her hand? She should go downstairs, get into her car, drive to South Fork and send the police.

She'd taken one step toward the stairs when a man's voice began to belt out a rousing rendition of "Under the Sea." What kind of thief or murderer sang selections from the soundtrack of *The Little Mermaid*?

Even though she'd deemed her stick worthless, Jilly took a firmer grip on the end and climbed the rest of the stairs, then tiptoed to the door and burst through.

"Aha!" she shouted, lifting the stick high over her head.

The place was empty.

"Were you looking for me?"

Jilly spun around. Her mouth dropped open and all she could think was *Oh, yeah!*

Dear Reader,

THE LUCHETTI BROTHERS continues this month with
The Husband Quest. For those of you who have been
asking for Evan's story, here it is.

Being the fifth boy in a family of six, Evan has never felt
necessary to anyone. So he's spent his life looking for
love…well, pretty much everywhere. His brothers refer
to him as the Luchetti family gigolo, never realizing the
term makes Evan feel even worse about himself than
he already does.

When he asks his girlfriend of the moment to marry him
and she laughs in his face, Evan decides it's time to change
his life—in South Fork, Arkansas.

Jillian Hart has been called many things—gold digger,
professional wife, serial bride. Following the death of
her fourth husband, Jilly is left with nothing but a broken-
down inn, but her first sight of Evan Luchetti gives her
an idea. They'll be partners in restoring the place,
then sell it and go their separate ways.

What ensues is a tale of love and laughter, a story about
finding your place in life and the person you want to live
it with. Introducing a cast of new friends and animals,
as well as a few visits with many of the old ones,
The Husband Quest was great fun to write. I hope you
enjoy it as much as I did. For those of you waiting for
Bobby's and Dean's stories, I'm working on them.

Lori Handeland

For information on future releases and a chance to win free
books, visit my Web site at www.lorihandeland.com.

The Husband Quest
Lori Handeland

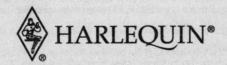

HARLEQUIN®

TORONTO • NEW YORK • LONDON
AMSTERDAM • PARIS • SYDNEY • HAMBURG
STOCKHOLM • ATHENS • TOKYO • MILAN • MADRID
PRAGUE • WARSAW • BUDAPEST • AUCKLAND

ISBN 0-373-71226-X

THE HUSBAND QUEST

For my brother-in-law and sister-in-law
Doug and Terry Handeland
Two people who are always such fun to be around

Books by Lori Handeland

HARLEQUIN SUPERROMANCE

922—MOTHER OF THE YEAR
969—DOCTOR, DOCTOR
1004—LEAVE IT TO MAX
1063—A SHERIFF IN TENNESSEE
1099—THE FARMER'S WIFE
1151—THE DADDY QUEST*
1193—THE BROTHER QUEST*

*The Luchetti Brothers

CHAPTER ONE

"ALL OF YOUR MONEY IS GONE."

Thinking there must still be water in her ear from taking a shower that morning, Jillian Hart tapped the side of her head.

"I'm sorry? I didn't catch that."

"Your money is gone."

Her late husband's lawyer, Jay Daggett, spoke slowly, as if she were a half-wit. Sadly, Jilly often had to act as if there wasn't a brain in her head. Men liked that, especially older, wealthy men. Her specialty.

"My money has gone where?"

"Into someone else's bank." Daggett, a short, stout, balding man of indeterminate age, shuffled his papers and put them in his briefcase. "Actually, several some-ones."

"Get it back."

"I can't. Henry owed everyone in town. His reputation kept them from collecting while he was alive and there was a possibility of his recouping the losses. However…"

Jilly was drawn to the peaceful, panoramic view of

the ocean visible from her house on Laguna Beach. "Now that he's dead, they want their money."

"Yes."

Her fourth husband, Henry Duvier, had died of a heart attack only a week ago. Considering he was eighty, that wasn't a surprise.

They'd been married five years—longer than any of her other marriages. Jilly had been fond of Henry, enjoyed his company and that of his friends. She'd hoped his assets would allow her to remain a widow for at least a year or two—something she'd never been able to do before.

Jilly turned her back on the ocean. "So you're telling me Henry's money is gone."

Daggett shook his head. "Everything. You'll need to be out of this house by Friday."

Not her beautiful beach house. She loved the sand, the surf, the endless expanse of blue. How would she sleep at night if she couldn't hear the soothing cadence of the water nearby?

"This makes no sense. Henry was a very wealthy man."

"Until he decided to become a movie mogul."

Damn. Jilly had known Henry's interest in Hollywood would bite him on the butt someday. Unfortunately, she seemed to be the one feeling the teeth.

Henry's ancestors had begun Duvier Publishing back when Gutenberg was a pup. Henry had spent his life making the family business even more successful. Then, when he was in his seventies, he'd sold out to a German conglomerate and retired to California.

But a lifetime of being a workaholic did not a good retiree make. Never having spared the time to create a family, Henry was not only bored, he was lonely. Which was where Jilly came in.

Some called her a gold digger; the society pages referred to her as a woman of means; the tabloids had long ago labeled her a serial bride. Jilly was both all and none of the above.

"There was just that one movie," she said.

Daggett peered at her over the rims of his glasses. "There were three."

Jilly sighed. In the manner of trophy wives, she was not expected to meddle in Henry's business affairs. She'd been in charge of his loneliness; his Hollywood friends had taken care of the boredom.

Henry had always wanted to be a producer. All he'd produced had been bombs.

"He used his money on *Aliens Are Easy*," Daggett continued. "Mortgaged everything for *Gunfight in Cleveland*. Your funds went into the *Beverly Hillbillies Return*."

Annoyance and disappointment flooded Jilly. She and Henry had made a good marriage, one based on trust and affection. But she should have followed her mother's advice and stashed her personal hoard in Switzerland. Instead, she'd let Henry manage the fortune left to her by husbands one, two and three. It had hardly seemed fair to deny him access to her money when she had access to his.

Fair? When had life been fair?

She'd been dragged from town to town as a child, on the whim of her mother's husband of the moment. Genevieve Hart had married once for love. Love had gotten her a child and poverty when her husband skipped off with every penny they had. He'd gambled it away, then promptly gotten himself shot by someone he couldn't pay.

Jilly had been five at the time, but she remembered the overwhelming sense of panic that pressed down on them, the countless times they'd had nowhere to sleep but the street, nothing to wear but the clothes on their backs, not a thing to eat but what they could beg or steal. She would *not* be in that predicament again.

"Is there anything left?" she asked.

"Just the Inn at South Fork. In Arkansas."

"Arkansas?" Her voice reflected the horror that was no doubt all over her face. "Why on earth would Henry buy something there?"

Daggett glanced at the single paper he'd left out of his briefcase. "The inn was supposed to be the setting for the hillbilly movie."

"And?"

"They never used it." He tilted his head. "I'm not sure why."

"The vultures couldn't leave me the villa in Tuscany?"

"They devoured that first. I suspect the inn wasn't worth the trouble."

"Great," she muttered.

Daggett shrugged. "Take it or leave it."

Jilly snatched the paper from his hand. "I'll take it."

What choice did she have?

JILLY SOLD THE ENGAGEMENT ring and wedding band from her third—or had it been her second?—marriage and bought a plane ticket to Little Rock. Then she rented a car and drove northwest—for a helluva long time—over roads that looked like something out of *Deliverance.* She kept expecting to hear banjos strumming behind the thick, green foliage that lined what passed for an Arkansas highway.

On the map, the drive to South Fork appeared to be a pleasant three-hour tour. In reality it took six hours over twisting, hairpin curves. She nearly ran over a skunk, two opossums, a raccoon and what she hoped was a dog but had a sneaking suspicion was a very large and well-fed coyote. She could have sworn she saw an alligator in one overgrown, flooded ditch. But she was too far north for alligators, wasn't she?

Jilly shuddered. She wouldn't last long in a place like this, and she knew it.

She might have been born poor, but she hadn't spent a night outside a mansion or a five-star hotel since her mother had discovered her one true talent.

Genevieve Hart was a very good wife. She was beautiful, street-smart and savvy. She could be whatever a man wanted her to be.

Her first husband had been a traveling salesman, the next a lawyer, followed by a doctor, then a CEO. At the moment, Genevieve was in Belgium on her honeymoon with a Polish count, and unavailable to help her destitute daughter.

"The one time I call her, and she's off becoming Countess Blah-blah-blah," Jilly muttered.

Well, she'd just have to handle things on her own. Drive to the inn, take a quick peek, then find a real estate agent, sell the albatross and use the money to fund another husband hunt.

Jilly sighed. She'd been anticipating some time alone. Since the age of twenty-two she'd been a wife. Before that she'd been preparing to become one.

Jilly had left her mother's house to attend the top boarding schools, then gone on to Vassar, every move calculated so Jilly could make the best possible marriage—over and over again. Because there were three rules the Hart women lived by:

Never, ever marry for love.

Poor men are for play; rich men are for keeps.

Old men are like fine wine. Once tasted, they don't last very long.

Jilly didn't believe in love. Love was for suckers and imbeciles. She'd never met a man she needed anything from beyond the answer to two important questions. How much was he worth and what decade had he been born in?

A sign popped up at the side of the road. Squinting

against the descending sun, Jilly could just make out the faded letters: South Fork, Arkansas—Unincorporated.

Were those bullet holes in the sign post? It flashed past too fast for her to tell.

"Couldn't be," she assured herself. "What did that sign ever do to anyone?"

She had no more time to ponder as South Fork seemed to appear out of nowhere. She was reminded of the musical Brigadoon, one of Henry's favorites. The town had popped magically out of the mist every hundred years.

Jilly had never cared for that movie. She didn't understand magic or mystery. Why waste time on something that wasn't real?

However, South Fork had the same mythical aura as *Brigadoon*. At the foot of the Ozark Mountains, the sleepy little hamlet was frozen in a bygone century.

Jilly slowed her rented Volkswagen Beetle—her mother would have a cardiac arrest if she saw Jilly driving such a bourgeois vehicle, but Jilly thought it was cute—and meandered down what appeared to be the only street in South Fork.

About ten buildings composed of graying wood made up the town. Each one had a sagging porch with a hand-painted sign perched on top that stated its purpose in the scheme of life.

Hillburn's General Store. Joe's Barbershop. Washington Primary School. The Main Street Tavern. United Baptist Church. The South Fork Jail.

She found it amusing, or maybe just sad, that the tavern stood right next to the church and the jail bordered the school. Perhaps the folks of South Fork merely found it convenient.

The only people on the street were a trio of old men gathered around a barrel on the porch of the general store. A game of checkers appeared to be in progress.

Were they kidding with this? She felt as if she'd stepped into Henry's hillbilly movie.

Jilly parked in front of the store and clambered out of the car, which wasn't easy, since she'd worn her best summer suit and favorite Italian shoes.

The three-inch slings and knee-length, sea-green skirt were not conducive to exiting a compact car gracefully. Without air-conditioning, her suit jacket, though stylish, was far too heavy. Thankfully, she'd worn a gray silk shell underneath. When she became desperate she could always ditch the jacket.

The two men playing checkers didn't even glance her way. The third, who had been observing them, now observed her.

Jilly plastered on her most charming smile. The old man smiled back. He had no teeth. Jilly's expression froze.

"Oh." He cackled. "Forgot 'em agin."

Reaching into his pocket, he pulled out a set of dentures, popped them into his mouth and clicked them together with a wink. "We don't get many visitors round here."

"Uh, yes, well…I'm wondering if you can direct me to the inn."

That got the attention of the checker players. The one on the left jumped up so fast he knocked the board off the barrel.

"What's that?" He cupped a hand to the side of his head.

"The inn!" her toothless friend shouted. "Turn on your hearin' thingee!" He slapped his own ear for emphasis.

"Damn thing makes the flies on the wall sound as loud as semi trucks," the man grumbled, but he fiddled with the plastic in his ear just the same.

"Did ye knock the board over?"

The second checker player squinted and began patting the top of the now-empty barrel. His Coke-bottle glasses remained perched on top of his shiny dome.

"If ye put on your spectacles, ye could see."

"Haven't been able to find 'em since this mornin'. I swear they walk away on me sometimes."

"They walked onto the top of yer head today." The denture wearer rolled his eyes at Jilly. "No fool like an old fool."

"I can beat him with my eyes closed." The sight-impaired man retrieved the glasses and settled them on his beak of a nose. He glanced at Jilly. The thick lenses magnified his eyes like Mr. Magoo's. "Well, ain't you a sight?"

She wasn't sure if that was a compliment, but she beamed at him, anyway. Couldn't hurt.

"The inn?" she repeated. "I'm afraid I only know that it's near South Fork."

The three men peered at each other, then back at her. Their smiles became frowns. "You don't want to go there."

"Why not?"

They exchanged glances again. Jilly was starting to get nervous. Had a tornado carried the place away? She wondered what the land would be worth. From what she'd seen so far, not much.

"You just don't."

"I own the inn. I need to take a look before I put it on the market."

"You're going to sell?" Toothless asked. "Good luck."

"Is there some sort of problem?"

"You might say that."

Exasperated, she sighed. "What is it?"

"No one's been able to stay there overnight for years."

Jilly had visions of bats in the bedrooms, skunks in the kitchen, holes in the roof.

"Sorry to tell ye this, ma'am, but the inn is haunted."

They nodded solemnly, as if they'd just said her best friend had died.

Jilly couldn't help it; she burst out laughing. Towns appearing from the mist, ghosts at the inn. What next? Unicorns playing peekaboo behind the trees?

"Haunted? Right. Sure."

Their grave expressions gave way to confusion. "What's so funny?"

"There's no such thing as ghosts!"

The old men's eyes met, and together they shrugged.

"Well," the one who did most of the talking drawled. "She is from out of town."

THE THREE WERE BROTHERS—Larry, Jerry and Barry Seitz.

Jilly stifled jokes about Larry, Curly and Moe, as well as comments referring to Larry, Darrell and Darrell. Somehow she didn't think they'd find her funny. Hardly anyone ever did.

Being funny was not something her mother approved of, and she'd squashed Jilly's attempts at humor very young. On the husband hunt, being pretty, attentive and vapid were important. Being smart and amusing were not.

When Jilly insisted that she had to see the inn, even if it was haunted, the men climbed into her Beetle without an invitation. They instructed her to head north out of South Fork.

"This here car—" Barry nodded at the dash of her bright-red Volkswagen "—it's foreign, ain't it?"

Larry and Jerry tsked in the back seat. She could see them in the rearview mirror, shaking their heads.

"Um…" Jilly considered. "German. Yes."

"We don't hold with that here."

"Germany?"

"Foreign cars." He pointed at the selection of automobiles parked in front of the buildings they passed on their way out of town. Now that he mentioned it, she saw that every one was American-made.

"This isn't mine," Jilly said. "I rented it."

"And I bet they were glad to see it go."

Actually, she'd nearly had to arm wrestle another customer for possession of the last Beetle on the lot. The dome-shaped Volkswagens were in high demand.

Jilly glanced at Barry, who was still frowning at the dashboard, and decided to keep that information to herself. He wouldn't believe her, anyway.

"How much farther is it?" She noted the fading sunlight.

"A mile or two."

Good. She'd be able to take a quick look around and be halfway back to Little Rock before dark.

They passed several houses. Coming into South Fork, Jilly had glimpsed a few mailboxes, but the residences had been too far back from the road to see. On this side of town, the homes were set on cleared land. The better to show off their horses, it seemed.

"Is there a reason people keep their horses in the front yard?" she asked.

Barry blinked, then frowned. "Where else would they keep 'em?"

"The barn?"

"Why would you have a barn at your house?"

Why would you have a horse at your house? she thought, but kept the comment to herself.

"Turn here!"

The shout came from right behind her, and Jilly jumped so high she nearly banged her head on the ceiling. A quick glance in the mirror revealed Jerry pointing at an overgrown dirt trail.

"Almost missed it," Barry said. "That's the one."

Jilly spun the Volkswagen onto the side road. Dust flew up and coated the hood of the car. Dense foliage slapped against the doors and windows. The sun disappeared behind a cloud and cool, gray shadows settled over the forest.

"You're sure this is the way to the inn?" she asked.

"Think so."

Jilly tensed. What if they didn't know? What if she went off a cliff? What if they were mad killers bent on taking everything she owned, then dumping her body in the backwoods?

The *Deliverance* banjos began to play again in her head.

Suddenly the trees parted, and her Volkswagen shot into a clearing. She almost ran over the horse.

"Watch out for Lightning!" Barry shouted.

Jilly hit the brakes and glanced, flinching, toward the sky. The sun was out once more, not a cloud to be seen.

"What lightning?"

"Lightning." Barry pointed at the ancient horse placidly cropping grass next to her right bumper. The animal hadn't even glanced up when she skidded to a stop near his nose.

"Did he used to be fast?" she asked.

"No." Barry got out of the car, pulling the seat forward so his brothers could follow. "He used to get hit by lightning a lot."

"He weren't exactly the smartest animal." Larry tapped his head. "Stood under the trees. Never did learn."

He slammed the door. Jilly contemplated the chestnut horse still grazing in front of her car. His back was swayed, his mane was going gray and he had streaks of white hair, almost like scars, in three separate places on his rump.

"They oughtta call him Lucky," she murmured.

Since the horse didn't appear to be moving anytime soon, Jilly turned off the car and got out. She took her first look at all she had left.

She was in big trouble.

The Inn at South Fork had seen better days—probably in 1865. The three-story structure was composed of peeling, yellowed paint and weathered wood. The porch steps had several holes, as did the windows. She didn't even want to consider what the inside was like.

Jilly turned to speak to the brothers, but the clearing was empty—except for her and the horse.

"Guys?" she called.

The only answer was the whisper of the wind through the trees.

"Fine." Jilly started for the inn. "I can do this myself."

The grass tickled her ankles. Wildflowers snagged her panty hose at the knees. Before she'd taken five steps, her heels had picked up enough mud to make walking difficult, and her jacket was smothering her.

She paused several yards from the inn and yanked off the coat and the shoes. She considered losing the panty hose, too, but when she glanced up, a shadow flitted behind the one unbroken pane of glass on the third floor. A sudden shiver raced down her spine.

A ghost? Or something worse?

"Ridiculous." Tossing her shoes and jacket onto the porch, she left her panty hose right where they were. "There's no such thing as ghosts."

The chill had been nothing more than a cool breeze across her bare shoulders, the shadow merely the sunlight flickering against the windowpanes. She hadn't seen anything, because there was nothing to see.

Jilly marched up the steps and into the house. Planning to take a quick tour and get out, she stopped dead just inside the door.

The place was much worse than she'd thought. Dust, broken boards, broken glass—was something living in the corner?

Standing in the center of what had once been a lovely foyer, Jilly fought the urge to cry. What was she going to do? The inn was all she had, and it was crap.

A shuffle overhead had the hair on the back of her neck tingling. Something *was* up there. Or maybe someone?

She glanced into the yard, hoping the brothers had come back—though what those three could do, she wasn't sure. Lightning stood at the bottom of the porch steps, staring at her.

"I don't suppose you want to go upstairs and check it out?" she asked.

His answer was a snort of air through his nose, which sounded suspiciously like equine sarcasm.

"That's what I thought."

Jilly pulled her cell phone from her purse. She wouldn't be able to afford it much longer, but for the next two weeks her bill was paid. She peered at the display.

"'Searching for service,'" she read. "The story of my life."

Picking up a good-size stick, Jilly headed upstairs.

The second floor consisted of bedrooms—a lot of them. She'd just decided she had no choice but to search each and every one, when a thump sounded above.

"Third floor," she whispered, thinking of the shadow she'd observed from outside.

Standing in the hallway, Jilly considered her actions. What was she thinking, coming up here with a stick in her hand? She should go downstairs, get into her car, drive to South Fork and send the police.

She'd taken one step toward the stairs when a man's voice began to belt out a rousing rendition of "Under the Sea." What kind of thief or murderer sang selections from the soundtrack of *The Little Mermaid?*

Even though she'd deemed her stick worthless, Jilly took a firmer grip on the end and climbed the second flight of stairs.

By the time she reached the third-floor landing, the singing had stopped. Had she really heard it at all? The brothers had insisted the place was haunted. However, she doubted a ghost would know a Disney ditty any better than a criminal.

Gauging the direction of the room where she'd seen the shadow, Jilly tiptoed to the door and burst through.

"Aha!" she shouted, lifting the stick high over her head.

The place was empty.

"Were you looking for me?"

Jilly spun around. Her mouth dropped open. Her eyes seemed to bug out. All she could think was, *Oh, yeah!*

CHAPTER TWO

THE SETTING SUN shone through the shattered window-pane behind him, creating a halo around his head. Jilly couldn't see his face, but she didn't need to. The rest of him was quite spectacular.

Long legs encased in scruffy, faded jeans… His work boots were equally worn and dirty. Drywall dust stuck to his bare chest.

Jilly had never seen a more spectacular specimen. Of course, she'd never had the opportunity to view, in the flesh, a male body under the age of sixty.

"Ma'am? Are you going to hit me with that stick or just think about it?"

He spoke with a flat Midwestern accent, obviously as out of place in this Southern town as she was.

Jilly blinked. "I, uh, who are you?"

"I could ask you the same thing."

"Jillian Hart. Duvier," she added.

She always forgot that last part. It was much easier to go by her maiden name when she'd had so many others.

"Duvier?" He cocked his head, and his face came into the light.

His eyes shone like blue neon against the sun-bronzed shade of his skin. His hair, which she'd thought short, was merely gathered into a ponytail at his nape. The elements had burned auburn highlights into the dark brown strands. She had a sudden and inexplicable urge to run her fingers through the locks and loosen the rubber band.

He was speaking to her. Jilly shook her head and the strange urges receded, though they didn't completely go away.

"Checking up on me?" he asked.

"I'm sorry?"

"Your…" he stared at her a minute "…grampa? He hired me to fix this place up."

"Henry?" The man nodded. "That's my husband."

His eyes widened, showing off incredibly long, dark, thick lashes. They belonged on a girl. Didn't that just figure?

"Husband? Huh." He shrugged and her gaze was pulled back to his chest. What would it look like with water running over the ripples and dips, soap washing away all the sweat and dust?

"Is he here?"

"Who?"

"Henry."

Jilly forced her eyes from the man's stomach to his face. He wasn't exactly handsome. The angles and planes didn't add up to a movie star, but there was something about him that made her both hot and cold all over. Probably too much smooth skin and sweaty muscles for her deprived brain to handle.

What on earth had gotten into her? She was not the kind of woman who swooned over a well-made man. She couldn't afford to. Besides, she believed in lust even less than she believed in love. Out-of-control need for sex? Ha. Never heard of it.

"What did you say your name was?" she asked.

"I didn't."

He reached for a powder-blue T-shirt that hung on a nearby ladder, then pulled it over his head. Jilly treated herself to a last ogle of his six-pack abs.

When the cotton covered him from neck to waist, he was still impressive. The tight material seemed to accentuate the firm, strong lines of his body—he must stand at least six-four without his boots. And the color made his eyes deepen to the shade of the Pacific at dusk. For an instant she missed the ocean very badly.

He held out a hand. "Evan Luchetti."

Jilly placed her palm in his. Another shudder went through her, but this time it was caused not by a chill wind but by his calluses flicking against her life line.

When he released her hand she stared at it, then folded her fingers inward in an attempt to keep the tingling sensation alive.

"Uh, sorry." Evan offered her a rag. "I've been working all day."

She took the cloth with the hand he hadn't touched, leaving the sweat and dust right where it was.

"When did Henry hire you?" she asked.

"Last month. Sent me a list of what he wanted done, and an advance. Though I've used most of that money for supplies. I don't suppose he sent a check with you."

"Um…" She wasn't sure how to say what he obviously didn't know. "Henry died last week," she blurted. "Heart attack."

Evan opened his mouth, then shut it again. Scrubbed a hand over his hair, leaving a streak of dust behind. "I'm sorry to hear that."

"Did you know him well?"

"Never met him."

"Then why…"

"Did he hire me?" Evan shrugged. "Said I was recommended by a friend."

"You're from California?"

He didn't seem the type. All the handymen there resembled actors or models—probably because most of them were.

"Illinois."

Which made no sense at all. She doubted Henry had ever heard of Illinois. In his world, the place didn't exist if it wasn't near New York or L.A. Of course, Henry *had* managed to buy an inn in Arkansas.

"I'm confused," Jilly admitted. "How did Henry hear about you in California? Are you some kind of handyman savant?"

He laughed. "You might say that. Word gets around. Henry talked to someone, who knew someone, who knew me. With enough time, I can fix damn near anything."

Jilly wondered if he could fix her.

SHE WAS STARING at his hands again. Evan wasn't sure what to make of her.

Not that he wasn't used to women staring. But they usually stared at his body, his hair, his eyes. She'd done that, too. However, she seemed to have a thing for his hands.

He glanced down, spread his fingers wide. They were just hands. More beat up than most; probably stronger, too. Scarred, hardened, chapped. A working man's hands in a lazy man's world, which only proved he didn't fit in anywhere. Never had and doubted he ever would.

"I don't suppose you have a check?" he repeated.

"I've got plenty of checks. Just no money to cover them."

"I'm sorry?"

"Me, too."

The urge to touch her arose at the sadness of her sigh. As if that were anything new. He'd made an art out of comforting lonely, sad women. Next to fixing things, it was his one true talent.

Back in his hometown of Gainsville, Illinois, Evan was the closest thing to a ladies' man they had. Even his brothers called him a gigolo.

They thought the term was a compliment. He'd never had the heart to tell them it made him feel dirtier than a pig in a shit puddle and not half as happy.

He liked women—all kinds. Their skin was soft, their hair smelled sweet and the sex…When Evan was having sex, he could almost convince himself someone loved him.

Which was what had gotten him here in the first place. Before he'd come to South Fork, he'd actually asked the woman he'd been seeing for months to marry him. Ashley had laughed in his face.

"As if I'd marry a man who's slept with three quarters of my friends. I have to live in this town, Evan."

Mortifying as her words had been, Ashley was right. So when Henry called the very next day, Evan had decided to change his life.

In Arkansas.

He shook off the self-pity. Most guys would kill to be him. Women throwing themselves at his feet, begging for a one-night stand, and all he could think about was a wife, five kids and a place to call his own.

"What do you mean there's no money?" he asked.

"Funny, that's just what I said." The woman took a deep breath. "According to Henry's lawyer, the only thing left is this place." She glanced around the room. "I know *I'm* excited."

Having been raised with a mother and a sister who excelled in sarcasm, Evan couldn't help but smile. Until he remembered that Henry owed him money, and Henry was dead.

"If you don't mind my asking, ma'am, why are you here?"

"I want to sell the inn."

"So did Henry."

Her cool green eyes swept over him, her gaze flickering like a feather across his face, his neck, his chest and, again, his hands.

She was a very beautiful woman. Average height, curvy in all the right places—she probably thought she was fat. Her hair was a rich, dark red. Most likely long and wavy, right now it was coiled into a fancy knot at the back of her head. She had freckles on her nose. Evan found himself wondering if she had freckles anywhere else.

"He did?" she asked.

He yanked his mind and his eyes from her chest. "What?"

She lifted a brow. She'd no doubt been stared at a thousand times before, but still Evan was embarrassed. The woman had lost her husband a week ago, and here he was thinking about the peaches-and-cream shade of her skin and the scent of jasmine that surrounded her.

He ran a hand over his face. Was it hot in here? She appeared cool and serene. He was sweaty, needy, exhausted. The usual.

"Henry planned to sell the inn?" she repeated.

"Yeah. I guess it was supposed to be used for a movie."

"Do you know why it wasn't?"

"The ghosts."

"Come now, Mr. Luchetti, you don't believe in ghosts."

"I didn't say I did. But the crew that was sent to check the place out had some odd experiences. Hear tell they didn't last one night."

"And you? Have you seen anything odd?"

"No rattling chains, no moaning at midnight—" He broke off. That had sounded a bit suggestive. He glanced at Mrs. Duvier. Her cheeks had turned pink.

"Well." She cleared her throat. "Why did Henry think anyone would buy this…uh, lovely establishment?"

"It will be lovely when I'm done with it." Evan frowned. "Or it would have been. Henry wanted me to restore the inn to its glory days."

"Which were?"

"Mid-nineteenth century. Before the Civil War, this was a high-class stage stop."

"Correct me if I'm wrong, but the stage no longer comes through here."

"The new highway will."

Her head cocked. "What new highway?"

"The one Henry planned to cash in on with a restored nineteenth-century bed-and-breakfast."

"Henry always was a clever man."

"Too bad it won't happen now."

"Too bad," she murmured, but he could tell she was thinking of something else.

She moved to the window, stared out at the setting sun. "What's with the horse?"

"He comes with the house."

"Is that an Arkansas tradition?"

"Looks like."

"You take care of him?"

"Yeah."

"Who did it before you came?"

"The Seitz brothers."

"See, hear and speak no evil?"

A burst of laughter escaped him. "I guess you could say that."

"I brought them out here to show me the place, then they disappeared."

"Scammed you for a ride." Evan crossed the room, then leaned past her to point out the window. "They live on the other side of that hill."

"Together?"

"They've always been together. Never been married. Never left home."

"Weird."

Evan stiffened. He still lived at home. Kind of. He'd taken over the threshers' shack on the back forty of his parents' farm. He was twenty-nine years old, never been married, and the address on his driver's license was the same one it had been at sixteen. More people than Jillian Hart Duvier would call him weird, but that didn't mean he had to like it.

He'd come to Arkansas to change his life. So far he'd only changed his zip code.

Three out of the six Luchetti children were married. His sister had a little girl, his brother Aaron a teenaged daughter and a child on the way, and his brother Colin had just added a baby boy to the mix. They'd named him Robert after the Luchetti brother in the Special Forces— the one who'd been missing on and off for far too long.

Evan understood why Bobby wasn't married—his life was too dangerous. Even Dean had a good reason for not taking a wife. He was genetically crabby.

However, Dean had managed to adopt a child. He and his son, Tim, made a family. Of the six Luchettis, only Evan was the eternal loser.

As he straightened away from the window, his forearm brushed Jillian Hart's bare shoulder. The catch of her breath made his belly tighten. He fought against the familiar shot of lust and the little voice that taunted, *You'll never change.*

She turned and tilted her head so she could see into his face. "I've got an idea."

Evan took several steps back until he could no longer feel the heat of her skin or smell the jasmine rising from her shiny red hair.

"Don't you want to hear it?"

He could imagine very well what her idea was. Lonely widow. Studly carpenter. He had the tools, she had the time.

The exhaustion returned in a dizzying wave. He was so damn tired of his life.

"Henry owed you money."

"Yes."

"I don't have any money."

"I got that."

"So I have a proposition."

They always did.

"What if we work together?"

Evan blinked. He'd never heard it put quite like that before.

"You do the physical labor."

Which was usually the case.

"And I'll help."

Uh-huh.

"Although I'm not very good at it."

He let his gaze wander over her centerfold body and lush lips. She had to be kidding.

"But I'm willing to learn."

That was new. Most women of his acquaintance wanted to teach him what they liked. He couldn't complain. He was a very fast learner and always open to fresh techniques.

"Let me get this straight," he said. "You want to—"

"Fix this place up. Once I sell it, I'll pay you back for your time and trouble." She stuck out her hand. "Deal?"

JILLY HELD HER BREATH, hoping he'd agree. She had nowhere else to go.

"Mr. Luchetti?" she prompted. "Deal?"

He lifted his incredible blue eyes to hers. "I'd agree to becoming partners."

"Partners?"

"You own the inn. I do the labor. We split the material costs. When we sell, it's fifty-fifty on the profits."

Jilly frowned. She wasn't sure fifty percent would be enough.

"Eighty-twenty," she countered.

"That's hardly fair. You do own the place."

"I meant eighty for me, twenty for you."

"In your dreams. Sixty-forty."

"Seventy-thirty."

"And you pay for the materials?"

Jilly considered the offer. She had a feeling it was the best she was going to get, so she nodded.

Evan slapped his hand into hers. "Deal."

She jolted—not only at the crack of flesh against flesh, but at the odd tingling that had begun again where their skin touched.

Jilly jerked away and surreptitiously rubbed her palm against her skirt. "Now, Mr. Luchetti—"

"Evan."

"Pardon me?"

"Mr. Luchetti is my father. If we're going to be partners, you'd better call me Evan." He lifted a brow. "Mrs. Duvier."

"And Mrs. Duvier is…not me. My friends call me Jilly."

Which was a joke. She didn't have any friends.

Acquaintances, yes. Friends? Hardly. The wives of Henry's associates had loathed her, seeing in Jilly their greatest fear—being replaced by a younger model. She'd never had the chance to meet any women her own age. In school she'd been an outcast, the stepdaughter of wealth plopped into a world of those who had been born to it.

"Jilly," he repeated. "Pretty name."

Why his words started a warm glow in the pit of her stomach, she had no idea. But then most of her feelings about Evan Luchetti confused her. She had a sneaking suspicion staying here was a bad idea, and staying here with him was an even worse one, but she couldn't think of anything else to do.

The money from the sale of a broken down inn would not take her very far. The money from the sale of a showplace was something else entirely. She could unload the rest of her rings to raise enough funds for the materials. She never wore them, anyway.

Her mother considered wearing diamonds from a dead man the height of gauche behavior. In this case, Jilly believed she was right.

"Where should I stay?" she asked.

"In town."

"There isn't a hotel, even if I could afford one."

He frowned. "You don't want to stay here."

"I'm not afraid of ghosts."

"What about outdoor…facilities?"

Jilly's chest went tight. "You're kidding."

"Nope."

"There has to be a bathroom."

"Why? The place was built in 1855."

"Well, put one in."

"I'll get right on that, but it'll take more than an hour."

"You've been here how long?"

"Two weeks."

"I'd think you'd put in a bathroom first."

"Maybe you would. I figured electricity would be a nice perk. It's a little hard to do anything without power."

"Let me get this straight. There's no plumbing and no electricity."

"No water or heat, either."

"Terrific."

"I shouldn't say there's *no* electricity. At one time someone started to put it in, but the wiring's iffy—needs updating. The kitchen has a few workable outlets, but the appliances were so ancient I had everything hauled away but the stove. Still want to stay?"

"I never said I wanted to. I have to."

"Suit yourself." He beckoned. "There's one other room that isn't a disaster."

Jilly followed him across the hall and glanced inside. "No bed."

"Which makes it just like all the others."

"What am I supposed to sleep on?"

"Sleeping bag."

"Never heard of it."

He laughed. "I've got an extra. Now, if you don't mind, I'd like to finish what I was doing before the light goes."

"Sure. No problem. I'll just…" She wasn't sure what she'd do.

"If you want to clean up, there's a creek out back and down the trail."

"A creek?" Her lip curled.

"Water's water around here." He shrugged. "You might want to change, too. That outfit's gonna get ruined."

He headed into the other room and seconds later the rhythmic sound of hammering commenced. Jilly glanced at her clothes. Dust on her skirt, dirt on her panty hose, Lord knows what on her shirt… She *could* use a wash.

Making her way downstairs, she took a tour of the second floor and then the first. There were eight rooms on the third floor, ten on the second. The ground level consisted of a kitchen, dining room and what might once have been a parlor near the front of the building.

As she went to the car, still parked on the far side of the pasture that doubled as the front yard, her mind clicked with ideas for turning the inn into a showplace.

Jilly excelled at decorating. Maybe because decorating was the one thing she'd been allowed to do in each of her marriages.

She'd almost reached the Volkswagen when plodding footsteps sounded behind her. More than two feet.

She spun around and nearly got a faceful of horse.

"Hey!" She jumped back.

Lightning sneezed all over her shirt.

"Thanks." Jilly held the soaked silk away from her skin. "I was wondering what I was going to do with this thing. It's pretty much junk now."

The horse threw his head up and down as if he was agreeing with her.

"This blouse cost a hundred and fifty dollars!" Jilly yanked her suitcase out of the car. She could have sworn Lightning snickered.

Opening the case, she squinted in the fading light. If she wanted to get to the creek and back before darkness fell, she'd better move.

Sighing, she contemplated the silk, rayon and linen, the high heels, short skirts and long-sleeved blouses. The only clothes she possessed that were even close to acceptable were those she wore when she did yoga exercises—gray sweatpants and a plain white T-shirt. Even her athletic shoes were out of place—lime-green with silver shoelaces.

Jilly shrugged and gathered the things together. She'd have to make do.

As she headed toward the grove of trees Evan had indicated, Lightning followed like an obedient puppy. She stopped at a fork in the path. "Which way?"

The horse butted her to the left. She stumbled and nearly fell.

"Watch it!"

Lightning stared at her with innocent brown eyes, as if he hadn't done a thing.

"This way?" she asked.

He sneezed all over her skirt.

"You really need to do something about those allergies."

Jilly headed to the left. The path disappeared into the trees and sloped downward. Seconds later the babble of water drifted to her. She must be going in the right direction.

Lightning followed more slowly, his hooves sliding on the smooth-packed dirt. The trees grew closer together. The path was barely wide enough for her to pass through. She could no longer hear the clip-clop of the horse behind her. When she glanced back, she couldn't see him, either.

But she could smell the creek, almost feel its cool caress on her skin. Sweaty, dirty and sprinkled with horse snot, Jilly couldn't wait to hit the water.

She picked up her pace. The downward slope became steeper. Jilly's nylon-covered heels slid, and suddenly, she had a hard time slowing down.

The trees parted, the path ended and there lay the creek, about twenty feet below. Jilly dropped her clothes and her shoes on the trail as she pinwheeled her arms. Heart pounding, chest heaving, she curled her toes over the edge.

Though she seemed to perch there for hours, it must only have been a few seconds before her center of gravity righted. She took one step backward, then another, until every inch of both feet rested on solid ground.

"Whew." Jilly took a deep breath. "That was close."

A thud was her only warning before the damn horse shoved her over the edge.

CHAPTER THREE

EVAN HEARD A faraway scream.

He wouldn't have heard anything at all if he hadn't finished pounding the last nail into the baseboard under the open window.

He stood and leaned out, just in time to see Lightning come out of the trees faster than he'd ever seen that horse move. The animal glanced at the house, then back toward the creek. He pawed the ground and whinnied.

Evan frowned. Jilly couldn't have taken the left fork. It was clearly marked as dangerous—or should have been. He'd had the Seitz brothers put up a sign yesterday.

"Hell."

Dropping his hammer, he ran—down one flight of stairs, then another, out the front door and across the backyard. Lightning was still pawing the ground. He'd dug a good-size hole by the time Evan raced past.

Evan took the right fork, raced down the path, burst into the clearing and saw Jilly bobbing in the middle of the creek. As he yanked off his shoes, the current pulled her under, so he dived in completely dressed.

Her red head popped up to his left. He kicked hard, pulled mightily with his arms and reached her just as she disappeared again.

Using the hold he'd learned in lifesaving, Evan tugged Jilly toward land. He'd fought his mother tooth and nail over taking that class. There were very few lakes in Illinois; who was he going to save? Right now he thanked the bullheaded stubbornness of Eleanor Luchetti, which had made her force all five of her sons and her only daughter into taking lifesaving classes.

Evan reached the bank quickly. Though deep in the center, the creek wasn't very wide. He was surprised Jilly hadn't been able to swim to the edge herself in the time it had taken him to get here.

She lay in the grass, eyes closed, skin ghost-white against the loosened tumble of her hair. Her clothes were ruined—panty hose snagged, silk shell rumpled and torn. Her skirt was hiked to midthigh.

He nearly went down on his knees and started CPR, then she coughed, choked and spit up half the creek. If she could cough she was okay, so Evan let her have at it.

Several moments later she collapsed on her back and stared up at the night sky.

"I take it you aren't much of a swimmer," he said.

"What was your first clue?"

Evan smiled. He liked her smart mouth. Reminded him of his little sister.

He missed Kim, had always gotten along with her better than any of his brothers. They were the closest in age, the furthest apart in temperament—Evan so laid-back his mom called him terminally asleep, while Kim had been wired from birth to excel at everything she touched. Back home, she had a new husband, new daughter, new life. He envied her.

Since his niece had been born, Evan had spent a lot of time baby-sitting, which was how he'd learned the words to every song in *The Little Mermaid.* Zsa Zsa loved Disney ditties, and Evan loved Zsa Zsa.

"Where's that horse?" Jilly demanded. "I'm sending him to the glue factory."

"What are you mad at Lightning for?"

"He shoved me over the cliff!"

"Did not."

"Then how do you explain me falling?"

"You're lame?"

She scowled. "I was perfectly fine until he bumped me from behind."

"What were you doing on the left fork of the trail, anyway?"

She sat up and her gaze slid away. "He told me to go that way."

"He who?"

She mumbled something.

"Did you say 'the horse'?"

"So?"

"Why would you follow a horse's advice over the sign?"

Her head came up. "What sign?"

"The one that says Danger. Cliff Ahead."

"There wasn't any sign."

Evan rubbed his forehead. That's what he'd been afraid of. Either the brothers had forgotten to do as he asked, or they'd done such a poor job of it, they may as well have forgotten.

He turned and headed back the way he'd come. Jilly followed, and moments later they stood at the fork in the path. The sign lay flat on the ground, covered with weeds and branches.

"I was supposed to see that?"

"In theory," he murmured.

"You lost me."

He very nearly had, and the close call still had him shaken. He glanced at Jilly and then couldn't look away.

Her lashes sparkled with droplets of creek water. There was a flush of peach across her cheekbones. Her hair was mussed and wild as it tumbled over her shoulders. The silky top she wore was plastered to her chest. Suddenly he couldn't remember what they were talking about.

He was such a *guy*. He might have sworn off women in his head, but his body had other ideas. Didn't it always?

"Hey!"

She snapped her fingers in front of his face. Thoughts of stripping her wet stockings down her smooth legs, then rubbing a towel all over her body disappeared.

"I have to apologize—"

"Yes, you do."

"If you'd let me finish, I can explain."

"I doubt that, but…" She spread her fingers wide and swept her hand out in a be-my-guest gesture.

"I should have put the sign up myself. But I let the Seitz brothers do it."

Understanding dawned. "Not too smart."

"I know."

What had he been thinking to let those old men take care of such an important task? He'd been thinking he wanted them out of his hair for five minutes, and what was so tough about putting up a sign?

Evan hunted around for a flat rock, then hauled the wooden post out of the brush and pounded it into the ground. "There."

He stood back to admire his handiwork. Not bad.

"You!" Jilly shouted.

Evan started and glanced over his shoulder. Lightning stood on the path, his nose hanging all the way down to his hooves.

"Where's the nearest glue factory?"

The horse's head came up. His ancient eyes met Evan's. Evan could swear the animal understood her.

"Leave him be," he said. "Lightning didn't push you in."

"How do you figure?"

"Follow me."

He set off down the left fork, but Jilly didn't move. "I'm not going down there again. You think I'm naive?"

"I just fished you out—I wouldn't let you fall in. Besides, if you die, I won't ever see my money."

She stared at him for a long moment, then shrugged and followed.

The trail narrowed; the trees bowed. By the time they reached the cliff, he was bent into the shape of an "r." A pile of clothes lay on the path. Evan gathered them together and handed them to Jilly.

"As you can see, the trail's too narrow for Lightning to get beyond the first few feet."

"But—"

Evan took her arm and led her back up the trail and toward the house. "It's been a long day. You've had a shock."

"I could use a hot bath and a cup of tea."

He shook his head. What was he going to do with her?

"Sorry, we're fresh out of water. How about a towel and a beer?"

She stopped dead at the edge of the front yard. "That…that *horse!*"

Evan followed the direction of her gaze. The contents of her suitcase had been strewn all over the pasture. Lightning grazed calmly next to the empty bag, as if he hadn't done anything wrong.

Jilly marched toward the animal. Evan caught her by the elbow and hauled her back. She was nearly hyperventilating. "Breathe," he ordered.

He was very good at dealing with hysterical women.

As a teen, his sister had always been on the verge of eruption. Lately, thanks to menopause, his mom usually was.

Jilly took a deep breath, then another. "Why did he do that?"

Evan wasn't sure. Lightning had never misbehaved before. The horse was a lump. He ate and he pooped and he stood there. He didn't shove people off cliffs, and he hardly ever threw their clothes all over the pasture. Either he really liked Jilly or he didn't; it was hard to tell with a horse.

"You go ahead and change." Evan gave her a little shove toward the inn. "I'll pick up your things and bring them inside."

"Thanks." She paused halfway between him and the house. "And thank you for saving my life. I think I forgot to say that in all the excitement."

"No problem."

"If there's anything I can do to repay you—"

"I don't suppose you'd consider sixty-forty?"

She tilted her head and her wet, red hair fell in hanks around her face, reminding him of the little mermaid. Except Ariel's hair was always dry or at least looked that way, even under the sea. Of course, that only happened in the wonderful world of Disney, not an Arkansas backwater.

"I'll consider it," she said with a smile, and disappeared into the house.

Evan started picking up clothes. Everything she had was high class, completely inappropriate for the temperature in Arkansas. A lot of it was grass stained, dirt smudged, water speckled; one particularly lovely blouse had the perfect imprint of a horseshoe on the back. Jilly was going to have a fit.

He stopped near Lightning. "What *were* you thinking?"

The horse shook his head, stomped his foot and whinnied.

"You're right." Evan glanced up at the inn. "She won't last a week."

JILLY FOUND A TOWEL in what must be Evan's room, since there was a sleeping bag spread across the floor, another in the corner and a knapsack nearby. She also found a battery-operated lantern. He was a regular outdoorsman.

His room was almost habitable. New drywall, baseboard; the hardwood floors were scratched but clean. The windows still had holes. She hoped they weren't large enough for birds or bats to get in.

Shuddering, Jilly carried the towel, the extra sleeping bag and the lantern into her own room. At least her windows were intact.

Quickly she undressed, dried off, donned the sweatpants and T-shirt, then wrapped her hair in the towel. She'd need to braid it before bed or she'd resemble Little Orphan Annie in the morning.

A scent reminiscent of moss and day-old fish rose from her skin. She should return to the creek with a bar of soap.

Jilly glanced at the window. The sun had gone down.

"Who knows what's in those woods?" she murmured, swearing she could hear banjos strumming in the trees.

A footfall on the stairs had her scurrying around the room, gathering her ruined clothes into a pile. Seconds later, Evan knocked.

"Come in."

Evan laid her suitcase, and judging from the amount of material sticking out the sides, all of her clothes, on the floor. "Sorry. There's a lot of dust and dirt and… other things on these."

Jilly sighed. "I wasn't going to wear them, anyway."

She glanced at her sweats. She was down to the clothes on her back. Panic fluttered in the pit of her stomach as old fears surfaced. When was the last time she'd had no clothes to wear, no food to eat, no place to stay and no money in her pocket?

The day she'd sworn never to be that way again— no matter what she had to do.

"How fast can we get this place ready to sell?"

Evan frowned. "Depends."

"On?"

"How much money you have to put into it and how much help you can give me. Ever use a power saw?"

She merely raised a brow.

"I didn't think so." He shrugged. "With just you and me, fixing this place up could take months."

Months? Here? With him? Jilly's shoulders slumped.

Well, she'd wanted some time on her own. Looked like she was going to have it in a very unlikely place. With a very unlikely companion.

"Is that what you're going to wear?" he asked.

Jilly glanced down. "What's wrong with it?"

"You'll boil."

He tilted his head, and his hair, somehow freed from the rubber band during their misadventure, brushed his shoulders. She'd never met a man with long hair. Most of those in her acquaintance were lucky to *have* hair.

"I've got an idea."

Evan walked out of the room, leaving Jilly alone with her thoughts. Not good, because her thoughts were of running her fingers through the sun-streaked strands, then under his dirty T-shirt, across smooth skin—

"Here we go."

She gasped and ducked her head, though she doubted Evan could see her flush in the flickering light of the lantern. He didn't seem to be interested in her face, anyway. He was coming at her with scissors.

"Hey!"

Going down on one knee, he grabbed a hunk of her sweatpants at midthigh. "Hold still."

Before she could protest, he clipped a hole in them, then grabbed hold of the fleecy material and pulled. His biceps flexed; her mind went gooey as her pant leg tore in two. The soft cotton slid to the floor, pooling around her ankle.

Evan lifted his head. "Better?"

His mouth was even with her belly, which quivered as his breath fluttered against her shirt.

She couldn't talk. She was too busy fighting the urge to lean forward and allow his incredibly lush lips to press against the place where her skin flamed.

"Jilly?"

He shifted to the other leg, and his shoulder bumped her thigh. Her breath hissed in at the contact.

"Sorry." He placed his palm on her bare knee. "Did I hurt you?"

She took an instant to be thankful she'd shaved her legs that morning, then shook her head.

"I'm fine." Her voice was a hoarse, sexy rasp.

He didn't seem to notice. Instead, he lifted the scissors and made short work of the other leg of her sweatpants. Within seconds she wore shorts.

Evan stood. Jilly's head tilted back. Their gazes met and the air around them stilled.

A trickle of sweat, or perhaps water, ran down his neck and disappeared beneath the collar of his damp shirt. The room felt like a sauna. They both smelled like the creek. So why did she suddenly want to press against him and absorb some of the heat?

"Do you want me to…?"

He stopped speaking and froze as she stepped closer. She could think of a lot of things she wanted him to do.

"Cut off the sleeves of your shirt," he blurted.

She inched even closer, and her knee brushed his. "Please."

Her voice was no longer hers. Her body didn't seem to be, either.

Evan took a quick step backward, then his fingers fumbled with the sleeve of her shirt, brushing against the side of her breast.

"Sorry," he muttered. "Uh, maybe you should take it off."

Jilly reached for the hem. He grabbed her hand. "Not now."

"I don't have anything else to wear."

"Well, um, I'll just make a slit and tear it like the pants."

"Fine. Sure."

He plucked the material away from her skin with his thumb and forefinger, as if he were afraid of touching her again. A snip later and his biceps bulged right in front of her eyes. She had to fight the desire to run her tongue along the muscles and mark them as hers.

The sound of rending cloth shot straight to her stomach, then dipped lower. She gritted her teeth, held herself still while he shifted and did the same to the second sleeve.

This time the brush of his nails, the chill of the scissors, the sound the cloth made as it ripped made her gasp, and his gaze flicked to hers. Instead of wary confusion, his heated eyes reflected the fire in her belly.

The scissors clattered to the floor as his hands closed around her shoulders. She had a moment to be glad the blades hadn't pierced one of their feet before his mouth captured hers.

His thumbs stroked the hollows between her shoulders and her collarbone in the same rhythm as his tongue stroked her lips. Their bodies hovered a wisp apart. Her heartbeat thundered in her ears. She wanted things she'd never wanted before, and she knew instinctively she could get every one from him.

His fingers held her face; his tongue dipped inside her mouth to entwine with hers. The towel tumbled off her head, and her hair cascaded around them like a curtain. She barely noticed.

The man could certainly kiss, or maybe she'd just never been kissed before.

Foolishness; she'd been married four times. She'd no doubt been kissed four thousand.

Too bad she'd never been kissed like this.

WHAT IN HELL was he doing?

The usual—seducing any female in the vicinity. Evan disgusted himself.

He had lost track of the number of women he'd taken to bed. He could count on one hand how many he had cared for. Count on…no fingers the ones who had cared for him—and that had to stop.

Stiffening, he broke the embrace. "I'm sorry. I can't do this."

Jilly, who despite his fumbling retreat was staring at him with soft eyes, her lips wet, red and inviting, blinked. "Do what?"

He shrugged, spread his hands. "This."

She straightened, going from luscious, willing country girl to put-upon, high society widow in an instant. "On the contrary, I bet you *can* do it. Very well."

"I didn't mean I couldn't." Evan rubbed a hand through his hair, shoving the damp strands away from his face. "I just swore that I wouldn't."

"What are you, some kind of priest?"

"No, that would be my brother."

"You have a brother who's a priest?"

She seemed shocked—as if he'd just said his brother was a serial killer and not a man of God. In truth, Aaron was neither one.

His big brother had planned to be a priest, but a single night with a stripper had resulted in a child. When that child had shown up on the doorstep of the family farm—thirteen years old and looking for her daddy— all hell had broken loose.

Evan, off working on someone's summer home, had missed all the fun. By the time he'd returned, Aaron had been married to the mother of his child and had absconded to Las Vegas to open a home for runaways.

"No," he answered. "My brother isn't a priest."

Jilly made an aggravated sound deep in her throat. "You aren't making any sense."

Evan glanced at her, and his body leaped in response. Tearing off parts of her clothes had been a very bad idea. Not only was it one of the most erotic things he'd ever done, but now her arms and legs were bare—soft, white and enticing.

He wanted to touch them—first with his hands, then with his mouth. He wanted to teach her all the things she didn't seem to know. He wanted to learn what she liked and how she liked it.

He had to get out of here before he forgot the vow he'd made to change his life. But it was so hard when he was…so hard.

Evan shook his head. Would he ever change? Could he? He wasn't sure, but he had to try.

"I'll see you in the morning," he said, and fled to his room.

"THAT WENT WELL."

Evan's door closed across the hall. He'd practically run away from her. Was she that unappealing? She might resemble Ellie Mae Clampett in this outfit, but was that bad? Obviously he thought so.

Or… A hideous thought occurred to her. Maybe she was only attractive to older men. She couldn't remember ever dating anyone her own age. She'd definitely never gone out with a man who was younger.

Jilly had just turned thirty-five; Evan appeared to be in his twenties at best. Why *would* he want her?

Sighing, she spread out her sleeping bag. It was only ten o'clock, but what else did she have to do but sleep—and think?

Seven hours later, she was still thinking. She'd tossed and turned, but hadn't slept much. Now she was hungry.

She sat up. The air was still and humid, and the bugs outside made more noise than a brass band. She missed the soothing cadence of her ocean. Without the murmur of the Pacific outside the window, she wasn't going to sleep well anytime soon.

She headed downstairs. A big guy like Evan had to have food around here somewhere.

Thankfully, the sun was coming up, spreading slivers of golden sunshine through the broken windows to light her path. She found the kitchen with relative ease, found the food even easier. The huge cooler was as out of place in this house as she was.

Jilly removed the makings for a sandwich—bread, turkey, cheese. No coffeepot. She just might have to kill someone.

How was she going to face Evan this morning after throwing herself at him last night? She had no idea what had gotten into her. She'd wanted nothing more than to tear off his clothes as he'd torn hers, put her hands all over his skin and have him put his mouth…everywhere. She must be more upset over Henry's death than she'd thought.

Jilly seized on the excuse. That was it! Losing Henry, of whom she'd become inordinately fond, had unhinged her mind. She'd be fine once she had a new husband. She always was.

A shuffle outside the open window frame above the counter drew her attention. Lightning stared back at her.

"What did I ever do to you?" she whispered.

The horse ignored her, pushing his nose, then his entire head, through the window. He pulled back his lips, teeth reaching daintily for her food.

Jilly snatched the sandwich away before he could eat, or sneeze on, it.

"Behave yourself!"

Jilly froze as a woman spoke behind her. Lightning took one look at the intruder and ran.

Jilly spun around. Her mouth fell open.

A tiny, skinny, withered old woman stood in the kitchen doorway. Where had she come from? Jilly hadn't heard the front door open, nor any footsteps on the plank floor.

She was dressed in a white cotton blouse, high-necked and long-sleeved, despite the heat. Her skirt hung to midcalf—the better to admire her ankle-high work boots. Her long, gray hair had been twisted into a bun.

"Do you like my house?"

Panic fluttered in Jilly's stomach. *Her* house? Was the deed contested? Jilly didn't have the money to go to court, but this place was all she had. She couldn't give it up without a fight.

"Who are you?" she asked.

"Figured you would have heard about me by now."

Jilly thought back over what she'd been told. The only thing she recalled was that the inn was…

Haunted.

CHAPTER FOUR

"TH-THIS IS your house?" Jilly asked.

"Used to be. Always loved the place." The old woman sat on a kitchen chair, then stuck her feet out in front of her and fanned her face with one hand. "Hot, ain't it?"

Jilly nodded, wondering if ghosts could be hot. Wouldn't they be cold? As in stone-cold dead?

She reached out and touched the woman's arm. Bony, warm, solid—she felt pretty real.

"You're alive," Jilly murmured.

"And kicking. Got a few good times in me yet, I hope. Whad ya think? I was a shade?"

"Shade?"

"Ha'nt." At Jilly's blank expression, she continued, "Spirit. Ghost."

"Oh! Yes. Well, not really. I don't believe in such things."

The woman lifted her snowy-white eyebrows. "You will."

Jilly straightened and tried to appear dignified, which wasn't easy wearing cut-off sweatpants and a torn T-shirt.

"I'm Jillian Hart." She offered her hand. "The inn is mine now."

The old woman stared at Jilly's hand with such a frown, Jilly surreptitiously peeked at her fingers, then winced. Her polish was chipped; two nails were broken. She needed a manicure in the worst way. However, until she made good on her husband quest, she'd be making do with a nail file and some polish remover.

"Sold the place to a man by the name of Duvier," the woman said. "Who might you be?"

"His wife. Henry passed on recently."

"Sorry to hear that. I'm Addie Tolliver."

She clapped her hand around Jilly's and crunched a few bones with her handshake. For a tiny, skinny old woman, Addie had the strength of an ox.

"Where's the youngun who's workin' here?"

"Youngun?"

"Pretty boy. Long hair. Nice butt."

Jilly's eyes widened. "Um. That might be Evan."

"Might be? Any other young men with a nice butt and an even better chest?"

Jilly put her nose into the air. "I wouldn't know. He's my partner."

"Partner? Well, that should be interesting. You plannin' on livin' here?"

"It's my place."

"And him?"

"There's nothing going on," Jilly hastened to explain. Though why she felt the need to explain to a stranger, she had no idea. Nevertheless… "We're fixing up the place to sell as a bed-and-breakfast. For the new highway."

"So I hear." Addie withdrew a cloth-covered rectangle from a voluminous pocket in her skirt and offered it to Jilly. "Made it m'self this morning."

Jilly glanced out the window. The sun had barely risen. "*This* morning?"

"Yep. Slept in, or I'd have brought two."

Jilly thanked Addie and took the gift, which was warm against her palm. Inside she found a loaf of fresh bread and a tiny jar of preserves. Her mouth watered as the aroma wafted across her face. Suddenly the sandwich Lightning had wanted so badly didn't seem so appealing.

Jilly glanced at the counter where she'd left her meal. The plate was empty.

"Damn horse," she muttered.

"Lightning was mine, too. I miss the old nag."

"Take him." Jilly set the fresh bread on a plate and dug a knife out of the jumble of utensils in a drawer.

"Oh, I couldn't," Addie protested. "He goes with the house."

"I don't mind."

"Lightning belongs here. He'd never leave. Ever."

Terrific, Jilly thought. "Would you like some?" she said.

"No, thank ye. Gotta be gettin' home. Patients to tend. Long day ahead."

"Patients?" Jilly turned away from the counter. "You're a doctor?"

"Addie's the local wisewoman." Evan stood in the doorway. Though he was fully clothed, Jilly's libido kicked in, anyway. She'd seen what lay under that T-shirt. She knew the taste of his mouth, the scent of his skin. Hell.

"Mornin', Addie."

Evan strolled into the kitchen, bending over the cooler and extracting a bottle of orange juice. Jilly couldn't help but admire the view. She glanced at Addie, who was ogling, too.

Addie's gaze met hers, and the woman grinned, then winked. Jilly couldn't help but smile back. He really was a beautiful sight. How could any red-blooded, breathing female not admire him?

"I brought your favorite." Addie motioned toward the bread. "Honey wheat."

"Thanks." Evan tore off a hunk. "Addie makes the best bread in the state."

"I wouldn't say that," she protested, but her weathered cheeks sported a pinkish tinge.

"Is there any way to make coffee?" Jilly asked.

"Sorry, don't drink the stuff." Evan took a bite of bread and chewed with obvious appreciation.

His teeth were slightly crooked, as Jilly's had been before she'd endured three years of braces and head gear. An investment, her mother had dubbed the wires. Jilly had just called them torture.

But as her mother always said, men don't make passes at girls who wear glasses, and rich men won't look twice at a young woman with an overbite. In the modern world the most telling indication of youthful poverty was a person's teeth.

Evan's were cute. Though crooked, they were white and strong, very clean. He still had every one of them.

Jilly walked to the window and made a great show of staring outside. "How can you live without coffee?" she asked.

"Much healthier than living with it."

"There's nothing wrong with coffee."

"I'd rather have juice or milk."

"Ugh," she murmured. "I need to buy a coffeemaker."

Crash. Bang.

Jilly jumped as Addie rustled around in a cabinet to her left. "Aha!" she cried, and yanked out a silver pot with a handle. "Here ye go." She shoved the thing into Jilly's hands.

Jilly stared at it. "Uh, what is this?"

"Percolator." When Jilly continued to frown, Addie added, "Fer coffee? No need to buy a new pot. I've had that 'un since I was just married. Never had a mite of trouble with it. Makes the best coffee you'll ever want t' taste."

"You're married?"

"Was," Addie said shortly. "He died pert near on the honeymoon."

"I'm sorry."

"Me, too."

"You never married again?"

"What fer? Matthew was my man. I loved him more than anything."

Addie's happy voice had grown sad. Her eyes were shadowed; her shoulders sagged.

Love was nothing but trouble.

"I'd best be on my way." She headed for the door. "You need anything, I'm over yonder." She pointed past the jumble of trees at the far end of the pasture.

"Thank you. We'll be fine."

"If ye hear funny noises and such, don't worry none. That's just Matthew."

She walked out the door and headed across the field. Lightning followed slowly behind.

"Have you heard noises?" Jilly asked.

"I've heard something." Evan took a swig of his juice. "A whole lot of somethings."

Jilly made an aggravated noise deep in her throat. "There's no such thing as ghosts."

Upstairs a loud thump sounded. Evan lifted an eyebrow.

"What fell?" she asked.

"Who knows? Stuff falls around here all the time."

"It's an old house."

"Exactly."

Jilly scowled. "How are we going to sell the place if everyone thinks it's haunted?"

"Not my department—the selling. Mine's the fixing, and we need to head to town for supplies."

"Right." Jilly set the ancient coffeemaker on the counter. "I'll just get my…things."

She ran to her room, hoping someone in South Fork was in need of a diamond or two.

EVAN LISTENED TO JILLY rustling around upstairs. He hadn't slept well last night. He'd been haunted by the taste of her lips and the echo of her sigh. His body had ached for hers, so he'd spent a lot of time talking to himself.

What kind of man was he that he couldn't be in the same house with a beautiful woman and not want her? Exactly the kind of man everyone thought he was.

A lothario. A gigolo. A pig.

All he wanted was to be a husband and a father, have a place to call his own and someone who loved him. He wanted kids to hug and play with. Little girls, like Zsa Zsa, who thought he was special. Little boys who thought he was a superhero.

But what kind of man harbored lascivious thoughts about a woman he'd just met? What kind of father would he make if he couldn't learn to keep his pecker in his pants?

The kind he did not want to be.

Ashley had hurt him by turning him down, but she'd also done him a favor. Evan hadn't been happy, but he wasn't sure why. Ashley's frank comments had revealed the truth. His life might have been most men's dream, but it was more of a nightmare.

Coming to South Fork was his venture into a new life. He would not begin by having an affair with his business partner. No matter how much he might want to. Wanting was what had gotten him into this predicament in the first place—nearly thirty with nothing to show for it.

The sound of Jilly's feet on the stairs preceded her entry by seconds. She wore the same shorts and shirt he'd torn apart last night, and the sight of them, the memory of what he'd done, made him hot all over again.

Evan slid away from the counter, intending to head out the door, but Jilly stepped into his path and held out her hand.

"What do you think?" she asked.

Her palm was full of silver, gold, diamonds. He blinked. "Those are real."

"Of course they're real. You think I didn't get them appraised the instant they were on my finger?"

Evan picked up one huge rock. The thing had to be three carats, not that he was much of an expert. Set in silver, the stone had at least ten smaller diamonds surrounding it.

"I know I won't get what they're worth," Jilly said, "but we should be able to buy what we need."

"You're going to sell them?"

She shrugged. "Why not?"

He chose another set in gold, with a waterfall of tiny diamonds falling away from a center stone that appeared even larger than the first.

"Second anniversary." Jilly smiled fondly. "Henry always did have exquisite taste."

Evan lifted his gaze from the ring to her face. "Sure did."

Her smile faded, and she took one step closer. Evan took two steps back. Why couldn't he learn to keep his mouth shut? Last night they'd shared a kiss that a few months ago would have led to several days in bed. But he'd put a stop to it, because he wanted to change.

Evan had promised himself no sex without love. Yet here he was, flirting again. For him, flirting was as natural as breathing.

Not so for Jilly. She lowered her eyes, blushing. Despite being a widow, and over twenty-one, she behaved as if she were a dewy-eyed virgin.

"How old are you?" he blurted.

Her gaze flew to his. "How old are you?"

"Twenty-nine."

Her eyes widened. "You seem younger."

Evan wasn't sure if that was a compliment or not. Probably not, since she snatched the rings from his fingers and stuffed the lot into the cavernous pocket of her sweat shorts.

"Well?" he pressed. "How old *are* you?"

"Old enough to know better," she muttered.

"Better than what?"

"Better than to tell anyone how old I am. Didn't your mother teach you it's rude to ask a lady her age?"

"No."

His mother had told him to settle down, behave and, recently, to be more discreet. None of her advice had been very helpful in the scheme of life.

"Well, it is," Jilly snapped.

"What's the big secret? Are you a lot older than you look?"

Her eyes narrowed. For an instant he thought she might kick him, before she shrugged and went through the door without answering.

"We'd do better to head to Little Rock with those," he called.

Jilly stopped halfway between the inn and his truck, then turned. "Why?"

"No one around here is going to have need for diamonds the size of a fingernail."

"Diamonds are a girl's best friend," she muttered.

"Maybe, but the women around here make do with the real thing."

"I told you they're real."

"I meant real *friends*. Giggling, slumber parties, girl talk. Remember?"

"I never giggle, rarely slumber at a party, and I can't recall the last time I talked to a girl."

"You're kidding."

"I rarely kid, either. There's no profit in it."

He stared at Jilly for several ticks of the clock, waiting for her to laugh. But she didn't.

"You've got no girlfriends?"

His sister had filled their house with laughing, shrieking teenage girls. Maybe that was how Evan had become so darn fascinated with the female species. Having temptation bounce past his bedroom in scanty attire from the age of twelve had given him some pretty amazing dreams—and some very early sexual experiences.

He was certain a psychiatrist would have a field day with his memories. His mother, if she ever found out he'd lost his virginity in the upstairs bathroom at age fifteen, would have a stroke, right after she kicked Mary Lou Kruppke's bony ass.

"Little Rock it is." Jilly neatly sidestepped his question. "I need to return my rental car, anyway. You don't mind if we share your truck, do you?"

Actually, he did. The shiny silver pickup was his baby, the first new vehicle he'd ever owned.

"In an emergency," he allowed. "Otherwise, you can always walk to town."

"Walk?" she repeated, as if he'd told her to dance naked under the moon.

That very image flashed before his eyes, and he forced it away. What was the matter with him? Sure, he liked women. He liked sex. He liked having sex with women. But he'd never been so aware of one before, so physically attracted from the instant he'd laid eyes on her. The only explanation was that in telling himself he couldn't have Jilly, his contrary libido had decided that he must.

Evan followed the Volkswagen to Little Rock, where they sold Jilly's diamonds, bought some coffee for the next morning and drove home. Nevertheless, the exercise took most of the day. By the time they returned to the inn, dusk was settling over the trees like a gray, misty fog.

The Ozarks were so far removed from Evan's home in Illinois, he felt as if he'd entered another world. In Gainsville, acres upon acres of corn and wheat spread in every direction, with fields broken up by houses, barns, silos and livestock. The colors of the earth were plain—amber grain, green grass, blue sky. Even the cows were black-and-white.

In South Fork, hill after hill spread into mountains of purple majesty. The sunsets faded from skies that were so much more than blue. Sunrise was scarlet fire bursting across a velvet night.

When it rained the horizon went gray-green. Steam rose from the grass and drifted across the fields in a silver haze. Whenever the rain fell he could swear he heard heaven sigh at the beauty of this place.

The inn was situated in one of the loveliest areas of South Fork. Once the highway went through, it might not be so lovely anymore. But without the highway, the inn would perish. A quandary. What in life wasn't?

Evan stared at the ancient three-story building. The

windows were dark. The wind whistled through the trees. The old boards on the porch creaked. The place did not appear at all inviting. At times like these, Addie's ghosts seemed very real.

He glanced at Jilly, who stared at the building without much enthusiasm.

"I'll go in and light a lamp," he offered.

"No." Her fingers trailed over his arm, stopping him, exciting him. "I like the dark. It's peaceful. Don't you think?"

Evan had never cared for the dark. Probably because, as the youngest of five brothers, he'd been the victim of too many pranks in the night.

Crickets chirped, an owl hooted, something rustled through the tall grass nearby. Probably a snake, though he wasn't going to tell Jilly that. She might not be like any other woman he'd ever met, but he still didn't think she'd appreciate a snake in the grass.

"We should have eaten in town," she murmured.

"I'm sure there's something in the cooler we can have."

"I'll buy groceries tomorrow."

"You sound as if you'd rather have a root canal."

She snorted. "Not quite. But I hate to spend money on anything but the inn."

"We've gotta eat or we won't be able to work."

"I know, but I wish we didn't."

Jilly climbed out of the car. Evan followed suit. She was halfway to the house when Lightning appeared and head butted her from behind. She flew forward. The unappetizing splat told him what she'd fallen in even before she said, "Horse shit!"

Evan helped her up, peered at her shirt. "Yep, that's horse shit all right."

She shoved him away and rounded on the horse, but Lightning disappeared at a gallop into the trees at the far side of the pasture.

"What does he have against me?"

Evan had never had a problem with the animal, never heard that Lightning was anything other than gentle.

"I think he likes you."

"Likes me? *Likes* me?" Her voice rose shrilly. "I'd hate to see what he does to someone he hates." She started for the house.

"Didn't a little boy ever push you in the mud? Kick you in the shin? Throw worms in your face?"

Jilly stopped and stared. "Why would they do that?"

He shrugged. "That's how little boys show affection."

"In that case, I'm glad I went to an all-girls school."

She strode into the house, leaving Evan to stare after her in the dark.

She'd gone to an all-girls school, yet she'd never had any girlfriends. He found himself feeling sorry for her, yet Jilly was the least sorry person he'd ever met.

CHAPTER FIVE

JILLY SMELLED LIKE horse dung, but she didn't want to go to the creek alone, and she didn't want to go with Evan. He didn't seem to like her.

She wasn't used to men not wanting her, and wasn't sure what to do about it.

"Nothing," she muttered, rifling through her suitcase searching for something suitable to wear. "He doesn't have any money. What on earth is he good for?"

Sex.

Straightening, she glanced around the room. The flickering light from the single candle only made the place more spooky. Had someone spoken? Or was it all in her head?

"My head," she stated. "I've got sex on the brain."

An amazing occurrence. She rarely considered the physical act. Men gave marriage, security and money; she gave herself. For Jilly that had always been a bargain best kept without too much thought involved. The old adage *Close your eyes and think of England* came to mind.

But since meeting Evan, talking to him, kissing him, she'd begun to consider sex as something more than a commodity. With the right person, maybe sex could be fun.

Too bad the person her body seemed to want wanted nothing to do with her.

The aroma rising from her T-shirt and shorts was far too ripe to ignore. She had to wash, with soap, and she wasn't going out there alone.

Sadly, Lightning had left her nothing to change into except a slinky white negligee. She lifted it, rubbed her fingers against the satin. Perhaps this would change Evan's mind.

She tucked the gown into a towel, grabbed scented soap from her cosmetics bag and marched across the hall, where she knocked on Evan's door.

Almost immediately, it opened. "Ready?" he asked.

Her heart increased in tempo. Could he know what she really wanted?

Evan's gaze dropped. "Guess so," he stated.

Jilly looked down. She carried a towel, soap, shampoo. Of course he knew what she wanted.

Together they left the inn. No stars, no moon; the clouds were out. Which made crossing the yard and meandering down the trail to the creek hazardous at best.

Evan took her hand before they'd walked three feet. "I've never much cared for the dark," he admitted.

Was he kidding? A big, strong man like him afraid of the dark? She didn't believe it. He was trying to make her feel better about asking for an escort.

The dark didn't bother Jilly. She didn't believe in

ghosts. But bats, alligators and…whatever that was making an odd grunting noise to her left? She didn't like those one bit.

They reached the creek without incident. Evan let go of her hand. "I'll be right here." He headed for a large boulder at the base of the cliff. Once there he turned his back, and she wasted no time stripping off her manure-encrusted clothes.

"Are there alligators in Arkansas?" Jilly dipped her toe into the water.

"Yes."

She snatched it back and peered into the murky blackness.

"But not here."

"You're sure?"

"We're too far north for a wild alligator to live in the creek."

Wild alligator? Was there any other kind?

Gathering her courage, Jilly waded in. She removed her hair from the French braid, then washed as quickly as she could, not liking the brush of fish—or at least she hoped they were fish—against her thighs, or the squish of mud between her toes. She especially hated the chill of the water, which made her nipples harden and her skin tingle.

Moments after she'd stepped in, Jilly stepped out. Drying herself quickly, she donned the white satin gown. When she went to look for the elastic band so she could rebraid her hair, it was gone. Jilly cursed.

"What's the matter?"

Evan's voice was closer than she expected and she started, then glanced up. He stood only a few feet away.

"I need to braid my hair, but I lost the fastener. I'll have a mess of tangles if I sleep with it loose."

Reaching up, he tugged on his ponytail. His hair spilled over his shoulders, across his face. He offered Jilly the rubber band. "Use mine."

His voice was hoarse, as if the cool night air had given him a sore throat. His hand trembled and guilt suffused her. He was cold, and she'd made him stand here waiting for her.

She plucked the rubber band from his palm and deftly braided her hair, ignoring her mother's voice, which said a rubber band would give her split ends. Mother had more rules than any sane person could recall. Funny how Jilly always managed to remember every one.

Or maybe not funny at all.

Jilly traced her fingers over Evan's rubber band, feeling dangerous and bad. Today a rubber band in her hair, tomorrow…what? Depraved sex with a poverty-stricken carpenter?

Her eyes strayed to Evan. He faced away from her again, arms wrapped around himself to ward off the chill. Just the sight of him made her nipples tighten and her body shiver.

"We should get back to the house," she said.

His answer was a grunt before he took off without

glancing back. Jilly scrambled to keep up, nearly tripping in the ankle-length sheath.

He didn't offer his hand, and she stumbled on the ascent. "Hey!" she called. "A little help here?"

He sighed, turned and hauled her up the last few feet. His eyes flickered over her, pausing at the neckline of her gown, then dipping a bit lower to linger. Jilly shifted and the satin brushed her nipples, tightening them further.

Evan spun around and headed for the inn at an even faster pace. Jilly lifted her skirt and struggled to catch up, which was the only reason she didn't see him stop dead several yards from the house. She slammed into him and would have fallen on her satin-clad butt if he hadn't caught her.

His hands, hard and rough, held her forearms. She liked how they felt against her skin. The scrape of countless injuries intrigued her. She wanted to learn about every one, trace the scars with her fingertip, lick them with her tongue.

Swaying toward him, she lifted her mouth, and discovered he wasn't looking at her but at the inn. She followed his gaze. The lamp he'd left burning in his room threw shadows against the wall next to the window. Shadows that looked an awful lot like a man.

Jilly stiffened. "We should call the police."

"Got your cell phone?"

"Damn." Even if she had brought it along to the creek, the thing didn't work in this neck of the woods.

"I'll get rid of him."

"No." She reached for Evan, but caught only the tail of his shirt. "Let's drive to town."

Evan grinned. "You want to go to South Fork like that?"

He had a point. "Fine. I'll stay here. You go."

"Like hell," he grumbled. "I'll take care of this."

He headed for the back door, Jilly on his heels.

Evan stopped, turned, tilted his head. His hair swung free, and she reached up to brush it away from his face. He caught her hand before she could touch him.

"Stay outside until I say it's okay to come in. In fact—" he reached into the pocket of his jeans and pulled out some keys "—get in the truck. If I'm not out in five minutes, head to town."

"Like hell," she repeated.

"I'm the youngest of five brothers. I know how to sneak up on someone, then kick their ass. At my house we called it fun."

"You got a gun?"

"I don't need no stinkin' gun," he said in a Mexican accent so bad she would have laughed if she hadn't been scared to death.

He sobered. "Guns kill people, Jilly."

"That's what I'm afraid of."

"Relax." He gave her a quick kiss on the forehead that only left her wanting more. "Burglars rarely carry guns. There's a much stiffer penalty if they're armed."

"Burglar?" Her heart pounded harder. "As in thief?"

"What did you think the guy was after? An invitation to dinner?"

"The money. I left it in my room."

Evan's face tightened. "Get in the truck." He put his hands on her shoulders and gave her a little shake. "Stay there."

He slipped into the house. Jilly took one step toward the pickup and paused. Slowly she backed up until she could see the single illuminated window on the third floor. A chill went through her.

The window was empty.

She bit her lip, glanced around the clearing. Nothing moved but the leaves on the trees. What if the intruder had come out the front door while they were talking? What if, even now, he was creeping up on her in the dark? Or…

What if he was lying in wait for Evan?

A tiny sob escaped her lips, and Jilly started for the house, but she stopped short of entering. Evan had told her to stay here. Wandering around in the dark would only confuse the issue. What if he hit her over the head with a two-by-four? What if she hit him?

Air being blown through horsey nostrils sounded an instant before something wet sprayed the back of her neck. Jilly turned and discovered Lightning's great big head right next to hers. She hadn't heard him approach. Not a clip or even a clop. She'd been too busy worrying about Evan and her money.

"If that money's gone we are so screwed," she murmured.

Lightning threw up his head in agreement.

For the first time she was glad the horse was there. At least she wasn't alone. Together they watched the house, until the door opened and Evan popped out.

"What happened?" Jilly asked. "Who was it?"

"No one."

"What?"

"I went through the entire house. No one was there."

"Did he run off?"

"Maybe. But I didn't hear anything. Nothing's disturbed. Your money's right where you left it."

"I don't understand."

"Me, either, unless…" Evan's eyes met hers. "Unless we just saw Matthew Tolliver."

"He's dead."

"Exactly."

"No. There's an explanation for everything, and a ghost isn't it."

"The place is haunted. Everyone says so."

"If everyone said the earth was flat would you quit taking long walks in the dark?"

"I don't, anyway."

"That's beside the point. The people here are—well…" She wasn't quite sure how to say "backward" without saying it.

He heard her, anyway. "The folks around here are a lot smarter than you think."

"Maybe so, but there's still no such thing as ghosts."

Evan looked up at the now empty third floor window. "I guess we'll find out."

"How?"

"The instant you say something doesn't exist, that's an open invitation to be proved wrong."

EVAN LEFT JILLY IN HER room and went to his. Was she trying to kill him with that gown?

So white it was nearly silver, the thing clung to every curve, leaving nothing to his imagination. She smelled even more strongly of jasmine; must be her soap or shampoo. Knowing that his rubber band was wrapped around her long red tresses made him want to wrap something else of his around something of hers—or the other way around.

Evan smacked his forehead against the door, but the urge didn't go away.

He took off his shirt, stripped down to his boxers. He couldn't sleep wearing much more than that. The inn was as hot as a kiln; he felt as if he was being baked hard from the inside out.

Crossing to the window, he stared at the backyard. Lightning was nowhere to be seen. Addie insisted the horse wouldn't leave the inn, which was why Lightning lived here and not with her. Evan thought it was a convenient excuse to pawn off the old nag.

Something shuffled behind him, like a shoe against the scratched wood floor. Evan turned, but the room was as empty as his life.

"Matthew?" he whispered.

The wind stilled as if listening for an answer, but

none came. Evan felt a little foolish talking to his sleeping bag.

Adrenaline pumping—both from the sight of an intruder and from a glimpse of Jilly in that satin gown—he paced. He wanted to go three rounds with something, maybe someone. Too bad Dean wasn't here.

As kids he and his brother had fought like cats in a burlap sack. If they'd had to share a room alone, they might have killed each other. But his mother, in her infinite wisdom, had put Aaron in with them. Whenever Dean wanted to throttle Evan, whenever Evan wanted to pummel Dean, Aaron would step in and with a few quiet words make all the anger go away.

Evan fingered the tiny scar on the back of his neck. Well, almost all. He and Dean had gone a few rounds when Aaron wasn't looking.

Since he couldn't beat the crap out of his big brother and take the edge off, a walk around the house would have to do. He'd check the locks—for all the good they did. Anyone who wanted to could climb in through a broken window.

What they needed was a dog, and Evan knew just where to get one. His mom had been trying to foist off doodles since the little yippers had been born. She hadn't had much luck, which meant there were still five at home. When he went to town, he'd call and have one of the dalmatian-poodle mixes sent to him ASAP.

Not a sound came from behind Jilly's door as he went by. At least someone was sleeping.

Evan crept downstairs, rattled the doorknobs, stared at the empty field, the shadowed trees, the dark, gloomy hills. He was so damned lonely he ached with it.

When had he started to search for love in all the wrong places? He couldn't quite recall.

He'd never truly been in love. No one had ever loved him. Well, his mother, but she didn't count. Just don't tell her that.

Everything had been fine until he'd begun to confuse sex with a deeper emotion, to hope that the women who wanted his body just might want him for more than a night, a week, a month. Only when he'd begun to hope had he discovered how foolish his hope had been. So he'd decided to start over where no one knew him as "just a gigolo."

Evan strode into the kitchen and ran smack into Jilly.

She dropped her cup on the floor. The plastic bounced; water splashed all over Evan's feet and half-way up his calves. She slid in the puddle, and Evan grabbed her before she fell.

"What are you doing down here?" he demanded, even as his thumbs skidded over the soft skin at the in-side of her elbow.

"Water," she rasped, her breath brushing his chest.

His body leaped in response, reminding him that he wore nothing but boxers, and she was still wearing that damn silver gown.

He tried to let go, but his fingers only clenched more

tightly. Her head tipped back; her breasts thrust forward; her thighs skimmed against his.

"Evan?" she whispered, and kissed him.

His head told him to run. Sadly, there was another part of him, a little farther south, that was telling him something else.

Touch her. Take her. Make her yours.

Of course sex didn't mean someone belonged to you, no matter how much you might want them to.

He was kissing her back before he knew what he was doing. His hands had a mind of their own, stroking her arms, clasping her shoulders, drawing her close, then closer still.

She didn't know how to kiss, and that in itself was arousing. He was so tired of women who told him what to do and how, wanting so much from him but never giving anything of themselves.

Along with his need for a new life had come a need for a new type of woman. He hadn't thought to find her in Jilly. She was a widow. Why didn't she know how to kiss?

His fingertips skimmed her face. She sighed, and he delved deeper, sampling every inch of her mouth. He loved kissing women. They almost always tasted as good as they smelled.

She went wild in his arms, touching his chest, pressing their bodies together. He drank her desperate cries, stilled her hips with his hands, lifted his mouth from hers and murmured, "Hush."

Her eyes glittered, despite the lack of light. A sheen of sweat shone across her breastbone. He wanted to fill his hands with the soft flesh of her breasts, dip his tongue into the valley between them, lay her back on the kitchen table and—

Whoa!

The thought brought him up short. He'd done that too many times before. He wasn't going to follow the same path. Here he would exert some control over the animal in his pants. He had to. Or lose what was left of himself.

If there'd ever been any self in the first place.

Evan had always been that fifth Luchetti brother. Talk about an heir and a spare; he was so far down the list as to be unnecessary. So he'd gone searching for a way to stand out. He'd found it. Right now "it" was standing out to an embarrassing degree.

"Jilly, I—"

"I don't know what's the matter with me," she interrupted. "You make me feel…things I've never felt before."

He frowned. What was she saying?

"Your body. Your hair. Your hands. All I think about when I close my eyes, and even when I open them, is having those hands all over me." She shook her head. "I can't believe I'm telling you this. I've never wanted…anyone."

"Never?"

"Sex was—is—a chore."

She stood so close he felt her chest rise and fall, the

shadow of a touch, the promise of so much more. He couldn't help himself—he stroked her cheek. She rubbed her face against his hand like a cat.

"Sex isn't a chore, if you do it right."

"Will you…show me how?"

"How?"

"To have sex and like it."

There was an offer no man in his right mind could refuse. A beautiful, single woman begging him to make her come. And he had to say—

"I can't."

A stricken expression passed over her face. "Don't you like…women?"

Her question startled a laugh out of him. "I like them too much. I've had sex with women like a drunk drinks."

"I don't understand."

"I'm never going to have sex without love again."

It was her turn to laugh, but when he didn't join in, the laughter trailed off. "You're serious."

"Very. Sex without love doesn't mean a damn thing."

"I don't want this to mean anything. I just want it not to be awful."

He frowned. That Jilly thought sex was awful upset him. He could be the guy to show her differently. He was so tempted.

Until she shook her head and headed for the door. "Hell, Luchetti, I don't believe in love any more than I believe in ghosts."

CHAPTER SIX

How COULD ANYONE not believe in love?

Evan stood in the darkened kitchen that still smelled like jasmine, and considered what Jilly had said.

She didn't like sex; she didn't believe in love. What had happened to make her so hard-hearted? He wasn't sure he wanted to know.

Except he liked her. A lot. He hated the thought of Jilly living her life without pleasure or love. But what could he do about it?

If he showed her the joy of sex, he'd only be betraying himself. Was that any way to change his life? If he started now with "just one more," how easy would it be the next time to give in?

Evan doused his head with cool water from a jug, then drank a little, too. It didn't help. His skin still prickled with heat, and his body still shouted for fulfillment.

He didn't sleep very well that night, but at least he slept alone.

JILLY TOSSED AND TURNED. Was she losing it? If she couldn't get a young, virile man, one who admitted to sleeping with far too many women, to sleep with her, how was she going to get anyone to marry her? Had she finally gotten too old for the game?

Impossible. Jilly climbed out of her sleeping bag. She had quite a few good years left. She just had to plan better.

Removing a pair of taupe linen slacks and a peach silk shirt, unfortunately long-sleeved, she hunted up the scissors Evan had left in her room. She wouldn't last an hour in this outfit, and since it was bound to be garbage by sundown, she might as well get a jump on the day.

"There," she said, satisfied when she'd cut the slacks off at midthigh and the sleeves at the seam. "That's the way to waste three hundred dollars."

Donning her new Arkansas outfit, Jilly went to the kitchen and tackled the percolator.

This proved a more difficult task. There were so many parts. How did they fit together? Where did the coffee go? Weren't there any filters? Confused, frustrated, caffeine-deprived, Jilly did the best she could, and ended up with brown water full of coffee grounds for her trouble.

Lightning stuck his head into the window above the sink and sniffed at her discarded cup. He snorted, spraying drool into the dregs.

"I agree," she muttered. "I can't make coffee. I can't cook. I can't seduce a man. What *can* I do?"

"Yoo-hoo? Anyone home?"

Jilly glanced at her watch. Not yet 6:00 a.m. Who

was yoo-hooing at this hour? The voice didn't sound like Addie's.

Two young women stood on the back porch. One was short and skinny, very young, the other tall and not so skinny, or so young. They had the same hair color—somewhere between brown and blond, the epitome of dishwater. No make up, bare feet, they sported cutoff jeans and plain dark T-shirts.

"I'm Naomi," the short one said. "This is Ruth. Wilder." The tall woman nodded solemnly.

Naomi handed Jilly a cloth-covered dish. "Welcome to South Fork."

"Thank you. Uh, would you like to come in?"

"Sure." Naomi practically ran Jilly over in her haste to get inside. "We'd have been here sooner, but Ruth likes to take her time in the morning."

"Take her time?" Jilly echoed, wondering when people crawled out of bed if 6:00 a.m. was considered late.

"She loves flowers."

Ruth handed Jilly a handful of wildflowers, as beautiful as any she'd seen arranged by a florist.

"Oh." Jilly caught her breath. "They're lovely."

Ruth smiled and ducked her head.

"She's shy," Naomi explained. "Always has been, even when we were kids. Ma and Pa named me Naomi because they were gettin' up in years when I came along. They knew Ruth would have t' follow me because they couldn't."

At Jilly's frown, Naomi spread her hands. "Book of

Ruth? Wither though goest. Ruth followed Naomi to Bethlehem. My Ruth just follows me everywhere."

The two women beamed at each other with obvious affection.

"You're…sisters?" Jilly guessed. Ruth appeared old enough to be Naomi's mother, hence the lengthy, biblical explanation.

"Yep. Though you couldn't tell it by lookin' at us, could ya? Ruth here takes after our ma, and I take after our pa."

Jilly lifted an eyebrow. She'd like to meet their parents, if only to see if they resembled Jack Sprat and his wife.

"Have a seat," she offered.

They did, then stared at her expectantly.

"Oh!" She whipped the top off the gift, uncovering fresh doughnuts still warm from the…oven? Stove? Microwave? How did one make doughnuts, anyway? It was as much a mystery to Jilly as the coffeepot.

She eyed the contraption balefully. "I'd offer you coffee, but I can't seem to figure this thing out. It's more complicated than a NASA spacecraft."

Naomi's face creased in confusion. "Where are you from?"

Jilly thought there might be an insult in there somewhere, but since she wasn't sure, she decided to just answer the question.

"California." Suddenly she realized she hadn't shared her name. "I'm Jillian Hart." She offered her hand. "Call me Jilly."

Naomi's handshake was as butterfly gentle as Ruth's

was All-Star Wrestling rough. But their smiles were welcoming and their friendliness seemed genuine. Jilly didn't know what to make of them.

"The brothers said you just got into town."

"Brothers? Oh, Larry, Darrell and his other brother, Darrell."

"Who?"

"Never mind." Classic television humor was obviously lost here.

"Everything all right so far?"

"No running water, no lights, no bed. But other than that—"

"Anything strange happen?"

Jilly looked up sharply. "Strange how?"

The sisters exchanged glances. Ruth appeared nervous. When a board creaked upstairs, she practically jumped out of her chair.

"You're asking about the ghost?" Jilly asked.

"There's more than one."

"I don't believe in the first one, and you expect me to believe there's a convention?"

Naomi shrugged. "No one's ever stayed here long. They up and leave—usually in the middle of the night. Some even say folks don't leave, they just disappear."

"I suppose a few of the travelers passed away in the rooms and their spirits never left. *Wooo*." Jilly made a spooky sound and wiggled her fingers.

"Travelers?" Naomi repeated. "What are you talking about?"

"This was a stage stop."

"That was forever ago. I suspect there are a few ha'nts from then, but mostly they're from the years Miss Dixie owned the place."

"Miss Dixie? Who was she?"

Ruth and Naomi exchanged glances again.

"What?" Jilly pressed. "You're acting like the place was a whorehouse."

Ruth choked.

Naomi's eyes widened. "How'd you know that?"

"It was?"

Naomi nodded. "Busiest place in the county. Until they ran Miss Dixie out on a rail."

"Because she was a..." Jilly wasn't sure how to say it politely.

"Madam," Naomi finished.

Jilly hadn't heard it put quite like that since Heidi Fleiss, but the title was nicer than most. She nodded.

"Well, they didn't actually run her out because of her business."

"Why else?"

"Miss Dixie employed colored folks to clean and serve and such."

"And they—whoever *they* are—ran her out because of that?"

"No. Miss Dixie didn't want her people walking home after she closed up. Especially during the dark of the moon. Witches and such are out then. Dangerous times."

Jilly opened her mouth to protest, then shut it again. What would be the point?

"Whenever her people worked past sundown, when the moon was hid, she'd let them sleep in the kitchen, then go home in the daylight."

"And this was a problem?"

"The Klan don't take to colored folks sleeping in the same place as white folks."

She should have known "they" were the Klan. Who else?

"What year was this?" she asked.

"Sixty-three."

"The ghost of Miss Dixie has been here for over a hundred and fifty years?"

"*Nineteen* sixty-three," Naomi clarified.

Jilly should have been surprised that the Klan was running people out of town in 1963, but she wasn't. She didn't bother to address the concept of a bordello in that era.

"Isn't that right, Ruth?"

Ruth shrugged.

"You two weren't even born then," Jilly pointed out.

"We hear stories. Our ma was Miss Dixie's niece."

"Where did Miss Dixie go when she left here?"

"Las Vegas."

Where madam-hood was legal. Good choice.

"Of course she came back," Naomi offered. "Right before she died, and then she stayed."

Jilly rubbed her forehead. "Miss Dixie is floating around my inn?"

"So they say, though I ain't never seen her myself."

"You seen any other ghosts?"

"Sure. Haven't you?"

Jilly considered the shadow at the window last night. An intruder, not a ghost, she was certain. The belief didn't soothe her nerves any.

"No." She headed for the coffeepot. "I haven't seen a thing."

"Place is full of ha'nts. Civil War soldiers, Miss Dixie, some of her gals, a few customers who expired under dubious circumstances. Matthew, of course."

"Things must be awfully busy in another dimension."

Jilly continued to fiddle with the coffeepot, but the thing remained a mystery.

"Here, let me." With deft movements, Naomi cleaned, then realigned all the movable parts.

"The grounds go in here." She demonstrated. "If you put them in the water, they just make a mess."

"Oh," Jilly mumbled.

Could she feel more stupid?

"Morning." Evan's voice caused heat to flood her cheeks.

She spun around and, if possible, blushed a deeper shade of crimson. His hair was loose and tumbled, the sight raising memories of a dream where she'd filled her hands with the dark strands, then buried her face in their softness.

"Hey, Evan," Naomi chirped. "You look tired. Didn't you sleep good?"

He glanced at Jilly, then quickly away. How on earth were they going to live in the same house after she'd thrown herself at him and he'd tossed her right back?

"You know each other?" Jilly asked.

"The girls have been keeping me in doughnuts since I got here. They're the best ever made."

Ruth giggled. The sound, coming from such a large woman, nearly made Jilly laugh herself. But she didn't want to hurt Ruth's feelings, even though the idea of her and Naomi bringing Evan doughnuts every morning at six, seeing him all warm and tousled before she'd ever known him, caused an odd burning sensation between her chest and belly. She must be hungrier than she'd thought.

The sisters brought Evan doughnuts; Addie brought him bread and preserves. How many other women brought food? And why did they feel the need to feed the man? Jilly felt no such need—probably because she felt so many others.

"Coffee's ready." Naomi poured three cups and handed them to the women. She obviously knew Evan didn't drink the stuff.

Jilly's stomach flared hotter, and she doused the flame with a huge, scalding sip, followed by a doughnut shooter.

Evan was right. They were the best doughnuts she'd ever tasted.

"Jilly's from California."

"So I hear." Evan snagged another doughnut. Where did he put them all?

"I didn't know anyone could be *from* California. Thought people just moved there. To be movie stars."

Jilly smiled. "California's the third largest state by area, but the first in population. Percentage wise, not very many people are in the movie business."

"Bright lights, big city." Naomi sighed. "I bet you can do just about anything you want there."

"If you've got the money," Jilly agreed. "What do you and your sister do?"

"Live with Ma and Pa."

Jilly couldn't imagine cohabiting with her mother. But then Genevieve was not an easy woman. A fact her husbands never discovered until too late.

"Once we find a husband of our own…" Naomi elbowed Ruth, who smiled brightly at Evan. He smiled back and took another doughnut. "Then we can move to a house of our own, too."

"Ever consider moving to another town?"

Ruth's eyes widened, and she shook her head frantically.

"Ruth loves it here," Naomi said, "and what would Ma and Pa do without us to help on the farm?"

"What'll they do when you marry?" Jilly asked.

"Same thing they do now, but with more help. At least one, maybe even both of us, will take over the place with our man. Your pa's a farmer, right, Evan?"

Naomi kicked her sister in the foot. Ruth obediently batted her eyes in his direction, but Evan wasn't paying attention. He was too busy with his doughnut.

"Dairy farmer," he said, once he'd swallowed.

"You plan to go back and farm, too?"

"Not me. There are five Luchetti brothers. I was never suited to cow-sitting. That's Dean."

The Wilder sisters exchanged glances. They were up to something, and Jilly knew what.

"Do you have boyfriends?" she asked.

Ruth snorted. Naomi shifted her shoulders and looked away. "I can't."

"Why not?"

"Oldest daughter has to marry first, Pa says. It's our way." Naomi brushed sugar off her hands. "We'd best get on home or Ma will have our hide. Gotta plant cucumbers in Gemini."

Jilly hadn't known that planting seeds was decided by the signs of the zodiac, but since she'd never planted anything, not even a flower, she'd take their word for it.

The women filed toward the door. Naomi glanced back. "Now that you're here, Jilly, I guess Evan won't need us to bring him breakfast."

"I wouldn't say that," Jilly muttered.

Though she didn't care for the way they stared at Evan, she didn't know how to cook any more than she knew how to plant.

"We'll stop by in a few days, see how you're getting on. What are you gonna do here, Jilly?"

"I, uh…" She wasn't quite sure. "Supervise?"

"You have any other clothes?" Naomi asked.

What was it with people and her clothes? She hadn't

fielded so many questions about them since she'd modeled the spring line for the League of Women Voters luncheon.

"Not really," she said. "I'll make do."

"Huh." Without further comment Naomi left, Ruth trailing behind her.

"Boy, have they got plans for you," Jilly murmured.

"What are you talking about?"

She hadn't meant to speak out loud, but now that she had...

"Ruth has to marry first. Husband takes over the farm. Your dad's a farmer. In my book, one plus one equals you married to Ruth."

Evan made a sound of exasperation. "You're nuts."

"I'm a woman. I know these things."

He stared at the door through which the sisters had disappeared. "I escaped from one farm. I'm not going to shackle myself to another."

"Escaped?"

"Oh, yeah. I did my time."

"You make the place sound like a prison."

"For me it was."

EVAN HEADED INTO TOWN for supplies. Not only did he need several items in order to get all the electricity up and running, he needed to get away from Jilly.

Despite a night spent telling himself they could be nothing more than partners, the first sight of her that morning had made his body jolt with awareness.

Talking about the family farm had taken care of any happy thoughts in a heartbeat. He'd lived there for twenty-nine years. He'd wanted to get away for twenty-five of them.

His father had never understood him. He'd always considered Evan lazy because he didn't work as fast as everyone else. John Luchetti loathed Evan's long hair, his love of women and his take-it-or-leave-it attitude toward the farm that was John's life.

Evan wanted so much more. Too bad he didn't know what the more was that he wanted.

He'd never felt welcome anywhere but South Fork. The hills spoke to him. The pace here was his pace. Slow and steady—do the job right or don't do it at all.

He didn't want to leave, but how was he going to stay? It wasn't as if they had a shortage of carpenters in this neck of Arkansas. They didn't even need one.

He could marry Ruth, or Naomi, or any of the other farm girls—if he wanted the life he'd already left.

"I'll pass," he muttered as he shut off the engine and climbed out of his truck in front of the general store.

The brothers Seitz were playing checkers, as they did every day. Evan wasn't sure what they lived on, since he'd never heard of them working. His father would have a stroke if he met them.

"How's it going at your place?" Barry asked, not even looking up from the board.

"Except for Jilly nearly drowning in the creek, not bad. You guys forget something the other day?"

All three frowned, then shook their heads.

Evan sighed. What was the point? The sign was up now. And Jilly knew better than to take the wrong trail even without it.

"So how long till you sell the place?" Barry asked.

"Too long."

"Suppose you could use extra hands out there."

"Can't afford them," he said quickly. "You fellas know where there's a pay phone?"

"None 'round here. But you can use the phone inside. Just leave fifty cents on the counter. Or a few dollars if'n it's long distance."

Evan nodded his thanks and left the brothers to their game, which appeared to be the same one he'd observed the last time he'd been to town. He'd never seen any of them play; they just talked about it.

"If I move that black 'un you'll have t' crown me," Barry said.

"I'll crown ye all right," Jerry informed him. "Upside the head if you move that piece."

Evan found himself smiling. Brothers were the same everywhere. No matter their age, race or zip code, they liked to fight just for the sake of fighting. Habits begun in the cradle died hard.

He slapped five dollars onto the counter and grabbed the receiver. Dialing long distance on a rotary telephone took awhile, but within minutes the phone rang, then was picked up, in Gainsville.

"Yeah?"

"Dean. Pal. Brother. Friend."

"What the hell do you want?"

Just because Dean had discovered the nature of some of his problems lay in undiagnosed ADHD hadn't made him a more cheery fellow.

"A doodle."

"Done. Where should I send it?"

"Arkansas."

"Still? Thought you'd be out of there by now. Who goes to Arkansas on purpose?"

"You'd be surprised, flatlander," he said, using the derogatory nickname fashioned by those north of the Wisconsin-Illinois border for all those south of it.

"Watch it. I might come down there and flatten you."

"As if you could."

Evan had been taller than any of his brothers before his sixteenth birthday, which had put a stop to a lot of the teasing but, amazingly, none of the wrestling.

"You're lucky I didn't call you a FIB," Evan sneered.

The acronym consisted of more swear words than not, and had caused more fistfights at interstate sports events than most people knew about.

"If you had, I'd know you were no longer allowed to step foot in the Land of Lincoln. When you coming home?"

Never whispered through his head. He missed his mother, his sister, his niece. But everyone else? Not so much.

"Could be a while."

Dean grunted. "Mom'll be pissed."

"Isn't she always?"

"Pretty much. She's still ticked that Colin got married on the sly. Although from the size of his wife's belly when we met her, he didn't have a moment to lose."

That was Dean. Ever ready with the embarrassing tidbits.

"Any other news?"

"Aaron's wife isn't supposed to pop until spring."

And ever ready with the graphic comments.

"Mom and Dad are fine," Dean continued. "Mom still explodes over nothing. Menopause is a bitch. Thank God I'm not a woman."

"Thank God," Evan echoed. The idea of his cranky brother as a female was frightening for more reasons than one.

"Dad still sticks his nose into the farm business more than I'd like, but he helps a lot with Tim."

A few years back their father had decided to go into semiretirement. He'd bought a robotic milking system that made running a dairy farm a lot easier, then turned the place over to Dean. Theoretically. He and Evan's mom still lived in the main house, while Dean and Tim had moved into the threshers' cottage on the far side of the cornfield the instant Evan had left it.

Tim, an orphan brought home by Aaron's daughter, had bonded to Dean and Dean to him. An amazing feat since Dean didn't like anything but cows. From what Evan had seen on his few visits home, Tim and Dean were so alike it was spooky. Maybe, as Aaron was always saying, everything did happen for a reason. Tim coming into Dean's life had certainly solved a whole lot of problems for both of them.

"Mom's getting real sick of women calling. Some of them have even showed up on the porch asking for you."

"Tell everyone I died."

Dean snorted. "Then there'd be a wake such as Gainsville's never seen. Squalling females, catfights— Wait a minute, maybe that's not a bad idea."

His brother's words startled a laugh out of Evan. "Catfight at a funeral. Only you would think that's funny."

"I never said anything about funny, just…interesting."

"What you find interesting has always been… interesting."

"Bite me. Where you want me to ship this doodle?"

"The South Fork Inn. South Fork, Arkansas."

"You wanna be a little more specific?"

"I don't think there is anything more specific. Believe me, you send it to South Fork, it'll get to me and Jilly."

"Whoa! Jilly? No wonder you don't want to come home."

"It's not what you think."

"How do you know what I'm thinking?"

"Something pornographic, no doubt."

"Give me a break. I haven't had sex in…I forget."

"No wonder you're so crabby," Evan muttered.

"Hey, just because I don't screw anything in a skirt doesn't mean I'm…"

"What?"

"Pathetic," he murmured.

Evan heard something in his brother's voice that worried him. "I never said you were."

"You'd be the only one."

"Something going on there you wanna tell me about?"

"Not in this lifetime, Romeo."

Evan wasn't surprised at his brother's refusal to share. Dean had been pals with no one in his life except Brian Riley, Kim's husband.

Even their friendship had been strained when Brian had gotten Kim pregnant not once, but twice. Dean had kicked Brian's ass. Evan still wanted to, but he had a feeling Kim might just kick him back. She was little, but she was mean. Having five older brothers did that to a girl.

"Any word from Bobby?" Evan asked.

Dean's sigh told him the answer even before Dean did. "None. Every time the phone rings or someone knocks on the door, Mom jumps a mile. Then, when it's just one of your bimbos…well, let's just say that if you ever do come home, I'd bring your own woman. The ones around here no longer have any heads. Mom bit them off. And women without heads? I wouldn't recommend them."

"Advice I didn't need."

"So who's Jilly?"

"My new partner."

"Thought you said there was nothing going on."

"There isn't. She owns the inn." Quickly he told Dean about Henry, the lack of funds, the sudden partnership. He left out the shape of Jillian's legs, the scent of her hair, the taste of her lips.

"Can I meet her?"

"Hell, no!" Evan snapped before he could stop himself.

Dean might be a pain in the ass, but he was a very handsome pain. The best-looking Luchetti of them all, except for Kim. Dean's personality, or lack thereof, was the only reason he was still alone. Evan wondered if there was a woman alive who could put up with Dean's sarcastic nature, but he didn't plan to find out with Jilly.

His brother snickered. "Nothing going on? Right."

"Really. She isn't interested."

"In you? Oh. Lesbian."

Evan choked. "No. Not by a long shot."

"Then what's the problem?"

Evan glanced around the general store. No one there but him and Old Man Hillburn, who was as deaf as Jerry Seitz—and he didn't have a hearing aid. Nevertheless, Evan turned away and lowered his voice. "She wants sex. I want love."

"You're a moron."

"I've been called worse."

"Join the club."

Evan frowned at the thought of anyone calling his brother worse than a moron. Evan could call him that, but no one else had better try it.

"Listen, Einstein, take what you can get while you can get it. Advice from a man who doesn't get any."

"Doesn't get any what, Daddy?"

The childish voice came through the phone line so clear, Evan started.

"Shit!" Dean cursed. "Get off the extension, Tim. How long have you been on?"

"Since 'you're a moron.' You owe me a quarter. You said the S word."

The line clicked, although Evan swore he could still hear furtive breathing.

"Dean?"

"Sorry. I'm just glad he didn't hear *lesbian*. I really don't want to explain that today."

"The S word?"

"I'm trying to stop swearing." Evan snickered. "And smoking."

"Wow. You really do love the kid."

"Yeah. He's probably the best thing that ever happened to me. Unconditional love is pretty cool."

"Isn't that something you get from dogs?"

"And kids. Until they figure out you aren't Superman. Let's hope Tim never does." Dean drew in a deep breath. "Now here's some advice, bro."

Evan waited, expecting pearls of wisdom about little boys and forever love. He should have known better.

"This Jilly? I'd nail her before she changes her mind."

CHAPTER SEVEN

JILLY, WHO HADN'T had a decent night's sleep since leaving her beach house, drifted off while waiting for Evan to return from town.

She was somewhat miffed that he'd left a note and taken off while she was in the creek. Then again, the less time they spent together the better. Just because he wanted something from her she couldn't give didn't make her want him any less. On the contrary, she only seemed to want him more.

A thud downstairs awakened her. The giggles brought Jilly out of her sleeping bag and to the window. She watched Naomi, followed by Ruth, scurry across the pasture. What were they up to?

Clothes started flying off the porch and scattering in every direction. Jilly glanced at her suitcase, still sitting on the floor in her room, and still filled with useless items she might as well sell at the nearest flea market. So whose things was Lightning tossing about this time?

Jilly hurried downstairs. The horse stood with his front feet on the bottom porch step. Considering the condition of the other three, it was a miracle he hadn't fallen through. His neck stretched, his lips nibbled.

"Freeze," she ordered.

Lightning's head swung in her direction. Green floral material dangled from his mouth.

"What do you think you're doing?"

He tossed his nose in the air, and the skirt flew ten feet, fluttering down to cover a patch of purple wildflowers.

"Okay, stupid question. *Why* are you doing that?"

A better question might be why was she talking to a horse? The only answer: because there was no one else.

Jilly wasn't used to being alone. She couldn't recall when she had been for more than a minute. Her mother had watched her like a hawk, then sent her to private schools where every hour was scheduled; no one was allowed to wander.

Once she'd married, her purpose had been to assuage loneliness. If her husband was off amusing himself, which wasn't often, since Jilly was the main amusement, she was surrounded by servants or shopkeepers or salon personnel.

She'd always dreamed of free time spent by herself. Now she had some, and she wasn't sure what to do. The inn was too quiet. She wanted to turn on some music or a television to break up the silence, but her only source of sound stood in front of her with his nose in a box of clothes.

"Get out of there," she ordered.

Lightning actually obeyed, moving away from the porch and into the pasture, managing as he went by to step on every piece of clothing he'd tossed in the grass. What was wrong with that horse?

Jilly picked up the mangled items then peeked into the box. A jumble of shorts, T-shirts, skirts and blouses filled the space. A note was taped to the side: "For Jilly."

She frowned. Why had Ruth and Naomi brought her secondhand clothes? She glanced down at her outfit. The linen had frayed; her top was not made for this climate. She really did need clothes more appropriate to Arkansas.

Lifting a worn gray tank top and a pair of cutoff jeans, Jilly crinkled her nose in distaste. She remembered too well wearing other people's clothes. Once Genevieve had gotten them off the streets, Jilly had never worn hand-me-downs again.

She fingered the denim, soft from countless washings. She could keep her pride and buy other things, but in truth, the money was better spent on the inn.

Tilting her chin, she marched inside and changed. The shorts were short; the shirt clung like Lycra. She resembled Ellie Mae Clampett a little more than she wanted to. But she was comfortable, cool, and she didn't have to worry about what Lightning pushed her into today.

Unfortunately, there were no shoes in the box. At least she still had her lime-green tennis shoes.

Or thought she did. When she went searching for them, they were gone.

"Maybe they're on the porch." She tromped first to the back, then to the front. No shoes in sight.

The day was heating up. If there was a thermometer, it would probably read ninety. She didn't need shoes. No one else wore them around here.

However, her chipped toenail polish was another matter. Just because she was short on funds didn't mean she had to walk around looking like a cretin. Jilly found her travel bottle of polish remover and scrubbed every last bit of Do Me Red from both her fingers and her toes.

Sitting back, she stared at her naked nails. Why did she feel as if her last link to the real world was gone?

"Stupid." Jilly capped the polish remover, then put it away. "If I want to go…somewhere, I only have to—" She broke off.

Walk. Barefoot.

"I could call…"

No one's name came to mind, even if her cell phone worked, or there was anything resembling a phone at the inn.

Jilly scowled at her toes, glared at her fingers, missing Do Me Red more than she could say.

"Too late now," she muttered, and got to her feet.

She strolled through the house, wincing whenever her sole crunched another bit of drywall or a discarded nail. She tried to remember if her tetanus shot was up to date.

"Do those things last five years or ten?"

She'd have to ask Evan. If he ever came back. She wouldn't blame him if he left her here to rot with the house.

He no doubt had women throwing themselves at him wherever he went. He'd probably OD'd on sex before he turned twenty-one.

Yet she'd never met a man who'd turn down a no-strings-attached night of passion. Maybe because she hadn't met the right man.

She pushed the disturbing thought aside and grabbed an old, broken door. When she tried to drag it outside, Jilly wound up with splinters in both palms and a scraped shin when she dropped the thing and the rough end slid down her leg. She barely managed to yank her foot out of the way before the door slammed to the floor.

The small earthquake made by the accident caused more boards to fall. Dust rained all around her and an old light fixture fell, smashing into a thousand pieces. She stared at her bare feet, then tiptoed toward the back door and slipped outside.

"I'm not going to be any help at all."

Why that upset her, Jilly wasn't quite sure. She wasn't meant for physical labor, she was meant for…unimportant things.

The thought, one she'd never had before, disturbed her. What *was* she good for? She'd majored in art history at college, with a minor in communications. Basically, she could talk about paintings done by dead people.

Inside the inn something else shattered. A large, heavy, unknown object shifted and fell.

Jilly glanced warily around. She could talk about dead people, she'd just never talked *to* them, and she didn't want to.

She headed across the yard. She hadn't gone ten feet when Lightning fell into step beside her. "If you knock me down again, so help me I'll…" She looked at him. He cocked his head, waiting. "I don't know, but something bad."

He pressed his nose to the center of Jilly's chest and shoved, gently this time, leaving a big, nose-shaped wet spot on her shirt. However, it didn't look that bad on this garment. In fact, she could swear the mark blended right in.

Jilly reached the edge of the pasture. Just past a tiny grove of trees, at the bottom of a hill, stood a cabin. Lightning pushed her from behind, harder this time, and she took several bumbling steps down the incline.

"Must be Addie's house."

Lightning lifted, then lowered his head, blowing air through loose lips. Jilly took that as a yes.

A quick glance at the inn made her decision easy. The place appeared deserted, lonely, haunted.

"How can it be deserted *and* haunted?"

This talking to herself really had to stop. Pretty soon she'd start answering.

Jilly headed down the hill, but Lightning didn't follow.

"Come on." She beckoned, whistled, clapped her hands. He presented her with his huge behind, lifted his tail and—

"All right, all right. I get the message." Jilly took off before she smelled more than flowers on the wind.

THERE WAS A BOX of women's clothes on the porch when Evan arrived home. Since it was marked "For Jilly" he carried it inside, calling her name. All he heard was the echo of his own voice.

He ruffled through the items, which appeared to be used. Evan had a lot of experience with used clothes. Before he'd turned sixteen he doubted he'd worn anything new. Of course, once he'd outgrown all his brothers, the tide had turned.

Holding up an out-of-date floral skirt, he found the imprint of a horseshoe in the center. "Uh-oh," he muttered. "Lightning strikes again."

He was glad he hadn't been around while Jilly was picking up the mess the horse had made. He checked outside, but Lightning was nowhere in sight and neither was Jilly. Maybe she'd ridden him somewhere.

Evan laughed at the thought of Jilly riding the sway-backed nag. He could see her on an English saddle, in full jumping regalia—boots, crop, top hat with a chiffon scarf.

When the image of her wearing nothing but those

three things caused him to smile dopily, he smacked himself in the head and carried the box to her room.

Someone, most likely Ruth and Naomi, maybe Addie, had gone through the church charity box and brought Jilly some clothes. He wondered how she was going to feel about that. He'd have to make sure she didn't hurt anyone's feelings when she gave them back.

A thump, followed by a crash downstairs, made him tense. Recalling last night's escapade with the disappearing intruder, he hurried in the direction of the sound, grabbing a good-size stick on the way.

Several voices spilled from the kitchen. Maybe he should hightail it to town, as he'd advised Jilly to do last night.

"I don't care if ye are older than me, I get the ham, you get the turkey."

Evan lowered the stick and stepped into the room. The Seitz brothers were helping themselves to his lunch meat. He glanced at his watch: 10:00 a.m.

"Early dinner, boys?"

Barry turned, beaming at Evan sans teeth. "We thought we'd eat before we got started. Saves time."

"Started what?"

"Work. You said you could use extra hands." Barry wiggled gnarled, arthritic fingers. "We got six."

Help like theirs he didn't need, but then again…if he was watching them, supervising them, what harm could they do?

"How did you guys get here?"

"Hid in the flatbed of your truck."

"Why didn't you just ask for a ride?"

"We stopped doin' that the last time we got turned down. If we ask, we never git."

The brothers had never learned to drive, so they bummed rides from everyone in town. Evan suspected they'd worn out their welcome half a century ago.

Larry and Jerry continued to make sandwiches. Actually, Jerry did, since Larry had lost his glasses again. How on earth was he going to pound a nail? The very thought made Evan wince.

"Don't worry about payin'," Barry continued. "We got nothin' but time. You give us food, and we're your men."

Evan eyed the size of their sandwiches. It might be cheaper to pay them.

"Any of you ever do any carpentry?" At Barry's negative head shake, he continued, "Plumbing? Electric? Drywall? Painting?"

"Painting!" Barry exclaimed.

Evan smiled. They had a winner.

"I always wanted to try that," the old man continued. "I could have done better paintings than that Picasso fella. I at least know where a person's head is supposed to go."

Evan sighed, scratched his nose, shrugged.

They were better than nothing.

A PLETHORA OF SOUNDS greeted Jilly as she approached Addie's cabin. Concentrating, she separated them into mewling, snorting, barking. She turned the corner and walked into a remake of *Dr. Dolittle*.

Addie stood in the middle of her yard surrounded by cats and kittens, several dogs, ten chickens and a pig that seemed to really, really love her boots.

One of the dogs spotted Jilly and started baying as if he'd seen the moon. Floppy ears, short legs, loud mouth—he'd be a basset hound if his fur wasn't the shade and length of a golden retriever's.

Glancing up, Addie smiled and made her way out of the animal throng. One of the kittens was stuck like a burr to her skirt and swayed with her movements, mewling pathetically all the way.

"Jilly, glad t' see ye. Got a few things t' do yet. Have a seat." She kicked an old cane-backed chair in Jilly's direction, pried the kitten off her skirt and deposited it on the pig's back. "Ye've caught me on critter day."

"You're a vet *and* a doctor?"

"I'm a healer. Don't make no never mind to me if my patients have fur or not."

She seized the pig's snout, yanked it open and peered inside. "Toothache," she pronounced, and grabbed a pair of pliers.

Jilly decided she really didn't want to see the rest. She turned her head and came nose to nose with an…

"Opossum!" she shrieked, and jumped off the chair.

Her cry was drowned out by the pig's squeal. When she glanced that way, all she saw was his tail disappearing into the brush, kitten still attached to his back.

Addie brushed her hands together. "He should be home in no time."

"He'll go home? Like a dog?"

"Pigs'r smarter than dogs, and Wilbur is smarter than most pigs. That's why Mack brung him over. Easier to make ham than extract a sore tooth from a pig. But Wilbur isn't just any pig. He's a pet."

"Does he stay in the house?"

"Only when it storms. He's gun-shy."

Jilly didn't know what to make of that statement. What a storm had to do with a gun, and why a pig would be shy of them was beyond her attention span for this morning.

"What about the kitten? Will he come back?"

"He belongs to Wilbur. Mom cat got hit by a car. Wilbur took the babies as his own."

"Pigs do that?"

"I never seen nothin' like it before. But then, like I said, Wilbur's kind of special."

Something furry sidled along Jilly's bare ankle. She leaped back, afraid it was the friendly opossum. His tail grossed her out. Instead, a baby raccoon started playing with her toes.

"Aw," she said. "How cute."

"He's yours."

"What? Me? No. I—I never had a—"

"Raccoon? They ain't hard to keep. Friendly critters. Like to cuddle and purr."

"Purr?"

"Yep. They make all sorts of sounds. And they're loyal. I'd take a coon over a squirrel any day. Squirrels are flighty. Not much upstairs. Coons are smart as dogs. Just need to learn 'em to stay off the main road. Folks sometimes run over 'em on purpose."

"I was going to say I'd never had a pet," Jilly muttered, inching away from the insistent raccoon.

"No pet? Where'd you live, girl? Timbuktu?"

"My mother didn't like animals."

Addie frowned. "How could anyone not like animals?"

"You'd be surprised." Sometimes Jilly had wondered if her mother even liked her.

"Now that you're here, let's get at it."

"At what?"

"Dosin' the chickens. I left 'em till last so's you could help."

"How did you know I was coming?"

"I just knew."

Well, what did she expect from a woman who believed in ghosts? Jilly threw up her hands in defeat. "What would you like me to do?"

"Hold the chickens while I pour the dose down their beaks."

Jilly eyed the filthy chickens scratching in the dirt. They smelled worse than…anything she'd ever smelled. "How about if you hold the chickens?"

Addie shrugged. "Suit yerself. That's the best part."

The rest of the morning and half the afternoon passed

in a flurry of motion. After dosing the chickens, they gave the dogs a flea bath, although Jilly really didn't see the point as the animals took off through the woods immediately after. Wasn't that where they got the fleas in the first place?

Jilly thanked her lucky stars for the clothes Naomi and Ruth had brought. Most everything she spilled blended right into the gray shirt, and the cutoffs could be easily washed. Not having shoes worked quite well, too, since anything she stepped in was dissolved with a bucket of water from the pond.

She worked so hard, strands of hair came loose from the rubber band. She tucked them behind her ears and kept on going.

The cats needed deworming. The opossum had intestinal troubles.

"I thought opossums were for eating," Jilly muttered as she tried to dump tonic into the frantically slashing snout of the animal Addie referred to as Peter.

"Shh." Addie cupped her hands over little opossum ears. "He'll hear you."

Jilly rolled her eyes.

"No one really eats—" Addie gave Peter a pointed glance "—them. Anymore."

"Who does Peter belong to?" Jilly asked.

"Me."

"You have a pet opossum?"

"Why not? He's quiet. Sleeps all day, carouses all night. Reminds of me of Matthew. How's he doin'?"

"Pretty fine for a dead guy."

"Death is only the beginning, Jilly."

Jilly held up the empty bottle of tonic. "Looks like the end to me."

"Don't make light of what you don't understand."

"Sorry." She met the older woman's eyes. "You're right."

Addie gave a satisfied nod. "Where'd that coon get to?"

Jilly glanced down and found the adorable bandit asleep on her foot. Addie followed her gaze and grunted. "Animals sure take a shine to you. Amazing, since you weren't around 'em much."

"They like me?"

"Peter's fussy about his friends. Not everyone could get that tonic in 'im. And Zorro don't hold with strangers."

Jilly took in the baby raccoon's mask and chuckled.

"Lightning isn't easy to get along with, either. He's old. Decrepit. Cranky."

"I'll say. He's tossed my clothes around the pasture twice."

"Sign of affection in a horse."

"He shoved me off the cliff and into the creek."

Addie frowned. "Couldn't have. Trail's too narrow."

"Well, somebody shoved me."

"Or some*thing*."

"Don't start that again. How could a ghost push me?"

Addie shrugged. "Place is full of ha'nts. You wonder why the inn's been empty for so long? Now you know. Most folks can't stomach all the company."

"I still don't believe in ghosts." When Addie opened her mouth to reply, Jilly added, "I know. I will."

She glanced around the yard. Peter lay asleep under the chair, kittens scampering after his tail. Zorro had waddled off and was now washing his hands in the rain barrel. While the scene should resemble wildlife run amok, everything looked just right. Jilly felt an odd tug in the vicinity of her heart.

"You got plans for tomorrow?"

Jilly thought about her pathetic attempt at cleaning up the inn. She'd broken more than she'd fixed. She was a liability, not an asset. Nevertheless, if Evan needed her, she'd have to stay.

"I'm not sure," she answered.

"If you can spare some time, I can use the help."

"All right."

"Hold on. Let me get your pay."

"Pay?"

"You don't think I'd let you work for free, do ya?"

Jilly shrugged. Though she hated to take anything from Addie, she could use every penny she could get.

"Here." Addie dumped a black kitten into her arms. "Enjoy."

CHAPTER EIGHT

WHEN EVAN LOOKED back on that first afternoon with the Seitz brothers, he would forever remember it as *The Three Stooges Go to Contractor School.*

He'd planned to finish the electricity. Between pulling Barry out of a hole in the floor and Larry out of a pile of lumber he'd knocked over, plus yanking a bucket off Jerry's foot, Evan got very little accomplished.

The only thing the brothers were any good at was cleaning up the messes they made. Like the window Barry broke when he put the broomstick through it, and the hole in the wall from Jerry's fist after he stubbed his toe on Larry.

With a headache from the sound of their bickering pulsing behind his eyes, Evan snapped, "That's it! Barry, you come with me. Jerry, clean the kitchen. Larry, sweep the parlor. Nobody works together in the same room anymore. Got it?"

Divide and conquer had been one of his mother's favorite parenting techniques.

By midafternoon, they nearly had the electricity up and running. Barry was a decent assistant. His not knowing much meant he followed instructions without question. Though the old man couldn't work alone and lessen the workload by half, he wasn't expecting to be paid, either. A lot could be forgiven of free labor.

Barry started to fade around 4:00 p.m., but he kept going. The thuds and mumbles from downstairs stopped, which made Evan nervous.

"Let's take a break," he suggested.

"If you really have to," Barry managed to answer, limping toward the stairs.

Evan followed him down to the first floor. "Go on out where it's cool." He indicated the front porch—where he could see Larry and Jerry collapsed in two chairs—with a jerk of his head. "I'll get us all a beer."

Barry's eyes lit up at the word, and his step became more spry as he headed for the door.

The kitchen was immaculate, as was the living room. Evan glanced through the back window. The debris had been stacked in a perfect pile next to his pickup. Maybe the brothers weren't so useless, after all.

He grabbed a six-pack from the cooler and joined the Seitzes, passing out the beer and taking a seat on the top step of the porch.

Lightning appeared, nuzzling first his arm, then nibbling at the top of a spare can.

"I don't think so." Evan whipped the beer out of harm's way. "I plan on drinking those, and I don't need horse germs, thanks."

Lightning lifted his head and sneezed in Evan's face,

then turned and walked away with as much dignity as an ancient, swaybacked nag could muster.

"Guess he told you," Barry said.

"I guess." Evan lifted his T-shirt and wiped his nose. "Wait a minute. There's Lightning. Where's Jilly?"

"Haven't seen her all day," Larry replied, squinting owlishly around the empty field.

Not that Larry would see her even if she stood right in front of him. His glasses were forever perched on top of his shiny bald head. Nevertheless, Evan began to worry.

"When did the horse show up?"

"Not sure. He wasn't here when we came, then *bam*, there he was."

Also not very informative when coming from Larry.

An unpleasant thought filled Evan's mind. He jumped to his feet and ran to the creek, but she wasn't there. He even walked downstream, terrified he'd find her body snagged on a log or under a rock. When he didn't, his fear increased. Maybe she'd been swept all the way to New Orleans. Why hadn't he gone looking for Jilly as soon as he'd discovered her missing?

Because he wasn't used to worrying about anyone but himself. And wasn't that sad?

He ran up the hill and into the house, then stood there helplessly. There wasn't any phone.

He'd been enjoying the quiet. No telemarketers, no calls from his mother or girls he no longer wanted to see. Suddenly the lack of a phone wasn't enjoyable, it was downright life threatening.

Evan raced to the front door, leaped off the porch and came to a screeching halt in the yard.

"There she is," Barry murmured.

The hush in his voice, the reverence, seemed to be felt by all of them as Jilly walked across the wildflower-strewn field.

Her hair was loose, flowing over her shoulders and down to her waist, like a river the shade of the setting sun. She wore a gray tank top and jean shorts so ancient they were nearly washed white. Both hugged her figure in all the right places.

Her legs were bare and seemed to go on forever before disappearing into the calf-high grass. As she came closer Evan saw that her nose was pink from the sun. Only the very tips of her hair remained caught in the rubber band, ready to tumble free at the slightest tug. His hands itched so badly to do just that, he rubbed them against his thighs.

In her arms she held a tiny black kitten. Dipping her head down, she whispered to it, and the kitten's ears twitched. So did Evan's. He wanted her to whisper like that to him.

Glancing up, Jilly smiled. "Hi."

Suddenly he couldn't breathe. He opened his mouth; no sound came out. When he cleared his throat, the kitten started and tried to scramble away. She snatched it back and soothed the animal with murmured words and gentle hands.

"Where'd you get that?" he managed to ask.

"He's my payment for helping Addie today."

"You got taken, little lady." Barry jumped up and so did his brothers. All three stared at the kitten as if it were the devil come to Arkansas. "That cat ain't worth the bag you'll need to drown it in."

Jilly's eyes widened, and she tugged the kitten closer to her chest, which appeared a whole lot larger than Evan remembered now that it was encased in worn gray cotton that was a size too small.

"You know dag blamed well you can't kill a cat." Larry smacked Barry on the back of the head. "That's as much bad luck as the black cat itself."

"What *are* you talking about?" Jilly demanded.

But the Seitz brothers were already hightailing it home.

"Addie mentioned something about black cats being considered bad luck around here," she murmured to Evan. "I didn't believe her."

"Do you believe *anything* you hear?"

"Nope."

Jilly took the porch steps two at a time, snagged a beer and collapsed into a chair. The kitten curled into a ball in her lap and promptly fell asleep.

"There are a lot of superstitious people in these hills." She popped the top on her beer. "Really?"

"Maybe you should take the cat back."

In the middle of a huge gulp, she choked. The kitten opened one eye, glared at Evan, then closed it again.

A few moments of coughing and Jilly was able to speak again, though her voice came out a bit hoarse. "You're superstitious?"

"Not really."

"I'm not taking the cat back. Addie said he's spooking the patients. She mumbled something about dumping him in Little Rock." Jilly put a palm over the tiny black head. The kitten began to purr loudly enough to wake Matthew's ghost, if it needed waking. "He wouldn't last a day in the city."

"I never took you for an animal lover," Evan observed, thinking of her behavior with Lightning.

"I never had any to love." She gazed down at the adorable ball of fluff. "Until now."

The expression on her face reminded him of his sister when she rocked her daughter. His heart did a slow roll toward his belly as he imagined Jilly on this porch, rocking their child. The picture was far too appealing.

"I thought you didn't believe in love."

She snatched her hand away and stiffened. "I don't."

"But you said—"

"Animals can't love, although I hear they're capable of great loyalty. I could use a little loyalty in my life."

She scooped up the cat and headed into the house.

JILLY WASN'T SURE what it was about the black kitten that made her want so badly to keep him. Maybe it was just that no one wanted him. She knew what that was like.

Most would say she'd been wanted all her life. Four husbands, each one adoring her. But they hadn't wanted *her*. They'd wanted what she represented.

Youth. Beauty. A certain status.

The kitten didn't know anything about such foolish concerns.

Evan followed her inside. "You're looking for loyalty? Why?"

"Lasts longer than love."

"Which doesn't exist, according to you."

"I'm not saying that people don't *believe* they're in love. They may even feel…something. But it doesn't last. Which means it isn't real."

"And loyalty is?"

"Of course."

She'd been loyal and faithful—a regular golden retriever of a wife. What had it gotten her?

Jilly glanced down at her bare feet, which were now gray with dirt and possessed an interesting array of cuts and bruises.

Barefoot. Down and out. That's what trust and loyalty had gotten her. Well, it was time for someone to show her some loyalty, and if that someone was a kitten, she'd take what she could get.

"I tried to clean up in here, but I made things—" Jilly stepped into the living room and her eyes widened at the tidy expanse "—worse."

"The brothers are the Three Stooges of contracting, but when it comes to cleaning up they do just fine."

"I can help tomorrow."

"Great," Evan said, but he didn't sound happy about it.

Jilly moved into the kitchen, also pristine, and rustled around, searching for something a cat would eat. She found a can of tuna, among other things.

"You went shopping," she said.

"Someone had to."

She winced. Was she completely useless in this partnership? "I could, if you let me use your truck."

"I don't mind."

She set the kitten on the floor, where it promptly tried to climb her leg while she opened the can of tuna. "Hold your horses."

A snort from the window revealed Lightning's opinion of her comment. "You really need to put some glass in there," she muttered.

"It's on my to-do list."

Jilly plopped the fish onto a paper plate and set it on the floor. "I'll make supper."

"Can you? Make supper, I mean?"

She scowled, but he continued, "There's no electricity yet. If you take care of the meal, maybe I can get us some lights before dark."

"No problem," she said, as Evan disappeared upstairs.

Unfortunately, everything he'd bought for supplies required cooking, or at least heating. So Jilly cut up slices of cheese, apples and pears, then arranged crackers and bread on a plate. The presentation was lovely, the color combination perfection, even if she wasn't very good at slicing and the cheese and fruit had a lopsided appearance.

Still, she was proud of herself. She'd managed to put together a meal from very little, and she hadn't required any help.

Stepping outside, she blinked at the tablecloth spread across the weathered boards of the porch. She'd have thought Evan had beat her here, except for the platter in the center where a roast was surrounded by red potatoes, tiny carrots and baby onions. The scent alone made Jilly's mouth water. Could ghosts cook?

Evan opened the door and stopped dead. "What the—?"

"Evan. Jilly." Naomi appeared at the bottom of the steps with a basket of fresh bread. "We made too much for dinner, so Ruth and I brought the rest over. Come and eat."

Her sister stood right behind her, carrying a chocolate cake. There wasn't even a slice missing.

Too much? Right.

"Oh, you made snacks." Naomi took the platter from Jilly's hands. "How fun."

Jilly's cheeks heated. She hoped no one figured out that her snacks were supposed to be the meal.

Everyone sat down, and within minutes the atmosphere was festive. Jilly had to admit the sisters knew how to cook. From the amount of food Evan consumed, he agreed.

Naomi and Evan chattered away. Ruth listened, laughing at the appropriate places. Jilly listened, too, and came to the realization that she was a lot older than she looked.

She was thirty-five, had traveled all over the world and been married four times. Naomi and Ruth had been nowhere but here, yet they spoke of movies she'd never seen, television shows she'd never heard of, bands she thought were a joke and not reality.

Was this what Henry had felt like whenever he'd tried to talk to her? No, because she'd made certain she knew all about his world, his era, his culture. As a result, she had no ideas of her own.

Jilly shrugged off a sudden depression. She'd never had a childhood. Too late now. So what if she didn't fit in here? She wasn't going to stay.

But realizing that she was too old for a man was a sobering experience. What would happen when she became too old for all of them?

Jilly snorted. That wouldn't happen. Look at her mother. Nearing sixty, she'd made the best marriage of them all.

"Something funny?" Evan asked.

Jilly lifted her eyes. Everyone stared at her expectantly. She definitely couldn't share her thoughts.

"No." She got to her feet, planning to clear the dishes, but as soon as she stood she nearly collapsed from the pain in her feet.

Evan caught Jilly before her knees hit the porch. "Hey, what's wrong?"

"Nothing," she declared. "I just couldn't find my shoes today."

He sat her in a chair and went down on one knee,

gently lifting her foot and taking a peek at the sole. His hair swung forward, obscuring his face, but the sight of him next to her in that position made Jilly's stomach clench. Too bad she'd left all her glass slippers in California.

"You walked to Addie's barefoot?" he asked.

"I didn't have much choice."

"We should have found some shoes to go with the clothes." Naomi bit her lip.

Jilly glanced at the girl. "The clothes—"

"Are great," Evan interrupted.

She shot him a glare. "I can speak for myself."

He lifted his hands in surrender, and Jilly turned to Ruth and Naomi. She'd planned to return the clothes. Until she'd worn them.

Jilly rubbed her fingers over the soft denim, hugged herself and felt embraced by gray cotton. These clothes were feel-good clothes, and she wasn't giving them up.

"They're wonderful," she continued. "I love them, and I appreciate your bringing them by."

Naomi and Ruth beamed at her. Evan gaped. Jilly wanted to lift his chin until his mouth closed. What had he thought she was going to say?

Naomi nudged Evan aside and took a look at Jilly's feet. "Tobacco," she pronounced. "Soaked in hot water. Poultice'll take the sting away."

"How about some Vicodin?" Jilly asked.

Naomi's forehead creased. "Can I gather that in the woods?"

"Never mind." Evan shot Jilly a scowl. "I don't have any tobacco."

Ruth held out her hand. In the center of her palm was a pouch.

"You're not supposed to be chewing, Ruth," Naomi scolded. "Remember what Pa said? Men don't cotton to women who chew."

Ruth lifted her brows in Evan's direction. He shrugged. "It isn't what I'd call an attractive pastime."

She tossed the bag into his lap.

"Hot water?" Naomi pressed.

Evan stood. "Guess now's as good a time as any to test the electricity."

"I'm fine, really," Jilly protested.

Everyone ignored her to tramp inside. Jilly was left alone on the porch. She could have gotten up and tottered after them, but what was the point?

She listened to the low murmur of voices as she watched the sun slide toward the hills. The cool breeze smelled of grass and water.

Her kitten scratched at the door, and Jilly reached over, opening it just enough for him to come outside. He jumped into her lap, twirled around twice, stuck his nose beneath his tail and began to purr.

Lightning was nowhere to be seen. He was probably down at the creek figuring out new ways to push her in.

"Eureka!" Naomi shouted, and her laughter filled the air. She was so young she made Jilly ache for a life she'd never had.

A soft glow beamed from the third floor. As Jilly watched, lights snapped on here, there, everywhere. Fifteen minutes later the three came out the door.

"We have ignition," Evan said.

"So I see."

Naomi carried what appeared to be a damp dish towel. The scent of tobacco wafted on the wind. She took one look at Jilly and gasped. "No wonder you're sick."

"I'm not sick. I stepped on too many rocks."

"The cat—"

"Don't tell me the kitten's bad luck. I already heard all about it from the Seitz brothers, and I'm not buying."

Naomi knelt and wrapped Jilly's feet with warm towels. She kept a wary eye on the kitten the entire time. When she was done she muttered what sounded like a prayer, or a spell. Then she patted Jilly's knee and stood. "You'll be right as rain soon."

"What did you say just now?"

"I can't tell you!"

"Why not?"

"Secret words. Hexes and spells passed down in our family. I can only tell 'em to three other women, then their power is gone for me."

"You were putting a hex on my feet?"

Ruth started to laugh; Naomi just smiled. "No, I was taking the hex off your cat."

CHAPTER NINE

THE GIRLS PACKED up their picnic and went home. Despite her annoyance at their obvious designs on Evan, Jilly liked them. They were generous, fun, genuine. The kind of women Jilly would have wanted as friends, if she'd known how to make any.

"The hex is off your cat, so you can rest easy."

Evan sat on the porch rail. The setting sun cast a crimson halo around his head. His face lay in shadow, but she heard the amusement in his voice.

"I *was* worried. What exactly does bad luck from a black cat entail?"

"Could be anything. I'm not exactly up on Ozark superstitions."

"I can't believe a place like this still exists in the twenty-first century."

"It's kind of nice, don't you think?"

"No electricity, no plumbing, no water. Ten miles to the nearest phone. *Nice* isn't the word I'd use."

"We've got electricity."

"Be still my heart."

He shifted and gazed out at the steadily descending night. "I like it here. No one knows me."

Jilly frowned. "You got something to hide?"

"Doesn't everyone?"

True. She didn't want anyone to know she'd eaten out of garbage cans and slept on the street. But what was *he* hiding?

She opened her mouth to ask as Evan stood, then dropped to his knees again at her side. She forgot everything but the slide of his fingers along the bones of her ankles. No man had ever touched her there. She didn't want him to stop.

She imagined him running those rough, clever fingers up her calves, over her knees, then continuing along the quivering flesh of her inner thighs. The thought had her shifting in her chair, and the kitten awoke with a sound halfway between a purr and a growl. He put his nose in the air and jumped to the ground, stalking into the night with his tail poker-straight.

"We'll have to bring him inside." Evan unwrapped the poultice from her feet. "He'll be coyote food if we leave him out here."

Jilly frowned. "What about Lightning?"

"What about him?"

"Coyotes won't bother him?"

"Coyotes aren't as dumb as they look. They pick on things more their size—or a lot smaller. One kick from Lightning and a coyote would be toast."

"He's old and slow."

"But mean." Evan cast her a quick glance. "Since when do you worry about the horse you wanted to send to a glue factory?"

Jilly shrugged. Since this afternoon when he'd been the only company she had. "He kind of grows on you."

"Uh-huh."

"Like fungus."

He patted the arch of her foot, and she resisted the urge to rub her sole all over his chest.

"You wanna try walking on these again?" Evan stood and held out his hand.

Putting her palm against his made her neck tingle. His hands were hard, hers too soft. Still, they fit together just right.

He tugged; she put weight on her feet and drew in a sharp breath.

"Does that hurt? Sit down." He gently shoved against her shoulder.

"No. I'm fine. They don't hurt at all."

Puzzled, she sat anyway, pulled one foot onto her knee and peered at the bottom. The scrapes and cuts were still there, but they were no longer red. If she didn't know better she'd swear they were fading.

"What did she put in that towel?" Jilly asked.

"Hot water and tobacco."

"You saw her?"

"Yeah. What do you think she put in there?"

"Bat's wings and rat's eyes."

Evan snickered. "Naomi isn't a witch. She's a hill girl. They know all sorts of cures. Some of them even work."

"I'll say." Jilly got to her feet once more.

Evan touched her elbow, and she froze, then lifted her gaze to his face. "We'd better call in the cat."

The homey chore caused warmth to return to her belly. Call in the cat. Lock up the house. Go upstairs and…retire to their separate rooms. Damn.

Jilly inched away. Why torture herself? Evan didn't want anything she had to give.

"I don't understand why Addie couldn't un-hex the kitten," she blurted.

"The way I understand it, each family knows certain spells to ward off specific things. Un-hexing black cats must not be in Addie's domain."

"She couldn't ask Naomi to do it?"

"You can't ask—they have to offer. Like I said, most of the spells are secret. One family doesn't know what another is capable of."

"Sounds like trouble to me."

"Could be."

Silence settled between them. Jilly peered into the night, but since the kitten was black, she wouldn't be able to see him even if he stood three feet away.

"What's his name?" Evan asked.

"Kitty-kitty?"

"You can do better than that. If you're going to keep him—"

"I am."

"Then he needs a name."

Jilly walked to the end of the porch. The stars were coming out; the moon hovered at the edge of the horizon. All was quiet. Peaceful. Haunted.

"Hobgoblin?" she blurted.

"Too long." Evan stood at her side.

"Purr puss."

"No self-respecting male cat would answer to that."

"Midnight."

"Original."

"If you're so smart, you name him."

"Can't. Your cat."

She sighed. "I'm out of ideas."

"Any words you like? Names that make you happy?"

She doubted Evan would approve of naming the kitten Cash, Villa or Diamond. Somehow Rockefeller, Gates and Sheik didn't fit either.

"Henry," she muttered.

"Your husband?"

"I miss him."

She did. He'd been a nice man. If he were alive, she wouldn't be here. Although *here* didn't seem quite so awful anymore.

"Henry," Evan repeated.

The kitten jumped onto the porch rail and mewed.

Evan laughed. "Henry it is."

Jilly picked up the cat and set him inside. Before she could follow, Evan snagged her elbow again. She glanced at him and the screen door slammed shut. They both started.

"Now that we have electricity, things will move faster," Evan said. "With the Seitz brothers helping I may be done in…three years."

Jilly gaped.

"Kidding. Ha-ha."

"Oh." She put her hand on her chest. "Don't give me heart failure. I don't have that much money."

He tilted his head, and his hair sifted against his jaw. She wanted to sample the texture of the strands, then trace her finger along his chin.

"I lost your rubber band," she whispered.

"I'll try and find you another one."

"Why?"

"You're the kind of woman who ties back her hair."

She stiffened. "I am?"

He was right, so why did his words bother her?

Evan's hand lifted, and he tugged one red curl. "Or maybe you *were*." He drew her closer, until the heat of his body washed over hers. "You're different today. The clothes, the hair, the feet."

"You like me like this?" She couldn't keep the surprise out of her voice.

"I like you like that," he whispered.

She couldn't ever recall a man saying he liked her. Desire, need, devotion? No problem. But simple affection? Never.

His fingers still held her hair. Her hip still pressed

against his thigh. Her breath came in short, fast bursts. Their noses were a mere inch apart.

"I want to be your friend," he said.

The lights went off with an audible click. Darkness descended like a cool velvet fog. The moon wasn't up yet. The stars spread little light. Jilly could barely make out Evan's shape in the night.

And then he kissed her.

He tasted of chocolate cake and sweet, fresh bread. His hair brushed her cheek, making her shiver. She lifted her arms and ran her fingers through the long, soft strands.

He smelled like soap and rainwater. His palms at her waist were hard, insistent, tugging her close, making her forget that they weren't supposed to be doing this. However, he was the one who'd said no, not her.

With that in mind, she shifted closer, pressed her belly against his erection and rubbed her breasts, barely covered in the ancient gray shirt, against his chest. Her nipples hardened at the friction, sending a delicious tingle from her head down to her bare, naked toes. So she did it again.

His hands slid lower, and he lifted her onto the porch railing. She clutched his shoulders, and he murmured her name. Lowering his head, he nuzzled her neck, then nudged her thighs apart and stepped inside.

He'd just settled in, hard to her soft, the pulsing heated part of him pressed to the aching empty part of her, when a thud on the second floor made them both freeze, then look up.

The lights came back on with a sudden flare that had Jilly flinching, and a shadow drifted past the window directly above them. Evan frowned and moved away.

She wanted to scream and yank him back, but figured that might wreck the mood. He glanced at her, and she saw the mood was already wrecked. He lifted her from the railing and set her on her feet. "I'm sorry. I said we'd be friends."

"I'm feeling pretty friendly."

His lips twitched, but the sadness in his eyes reached out to her. "I can't, Jilly."

"No sex without love. I remember. I should be the one saying I'm sorry, but when you touch me—" She broke off.

When he touched her she wasn't sorry.

She really didn't want to articulate how out of control he made her feel. How out of control she wanted to be just once in her life. With him.

Several thuds sounded, one after the other, as if a heavy object had been thrown down the stairs.

"Matthew again?" Evan murmured.

"More likely Henry than a ghost."

"The cat and not the dead husband, right?"

"What do you think?"

The lights went off again. Into the sudden silence a coyote howled. The sound made Jilly shiver, even though the night was anything but cold.

"Still don't believe in ghosts?"

"Your electricity failed."

"Someone, or something, had to hit the main switch, and I don't think it was Henry."

"Another intruder?"

"There wasn't anyone here the last time."

"But we saw…something in the window. Don't tell me you think Matthew Tolliver still lives—or rather doesn't live—here."

"I don't know what I think, but something weird's going on."

"There's a short in the wiring. That's all."

"Maybe." He grabbed her hand. "Let's find out."

Evan led the way into the house and up the stairs. It was even darker inside, and Jilly was thankful he grasped her tightly. Her night vision was slim to non-existent. She'd have run into every wall and tripped on the steps.

"For some reason the main switch is on the third floor." Evan stopped in front of a door about midway down the hall there. "In the linen closet."

He opened it. A whole lot of blackness spilled out.

"How are you going to fix the lights in the dark?"

He released her hand and reached inside. Seconds later a bright beam spread across the floor.

"Always keep a flashlight near the fuse box."

Running the golden ray up the wall, he positioned it on the switches. "Huh," he grunted.

"Huh what?"

"The main switch is off."

"Which means?"

He reached forward and *click*—all the lights came on. "There isn't a short."

Something stirred Jilly's hair, like a breeze, but there weren't any windows. A wisp of air floated past her cheek, and she could have sworn she heard a whisper.

She spun around, but nothing was there.

EVAN ENDURED ANOTHER restless night. He'd had a hard time getting Jilly to bed. She might not believe in ghosts, but she was spooked by the lights. To tell the truth, so was he. They shouldn't be going on and off like that. He hoped the place didn't burn down around them.

She'd finally settled in, with Henry on her pillow— as if the kitten would protect her. Then again, the cat would be a better defense against the unknown than Evan. He couldn't even protect her from himself.

What had gotten into him? Asking her to be his friend, then sticking his tongue down her throat? Why didn't he just whisper, "Trust me," then screw her blind?

He was starting to sound like Dean.

Hell, he should at least be honest with himself. He'd done a lot of things he wasn't proud of, said a lot of things that weren't true, just to get in a woman's pants. One of the reasons he'd vowed not to do so anymore.

The next woman he slept with would be "the one," and she'd sleep with him because she knew that, too, not because he'd seduced her—or the other way around.

Once Evan fell asleep, morning arrived too quickly.

With no curtains on the windows the sun glared in his face before 6:00 a.m. Waking with the roosters, just like home.

He dry-brushed his teeth, scraped his hair into a ponytail, then realized he had nothing to tie it back with. He needed to beg, borrow or steal a rubber band soon, or maybe get a haircut. He'd grown it long to annoy his father; now the unruly strands were just annoying him.

Evan hurried downstairs and into the kitchen. He stopped at the sight of the Seitz brothers drinking coffee and eating eggs.

"Sleepyhead's up," Barry announced.

Larry squinted despite his thick glasses. Jerry didn't lift his head, probably because he hadn't heard a thing. Jilly, stirring the contents of a frying pan on the stove, glanced over her shoulder and smiled.

"Morning. Hungry?"

Seeing her there, cooking, her feet bare beneath a colorful, calf-length skirt, gave him domestic fantasies again. She was killing him.

"Sure." He sat at the table. "How long have you been up?"

She turned, and he clenched his teeth to keep his mouth from hanging open. The white cotton T-shirt was at least a size too small and outlined her breasts and trim waist like a second skin.

"An hour?" She glanced at Barry for confirmation. "I haven't been sleeping well."

"Join the club," Evan muttered.

"I came down for coffee and Barry, bless him, already had the pot perking."

"When did you guys get here?" Evan asked.

"Not too much before five. I didn't figure you for a layabout."

"Layabout? I've been getting up with the cows since I was six."

"Cows must get up mighty late in the north."

Evan let the matter drop. He wasn't going to win.

Henry jumped into Barry's lap. The old man patted him on the head.

"Thought that cat was bad luck," Evan observed.

"Naomi took the hex off."

Evan looked at Jilly and together they shrugged. He took a bite of scrambled eggs. They were really good.

"Barry showed me how to make them," Jilly said.

"You didn't know how?"

"I've never had to cook a day in my life."

"What did you eat?"

"Whatever the chef made, or what I could order off the menu."

Evan's chef's name had been Eleanor Luchetti. The only time they'd ever gone out to eat had been Mother's Day.

Jilly's life was as foreign to Evan as his was foreign to her, but she was trying. From the flavor of the eggs, she was succeeding. He admired that.

Because soft feelings for Jilly would only land him right back where he'd been last night—with a hard-on that wouldn't stop—Evan put those thoughts out of his head and pushed away from the table.

"Let's get to it, boys. Plumbing is next."

The brothers stood. Barry tripped over Henry. Larry bumped into Jerry.

"Watch where you're going!"

"You watch where you're going!"

The three started shoving each other like eight-year-olds. Evan grabbed them and pulled them apart. "Clean up the second floor," he said to Larry, pushing him toward the door. Then he turned to Jerry. "You take the garden."

Jerry cupped his ear. "Eh?"

"Garden," Evan roared, and pointed outside.

"Oh, sure."

"Barry, you're with me." Evan started out of the room.

"What about me?" Jilly asked.

Her hands were full of dirty dishes. She had toast crumbs stuck to her shirt. The kitten wound around her ankles, begging for scraps. Evan wanted to beg for some, too.

Why did he keep imagining her right here, like this, with two of his children clinging to her skirt? These fantasies were almost as bad as the sexual ones, because they promised a lifetime instead of just one night.

"We'll be fine." He turned away before he surrendered to the urge to brush the crumbs off her shirt, let his palms linger at her waist, lift his thumbs to the swell of her breasts and—

"Why don't you help Addie?" he blurted. "I'm sure she could use an extra hand."

"But we agreed—"

"We agreed that you'd provide the money and I'd provide the labor."

"You'd be done faster with another set of hands."

"That was before I got six Seitz hands for free."

Something flew past the kitchen window and landed with a thud on the ground outside.

"Hey! You almost hit me, you old fool."

"Sorry," drifted from the second floor.

"Don't throw the garbage out the window," Evan shouted, and rubbed his forehead. "What time is it?"

Jilly laughed. "Maybe my two hands would be better than those six."

Probably. But he didn't want to kiss the Seitz brothers—in every room of this house, down by the creek, out on the porch.

"I'll see you later," he muttered, and nearly ran from the room.

As JILLY CLEANED UP the kitchen, the sun streamed through the windows and warmed the air with a drowsy heat. Henry chased dust motes through the rays. Jilly found herself humming as she washed the dishes. A strange contentment filled her, and she wasn't sure why.

When the place was in order, she glanced around and experienced a sense of pride. She'd made a meal, made a mess, then cleaned it up, something most women did every day. Why did she feel as if she'd just climbed Mount Everest alone?

Because she was an idiot. She'd cleaned the kitchen. Big whoop. Evan didn't need her. He didn't want her, either.

Her watch read 7:00 a.m. What would she do all day?

She glanced at Henry, but he'd fallen asleep in the center of the kitchen floor. Jilly smiled. He was so cute. Much cuter than the original.

She bounced on her toes. Her feet were fine. Whatever Naomi had done had worked wonders. She could walk to Addie's, so she did.

Once again Lightning followed her, but this time he didn't try and knock her over, but plodded along at her side like a lifelong companion.

She eyed his back. "I don't suppose you'd want to give me a lift to Addie's?"

He galloped away.

"You're right," she called. "The walk will do me good."

The most Jilly had ever walked had been in a shopping mall. She had to admit a stroll through the pasture beneath the summer sun was more relaxing.

She listened to the birds sing and the chipmunks chatter as she eyed the wildflowers and the tall, swaying grass. If she stopped and listened closely, Jilly could hear the water rushing over the stones in the creek. The sound reminded her of the ocean—the only thing she truly missed from California.

"If I move to the other side of the inn and leave the window open, I could hear the water," she murmured to herself.

Maybe then she'd be able to sleep.

Zorro and Peter waddled out to meet her. Peter's tail only grossed Jilly out for an instant. Zorro latched on to her skirt and started to climb.

"Lift him off and tap his paws so he knows he ain't supposed to do that."

Addie stood in the door of the cabin holding a baby—of the human variety, Jilly hoped.

"But be gentle," Addie continued. "He'll bite if you're rough."

Jilly glanced at the raccoon, who had clambered to her waist while they spoke.

"Hurry up," Addie urged. "Afore he tears your clothes."

Gingerly, Jilly plucked Zorro from her person and tapped his fingers with her own. He chittered in disappointment, but when she set him on the ground, he merely followed in her wake, batting at the hem of her skirt.

"Pretty soon you won't even know he's around," Addie said.

Somehow, Jilly doubted that, but she let the matter drop.

"I came over to help."

"Figgered you would."

"Why?"

"What else ye gonna do all day?"

"I could help Evan with the inn."

"Pshaw. That's men's work."

Jilly had never been much of a feminist. How could she be? But she took issue with that. "I could do it."

"Of course you could. Women can do damn near anything a man can. Except lift really heavy things. But who'd want to if'n you don't have to?"

"I agree."

"The list of things a woman can do that a man can't…" Addie tsked. "Mighty long."

Jilly smiled. "Like what?"

Addie dumped the bundle in her arms into Jilly's. "Like that."

Jilly bobbled the baby. "Hey, watch it."

"Rock her. Over there. I want that kid to stay asleep till her ma comes. Anna Mae can raise a hellish racket."

"Is she sick?"

Jilly sat in the rocking chair next to the front door. Zorro started to play with her toes. Jilly was too interested in the baby to care. She shifted the blanket so she could see the child's face. Why did every newborn resemble Winston Churchill?

"Summer complaint. Used t' treat it with tea made from wild artichokes. But it never did much good. I use chamomile now. Soothes the belly."

"What is summer complaint?"

"Colic."

"They still have that?"

Addie gave her an arch look. "You aren't around babies much, are ye?"

"Never."

"Where you been that you haven't held a baby?"

Where *had* she been? Paris. London. Milan. New

York. San Francisco. Chicago. She was certain there were babies in those cities. Somewhere. But they usually didn't turn up at Bloomingdales. If they did, Jilly hadn't been paying attention.

"Never mind." Addie shooed Zorro off to play with Peter. "We'll have a full day today. Might be summer, but folks still get sick. And they get hurt even more during Gemini."

"Gemini?" Jilly recalled the Wilder sisters mentioning something about Gemini before. "You mean the Zodiac sign?"

Addie nodded. "'Round here we go by the zodiac sun signs for a whole lot. Plantin', healin', marryin'."

"Because…?"

"Because that's the way we've always done it. The sun signs came about fer a reason. Now, today yer gonna see a lot of sickness, some blood, too."

"I've never done any first aid," Jilly said.

"Me, neither. I'm a healer, plain and simple. My mother was a power doctor, and I use some of her spells."

"What's a power doctor?"

"Power comes from above. My ma could lay on the hands and take away a fever. Never worked for me. I mostly use the medicines."

Addie cracked her knuckles, then stared at her veined hands as if wishing they could impart healing as her mother's had.

"In the old days there were all sorts of healers. Chills

and fever doctors, yarb doctors—for poultices and such—rubbin' doctors, nature doctors. Nowadays, there's those that had schoolin' and those who learned the hard way. Folks in the hills trust me. Certain things I can fix. What I can't, I send 'em to the town doctor fer. They wouldn't go less'n I told 'em to, so I figger I'm doin' a service, savin' lives, too."

Addie's voice and eyes were so earnest, Jilly found herself nodding in agreement.

"You just rock the baby till I tell ye t' stop. The movement helps her belly. The more she sleeps the better for us all."

Addie disappeared inside. Jilly sat on the porch and rocked. The sun beat down, warming her feet, making her drowsy.

She drifted, dreaming of Evan's kiss, his touch, the dark hair with the auburn streaks drifting all over her body. She imagined making eggs at dawn, drinking coffee in the kitchen as the sun blazed over the horizon. She wanted to work hard at something important and feel good about herself at the end of the day.

Anna Mae shifted in her arms, turning toward Jilly's breast and nuzzling in close with a soft sigh. Jilly tilted her head.

Funny, the kid didn't look like Winston Churchill anymore.

CHAPTER TEN

JILLY ROCKED THE baby until the infant woke up squalling. Addie'd been right. Anna Mae could raise the roof with her screams.

"Here." Addie appeared in the doorway. "I'll take her."

"No." Jilly stared at the beet-red baby face. The little girl was twisting and turning, writhing as if in pain. "I don't mind. What should I do?"

Addie studied Jilly, then motioned for her to stand, which she did. "Hold her against ye, tight like. Her belly to yer chest. Rub her back and sway." She demonstrated.

Jilly did as instructed. The baby kept crying, but she stopped squirming.

"May take a while, but keep at it. If yer ears start ringin' and yer eye starts twitchin', I'll take 'er."

The wailing didn't bother Jilly. The child's obvious discomfort did.

She swayed with that baby for forty-five minutes before Anna Mae stopped crying and fell back asleep.

"Should I put her down?" she asked Addie.

"Lord, no. She'll wake right back up. Her ma'll be here directly."

When Anna Mae's mother arrived, Jilly didn't want to let the child go. She was so soft and cuddly, so warm and trusting. Her little mouth hung open, and her eyelashes created a spiderweb of shadows against her pale cheeks.

"Thank ye." The young woman slipped the baby out of Jilly's arms, handing her a burlap sack in return.

Jilly glanced inside and nearly dropped the sack. "What's with the dead chicken?"

"Payment." She settled Anna Mae into her car seat. "For your time and trouble."

"I'd rather have cash," Jilly muttered as the car drove away.

"Not much of that in these parts." Addie had come out of the cabin.

"Why not?"

"Just ain't. Folks use their paper money at the store. What they can pay fer in trade, they do."

"Here's your chicken." Jilly held the bag out to Addie.

The old woman turned away. "That's yours."

"What am I going to do with it?"

"Make dinner."

Jilly peered into the bag again. The thing inside looked like nothing she'd ever found on a plate.

"Never mind," Addie ordered. "We got customers."

Jilly looked up and saw an elderly couple approaching on foot.

"Wife's got the flux," the man said. "And my bold

hives ain't so good, either." He squinted at Jilly. "Who in blazes are you?"

"My new helper." Addie led the old woman to a chair. "Lives at the inn."

The man's white eyebrows flew upward. "With Matthew?"

Jilly opened her mouth to deny living with Matthew, but Addie answered, "Of course," before she could say a word.

"Get my medicine bag, Jilly. Directly inside the door."

Jilly decided not to bother arguing. Matthew lived at the inn, and no one around here was going to believe otherwise.

She stepped into Addie's cabin and was struck speechless. Herbs hung from the ceiling. Bottles filled with tonics in every color of the earth lined several shelves and the mantel. Books and notebooks overflowed several tables. The entire place was devoted to the healing arts. Even the stove held bubbling pots of brew.

Jilly should feel uncomfortable, like Gretel blundering into the witch's lair. Instead she felt as if she'd stumbled upon something wonderful.

Until the alligator crawled out from under the bed. Jilly shrieked and ran outside.

"What's wrong with you?"

"There's an alligator in there."

Addie's gaze slid past her. "He's out here now."

Jilly turned. Yep, there was an alligator eyeing her

toes as if they were his next meal. She jumped onto the nearest chair as if she'd seen a mouse. Addie and the elderly couple stared at her with puzzled expressions.

"What is *wrong* with you, girl?"

"I don't care for alligators near my bare feet."

"Fergus can't hurt you. His teeth are gone."

As if to illustrate, Fergus opened wide. He was as toothless as Barry Seitz.

"What's he doing here?"

"He used to be the star attraction at Hugenot's Alligator Wrestling Emporium."

"I'd think a toothless alligator would be a big plus in wrestling."

"Nah. No one's scared of 'im then. What fun is that?" Addie shook her head. "Hugie was gonna have 'im stuffed, put on display out front. But I convinced 'im Fergus would be better off here with me. Much easier to get alligator dung this way than tracking 'em through a swamp."

Jilly knew she'd be sorry, but she was too curious not to ask anyway. "Why do you need alligator dung?"

"Gets rid of freckles."

Jilly wrinkled her freckled nose, which suddenly itched quite terribly. Addie's eyes narrowed. "Want some?"

"Uh, no. I kind of like them."

Addie shrugged. "Suit yourself."

The day was a revelation. After an hour or so, Jilly got used to the sight of Fergus walking slowly about the place. She learned to step over Peter. She ignored Zorro hanging off the edge of her skirt, and she discovered something.

She was good with sick people.

That might have something to do with four marriages to men on the far side of sixty, but still, she liked helping. She was fascinated with the natural cures Addie prescribed, and riveted by the secretly whispered spells.

How could a woman who believed in nothing but what she could sell be intrigued by Ozark mountain magic?

Jilly had no idea, but she was.

Old and young thronged to Addie's cabin. Jilly learned things she'd never thought to know. They used ragwood tea for the flux, which turned out to be nothing worse than diarrhea, thank goodness.

The bold hives were just hives, which Addie treated with plain calamine lotion. Common sense appeared to play a large part in doctoring.

Skunk oil for croup, horehound for colds, onion tea for pneumonia—Jilly hoped she never got sick.

She worked and she learned; she soothed and she dosed; she conversed with everyone. But her favorite patients were the children. All shapes and sizes, sexes and ages, they were fun, and they liked her for no other reason than that she was there.

As the afternoon wore on, the crowd thinned out until only Addie, Jilly and the critters remained.

Jilly collapsed in the rocker. She'd gotten her wish.

The day was over and she was exhausted—because she'd actually done something and not been bored out of her skull.

Her white T-shirt was a mess. Her skirt wasn't much better. Her feet were filthy. She wasn't sure, but she thought there was baby barf in her hair. Life was good.

"You'd best head on home." Addie dropped the sack with the dead chicken into her lap. "If you get that on the stove right away, you can eat afore dark."

Jilly hoisted herself to her feet. "Where's Fergus?"

She hadn't seen the alligator for a while, and she didn't relish running into him on the way home. No matter how friendly he was.

"Must have gone for a dip in the pond."

"The cement pond?" Jilly snickered.

"I don't know what yer talkin' about, girl. Ain't no cement in my pond. Just good old-fashioned dirt."

"It was a joke. The *Beverly Hillbillies*. From television?"

Jilly hadn't watched the show very often. However, she seemed to remember it all too well. Probably because she'd been dropped into one of the lost episodes.

"Don't hold with the idiot box 'round here. It'll rot your mind."

Addie was probably right. Jilly hadn't missed television yet, and it had been her main occupation during many a long, lonely day. What was happening on *Days of Our Lives*? She no longer cared, because her own day was suddenly full of life.

Jilly studied Addie's cabin. She thought of the stove—wood—and the lamps—kerosene. "You don't have electricity."

"Don't hold with that, either."

"Plumbing?"

Addie jerked a thumb toward what appeared to be a wooden port-a-potty partially concealed by trees.

"Running water?"

"Runs just fine. From the pump out back."

"How old are you?" Jilly asked.

"How old are *you*?"

Jilly had been offended when Evan asked her the same thing. However, this time she'd started it, so she answered. "Thirty-five."

"Huh. Better get movin' if you want any kids. Time's a-wastin'."

Jilly hadn't given much thought to children. How would she take care of them, when she had enough trouble taking care of herself? But today she'd taken care of a lot more than herself. She'd taken care of everyone else.

"I'm ninety this Christmas," Addie said.

"And you don't look a day over seventy-five."

"Funny. You're a regular Jack Benny. Now get on home. I should be fine tomorrow. I won't need you to come."

Jilly's happy mood deflated. "But…I want to."

Addie peered into her face, then patted her on the arm. "Well, then, that's different. See you at seven. Sharp."

EVAN HAD JUST GOTTEN RID of the brothers and finished washing in the creek when he heard a vehicle stop in front of the inn. He tossed his clothes on and hurried up the hill. Old Man Hillburn's son, Ustis, climbed out of his delivery truck.

"Hello!" Evan called.

The man just raised a hand and didn't answer. By the time Evan crossed the yard, Ustis, a contender for heavyweight champion of Arkansas, had hoisted a dog crate out of the back end.

"I would have come into town," Evan said.

"You don't got no phone." Ustis spoke in a slow bass tone reminiscent of Barry White. "'Sides, Dad couldn't stand the yapping any longer. What in tarnation is that?"

As if he'd understood, the animal began to yip in an annoying falsetto.

"That…" Evan sprang the lock on the cage. The door slammed open, whapping Ustis in the shin. A fluffy, spotted dog shot out. "…is a doodle."

He raced in circles, then proceeded to jump on Evan. Ustis stopped hopping on one foot and settled into rubbing his injured leg. The doodle took the opportunity to slurp at his face.

Ustis straightened abruptly. "Remind me never to get one." He climbed back into his truck and sped away.

Evan snagged the dog, which was no longer a puppy, but over a year old, and lifted him into his arms. "Settle," he snapped in a no-nonsense voice he'd learned from his mother.

The animal froze, blinked, then started squirming again. "That went well," Evan muttered.

Suddenly the doodle's head went up, his ears perked and he growled.

Evan looked around just as Jilly stepped out of the woods. Loose skirt, bare feet, filthy white shirt, her hair snarled around her face. A baby raccoon chased her skirt. Why did he find that attractive?

Something trailed a few feet behind her in the grass. It appeared to be an...opossum?

Evan was so amazed he forgot about the doodle. Big mistake. The dog made a mighty lunge. Evan tried to grab him, afraid he'd break a leg. The animal wasn't a cat, but tell him that. He hit the ground running, yapping, and headed straight for Jilly and her friends.

"Watch out!" Evan shouted. He doubted the dog would hurt her, but who knew what the wild animals might do when confronted with a psychotic doodle?

The opossum ran. Except he wasn't very fast. The dog would have caught the critter if Jilly hadn't stuck out her foot. The doodle tumbled head over tail in the grass and came up barking. By then the opossum had disappeared into the brush.

The raccoon clambered up Jilly's skirt, reaching her waist before she snatched him up and placed him on her shoulder, where, from the safety of the greater height, he scolded everyone in the vicinity.

When the doodle realized the opossum was gone, he came back to Jilly and proceeded to dazzle her with thigh-high leaps, barking all the while.

She ignored him and continued toward Evan. He couldn't help it; the sight of Jillian Hart with a chittering raccoon on her shoulder cracked him up. Evan started laughing, and he couldn't stop.

"What's so darn funny?"

He glanced at her, pointed at the raccoon and snickered some more.

"This is Zorro," she said. "I think he's going to be living with us."

Evan managed to stop snickering. "Who are you? Snow White? Next thing I know you'll be singing birds from the trees."

"I wouldn't hold my breath. Hey, stop that!"

The doodle was yanking on the burlap sack in her hand.

"What's in there? More cats?"

"Dinner."

Evan frowned. "Fried chicken?"

"Raw chicken. I'd better get it on the stove."

"Where'd you get a chicken?"

"Payment. I helped Addie today."

"Helped her what?"

She shrugged. "Help."

"Addie's a healer." Evan hurried after Jilly when she headed for the house. "What did you do?"

"Little bit of this, little bit of that. It was interesting."

Evan was confused. "Healing is mostly about… magic."

She snorted. "No such thing."

"Did you tell Addie that?"

"Of course not. Her cures work, though I doubt it's because of the spells she mumbles."

"Then what?"

"The herbs. The potions. Her family has been perfecting them for generations. Like a backwoods pharmaceutical company. I have no doubt that some of her cures work better than anything you'd get at the drugstore."

"And the spells?"

"People believe. The placebo effect is well documented."

She still denied the existence of anything supernatural. Jilly was going to learn more from Addie than the ingredients to a tonic for warts.

She opened the door of the inn, and something streaked out. Something black.

"Wait!" Evan shouted, but it was too late. Henry ran smack into the dog.

The kitten arched like a Halloween cat. His hiss was very impressive. The doodle tilted his head, and this time his growl was more like a snarl. He learned fast. Jilly reached for Henry.

"No," Evan murmured. "Let them go."

She glanced at him, concern creasing her features. "Are you sure?"

Having spent his life on a farm, Evan knew a little bit about dogs and cats. "Positive."

The two humans held their breath. The kitten and the overgrown puppy stared into each other's eyes. The cat grumbled, low and serious. The dog made a fast move, and Henry slashed him across the nose with unsheathed claws.

The doodle yelped, then turned tail and ran. The kitten started cleaning his butt. Jilly set the raccoon on the floor, then turned to Evan.

"You have to let them set their own rules," he said. "Interfering only makes the transition take longer."

She gazed past him. "You think he'll ever come back?"

Evan spun around. "Which way did he go?"

"Toward Ecuador. You might catch him around Mexico, if you hurry."

Evan cursed, which made Jilly laugh. "Supper in a few hours. Don't be late."

The screen door banged shut behind her. Evan headed for the most likely places to find a frightened farm dog. But he wasn't in the bushes or the grove of trees on the hill. He hadn't gone down to the creek or scooted under the porch.

Whistling and calling only brought Lightning from wherever it was he'd been all day. "Seen a doodle?" Evan asked.

The horse snorted and nudged him toward the hill.

"I already looked there."

Lightning was insistent, so Evan preceded him to the edge of the yard. There the animal shoved him so hard Evan stumbled several steps down the slope.

"You think Addie's seen him?"

Evan didn't wait for Lightning's opinion. He hustled down the hill and across another field. Fergus was in the yard. He appeared happy—and full.

"Hell," Evan muttered. "Addie!"

She appeared at the door. "What's all the bellering?"

"You seen an overgrown puppy around here?"

Her gaze went immediately to the alligator. "No. But that doesn't mean one wasn't around."

Evan's heart started pounding too fast. If he had to tell Dean one of his doodles had been eaten by an alligator, he wouldn't put it past his brother to come down here and beat the crap out of him. Dean might be ornery, but he loved his animals. He never would have given Evan one if he hadn't trusted him to take care of the thing. One hour in Evan's company and the doodle was alligator bait.

"What's it look like?" Addie asked.

"Fluffy. Black-and-white. Hyper."

"Come inside. I'll see what I can see."

Evan wasn't sure what that meant. He was itchy. Antsy. He needed to keep moving. But first… He eyed the ancient alligator.

"Evan?" Addie stood in the doorway. "What are you doing?"

"Trying to figure out how to get Fergus to open wide."

Addie made an annoyed sound and marched into the yard. She leaned down and grabbed the alligator's mouth, then pulled. The huge beak gaped.

"Fergus doesn't have any teeth, remember? You think I'd let him sleep under my bed if he had a mouthful of pearly whites?"

In his panic, Evan had forgotten that important piece of information. "He didn't eat the doodle."

"Not unless he gummed 'im to death. Fergus doesn't eat anything but mush anymore." She let the alligator's mouth slide closed. "What's a doodle?"

"Dalmatian and poodle mix."

Addie snickered. "Doodle. I like it."

"Want one?"

"Not me. I'm parcelin' off my critters."

"I did notice Jilly came home with more than she had when she left."

Addie smiled fondly. "I been waitin' years for her to show up."

"Years? I don't understand."

"I got no one to take over when I die. But my ma told me someone always shows up to receive the knowledge. You just have to wait."

"The knowledge? You mean your spells and your cures?"

"What else?"

"And you think Jilly…?" He shook his head, remembering her comments about placebos and magic. "Addie, I wouldn't count on her."

She frowned. "Whadda ya mean?"

He hesitated, uncertain how to tell a woman who'd spent her entire life healing that Jilly thought her cures were little more than sugar pills and mumbo jumbo. He opted for another truth instead.

"Jilly plans to fix up the inn and sell it. She isn't going to stay."

"That's what you think. I know better."

Evan was about to argue further when he heard a faint yip from the top of the hill. Dog- and horse-shaped shadows frolicked in the grass.

"You'd better get home," Addie said.

He nodded and headed for high ground. It wasn't until he scooped up the doodle and patted Lightning's head that he realized Addie had called the inn his home.

Evan stared at the warm glow of electric lights in the windows, listened to the rustle of wind through the grass and the tumble of water in the creek. He'd lived nearly thirty years in Illinois, but the place had never called to him as this one did.

He liked the hills, the trees, the critters—in the woods and in the yard. He liked the people, the town. He liked the way the sun set and the way it came up in the morning.

But most of all he liked the inn. The dwelling had stood for over a hundred years and would no doubt stand for a hundred more. Evan wanted Luchettis to be here even then.

He walked toward the porch with his dog in his arms,

and he understood what it felt like to belong somewhere.

Jilly appeared at the screen door and lifted her hand.
How was he going to convince her the inn should be
his?

With the only thing she seemed to want. Cold hard
cash.

Too bad he didn't have any more of that than he had
of true love.

CHAPTER ELEVEN

JILLY PEERED AT THE FIRST chicken she'd ever made, which didn't resemble anything the Colonel would serve.

The outside was brown, the inside still red. She'd cut off enough meat for them to start with, then shoved the bird back on the stove.

"I'm sure the chicken will be wonderful." Evan smiled and took a bite. His smile froze.

"What?"

Jilly took a bite, too. She chewed, then grabbed her napkin and got rid of the mouthful. "Why is there hair in my chicken?"

"Did you singe it?"

"If I knew what that was, I could answer you."

"You need to stick the chicken in a pot of hot water and remove the skin—"

"Ew."

"Or use a match, maybe a lighter, to burn off the hair."

"Chickens have hair? Under their feathers?"

Evan shrugged and moved on to his mashed potatoes from a box.

Jilly was disappointed. She'd enjoyed cooking dinner. She'd felt like she was accomplishing something, only to find out that chickens have hair. It just wasn't fair.

"Sorry," she said. "I've never cooked before."

"You made eggs this morning. They were good."

She was unreasonably pleased, even if you had to be a moron to screw up scrambled eggs—or so Barry had told her.

"Your mom must be a very good cook," she said.

Evan glanced up, mouth full of canned green beans. Jilly didn't think she'd ruined those. Though she had forgotten and left them on the stove until they resembled green beans in a baby food jar rather than the picture on the can.

"Why would you say that?"

"Luchetti." She shrugged. "I love Italian food."

Evan laughed and took a sip of milk, then swallowed thickly. She had a sneaking suspicion he'd swallowed the beans almost whole—or as whole as they were after being heated to within an inch of their lives. Did a green bean have a life?

"My mom isn't Italian, she's…I'm not sure what."

"You don't know?"

"Nope. No one cared about any ancestors before the ones who'd lived on our farm."

The girls in Jilly's schools could trace their lineage back to the *Mayflower*, and often did, just for fun. That Jilly knew nothing about her great-great-great whatever had earned her no small amount of scorn. She found it comforting to meet someone else who didn't know where they'd come from and didn't care.

"What about yours?" Evan asked.

"No idea. I like to look forward instead of back. So in my near future, I'm going to learn how to cook."

Evan blinked. "You don't have to."

"I want to. I've never done anything but—" She broke off, frowning. "I'm not exactly sure."

"Come on. I'm sure you've done something."

"I've been a wife. Pretty, witty, there, which isn't much of a talent, but it's the only one I have."

"I doubt that," Evan said. "I doubt that a lot."

She smiled. "Thanks. That's probably the nicest thing anyone's ever said to me."

"Then you need to meet more people."

They stared at one another for several ticks of the clock. She really liked Evan Luchetti. He was a very nice man. And he didn't look half-bad without a shirt.

Her gaze dropped to the hollow of his throat. He swallowed again, and her own mouth went dry. What would he taste like if she pressed her lips, then her tongue, to the smooth wash of skin at the curve of his neck?

The damn doodle started yipping from the safety of his dog cage, where Evan had confined him after he'd tried to leap onto the table and sample the chicken—twice.

Jilly started, and all thoughts of licking Evan's neck fled. She turned and discovered Henry sitting on the other side of the prison door. His tail twitched and he yawned, then lay down, staring at the madly barking mutt with interest.

"You are so mean," she murmured.

The kitten glanced at her with impassive yellow eyes.

"I don't think he cares."

"Let's open the cage and see if he cares."

"Better not. I've had enough action for one night."

Their eyes met. Jilly blushed. Evan stood and started to clear the table.

"Wait. You didn't have enough to eat."

"Sure I did. Besides, there's chocolate cake left."

Naomi and Ruth's cake. Of course he'd want to eat that. If Jilly tried to make a cake it would no doubt be raw in the middle, just like her chicken.

They walked into the kitchen. Zorro perched on the counter, paws buried in what was left of the cake.

"Uh-oh," Jilly murmured.

The raccoon took one look at them and scooted out of the kitchen, leaving chocolate paw prints across the counter and the floor.

Jilly glanced at Evan and fought the urge to laugh at his bereft expression. "I bet I can salvage a piece."

"I'll pass."

"Sorry."

"We'd better invest in some good Tupperware. Raccoons can get into almost anything."

Just then the sounds of the cage door banging open and the scrabbling of claws erupted.

Evan and Jilly hurried through the doorway in time to see Henry's tail disappear up the steps, with the doodle a nose behind. Zorro chittered from on top of the dog cage.

"I see what you mean," Jilly muttered.

Something crashed on the second floor. Evan grabbed her hand and together they ran upstairs.

On the landing, they paused. "Shh." Evan put his finger to his lips.

A growl, a hiss, more feet than two pounded across the floor.

"You go that way, I'll go this way," he whispered, then dropped her hand.

She resisted the urge to grab his. She wasn't scared, but she liked holding on to him. He made her feel young again. Or maybe just young—since she hadn't ever been young in the first place.

Jilly crept through the bedrooms on the right side of the hall while Evan crept through those on the left. She found a lot of dust but no doodle and no Henry.

Back at the stairs, Evan pointed upward and motioned for her to stay where she was. If the animals came back down, she'd be waiting for them.

Jilly moved closer to the staircase, slid to the side so they wouldn't see her until it was too late. She stifled a giggle. This was almost like playing hide-and-seek. Not that she'd ever played, but she'd wanted to.

Her mother wouldn't let her associate with the street kids or the poor kids, considering them beneath her.

Once Jilly was enrolled in private schools she'd been below everyone. And besides, no one there had been so bourgeois as to partake in hide-and-seek.

Jilly held her breath and listened. Nails against wood. A kittenish squeal. The bark of a dog. Zorro still chittered madly downstairs.

Evan's sure, steady footsteps moved back and forth. He called, "Henry!" then, "Here, doggy, doggy!"

Maybe they should be playing name-that-doodle instead of hide-and-seek.

Jilly snickered, then put her hand over her mouth. She couldn't remember ever having so much fun.

A thud from the bedroom directly in front of her had her creeping on tiptoe toward the door. Slowly she turned the knob. Expecting something small and furry to shoot out, she stood back. Nothing happened.

She pushed open the door and stepped inside. The room was cold. Really cold. Shivering, she moved toward the window, and the door slammed shut behind her.

Jilly spun around. The moon shone across the floor, a pretty, silver beam revealing nothing. So why did she feel as if something was there?

"Insanity," she muttered. "Must run in the family."

Her words echoed in the empty room. Until the footsteps started. Hollow, faint, nevertheless she could have sworn someone was walking toward her.

Jilly shook her head, tried to clear her mind. She didn't believe in ghosts. She was merely hearing Evan's stride from upstairs, and the door had closed on a draft. It wasn't as if the windows were anything more than decoration.

She glanced outside. The leaves on the trees hung limply, without a breeze.

"But that doesn't mean there wasn't one," she said, and opened the door.

As soon as she stepped into the hall, the thunder of footsteps sounded on the stairs.

"Here they come!" Evan shouted. "Grab one."

She watched, mesmerized, as the doodle sped by, with Henry on his heels. The dog had amazing speed. Until he misjudged the steps, put on the brakes, slid across the wood floor and banged his head into the wall.

The canine didn't even slow down, just stepped to the left and raced onward to the first floor.

"Hey!" Evan landed next to her with a thud, as if he'd jumped over the last three or four steps. "We could be at this all night unless you help." When she didn't answer, he frowned. "You okay?"

Jilly glanced through the open door, but nothing was there. Never had been. The footsteps she'd heard had been Evan's. She had merely let the imagination she didn't have run away with her.

"The dog hit the wall," she said.

"Just his head. Won't hurt him a bit."

Evan grabbed Jilly's hand again and tugged her toward the stairs, grinning all the way.

"What's so funny?" she asked.

"I feel like I'm back at the farm."

"You chase animals through your house?"

"Never. My mom would smack me with the polenta stick. If she hadn't broken it on Dean's butt."

They reached the first floor. No dog, no cat, no raccoon to be seen. But they were here somewhere. They had to be.

"Your mom smacked you with a...what?" Jilly was still having a hard time focusing.

"Polenta stick. To make polenta."

"I thought your mother didn't cook Italian."

"I said she *wasn't* Italian. Besides, she didn't use the stick for polenta. It was the perfect size for a good whap."

"She hit you?" Jilly was horrified.

Evan glanced over his shoulder with a frown. "Not *hit* exactly. A little tap to get our attention. And only when we needed it. Which was...a lot."

"I don't approve of corporal punishment."

"When you've got six kids all born less than a year apart, then you get to talk."

Jilly's mouth fell open as she contemplated the time line. "That's insane."

"She was, and she'd be the first to admit it."

Jilly couldn't imagine all those children so close together. That Evan's mother wasn't in a mental institution was one miracle. That she'd broken a single polenta stick on someone's backside was another.

Suddenly the doodle shot out of the kitchen, heading for the front door. Either he was blind or just plain stupid, because he smashed into the screen and fell on his face. Evan scooped him up. "That's it for you, Mario. Sleepy night-night."

He popped the dog into the cage and turned to Jilly, still grinning.

"Sleepy night-night?" she asked.

He shrugged. "Sounded good at the time."

"Who's Mario?"

"Andretti. I always liked that name. What do you think?"

She glanced at the doodle, then back at Evan. Naming the dog together smacked of a relationship they didn't have. Nevertheless, the act felt too right to deny. Besides, they had to call him something.

"Mario. I like it."

EVAN WASN'T SURE what had gotten into Jilly, but she practically clung to him for the rest of the evening. They had coffee on the porch and chatted about the folks of South Fork, what she'd learned that day, what he'd accomplished. This was the life he'd always dreamed of having, except with a woman who loved him.

Jilly was interesting. She knew how to listen and how to make conversation. She wasn't hard on the eyes either.

Henry sat in her lap, his eerie yellow gaze unblinking. If Evan hadn't known better he'd swear the cat *was* Henry, and that the old man was sizing him up.

"Naomi and Ruth didn't come over tonight," Jilly murmured.

"They brought lunch."

Frowning, she stroked Henry and didn't comment.

"You still think Ruth is after me?"

"Of course."

"You're wrong. They're just…friendly."

"Friendly like a fox in the henhouse."

"I don't know what that means."

"Watch yourself," she muttered. "You'll end up on the wrong side of a shotgun wedding."

"You seem really concerned about my love life."

She shrugged. "I just want you to finish my inn before you get your head blown off."

He hesitated, trying to find the right words. "You ever think of staying here?"

"Here?" She snorted. "Not."

"But you could. Why not run the inn yourself?"

"Hmm, let me see. I don't know how to cook. I certainly can't clean. I've never run a business."

"Ever try?"

"Of course not."

"I bet you could do anything if you put your mind to it."

Her startled green eyes met his once more.

"Hasn't anyone ever told you that?"

"Close. My mother told me I could get any man I wanted to—if I put my mind to it."

Evan frowned. Her mother sounded…odd.

"Until now," Jilly continued, "she was right."

Evan glanced away. Her words were further proof that she wanted him, but didn't need or love him.

"Jilly—"

"I know. You want love. I can't give it."

"Can't or won't?"

"What's the difference? The day I believe in ghosts, is the…" She glanced up at the inn, then frowned and straightened her shoulders. "That's the day I fall in love."

Standing, she held the kitten close to her chest. "I'd better get to bed. You coming up?"

"In a little while. I have to secure the dog cage so Zorro doesn't let Mario out again. I don't feel like chasing them in the middle of the night."

"Where is Zorro?"

"Saw him toddling off with that opossum you brought home."

"Peter?"

"I didn't ask his name. I suspect they have places to go, chickens to eat."

Her eyes widened. "Raccoons eat chickens?"

"You'd be surprised what they eat."

Jilly went into the house shaking her head. A few minutes later, the glow of her bedroom light splashed across the lawn. Evan stood, then walked a few feet into the yard, where he stretched. He planned to go inside and steal the twistie-tie off the bread, then secure the dog cage, but he made a mistake.

He looked up, and then he couldn't look away.

She was brushing her hair, which wouldn't have been that interesting, except she wasn't wearing a shirt. He couldn't see much; she had her back to the window. But what he saw made his mouth go dry and his body tighten.

She had beautiful arms—smooth and white. The muscles rippled as she lifted her hand, then stroked the brush down the silky red tresses, which reached her waist.

She still wore her skirt, which for some reason was more erotic than if she'd been completely naked. Bending over, she disappeared from view. Seconds later she reappeared, tossing her hair back and turning.

Evan dived for the safety of the porch, but not before he got an eyeful. He'd thought her back was beautiful—because he hadn't seen her front.

Embarrassed to have been watching her like a lustful adolescent, he took one step toward the door and knew he couldn't go inside.

Instead, he practically ran to his truck and drove away, purposely keeping his eyes on the road until the lights of the inn faded behind him.

JILLY HEARD THE TRUCK start while her head was covered with a faded purple nightgown. She yanked the neckline over her face, scraping her nose, then hurried to the window. All she saw were taillights disappearing into the distance.

Worry filtered through her. Where was the fire? And if there was one, how had Evan found out about it? They didn't have a phone.

The lack of that modern convenience had disturbed her at first, but it was amazing how quickly she'd forgotten about their isolation, how little she missed the tinny ringing of a telephone. She wasn't lonely here. There was too much to do, too many people and animals to help.

Jilly glanced around the sparsely furnished room. She wasn't lonely, but she was a bit uneasy after the odd incident in that spare bedroom. She'd convinced herself it was only her imagination. However, when she was alone, like now, she wasn't so sure.

Henry, who had been lying on her sleeping bag, staring at the corner, suddenly hissed. The hair on his back stood straight up. Jilly squinted though the shadows. She didn't see anything.

The kitten growled low, like a junkyard dog, and took off, tail pointed at the ceiling, fur spiked in every direction as if he'd stuck his paw into a light socket.

"What's your problem?" she muttered, just as Mario started barking.

Even though she knew the dog was barking at the kitten, Jilly jumped. Hell, Henry was probably doing the cat tango right in front of the cage. Still, the rhythmic sound made her own hair tingle along the base of her neck. She really wished Evan hadn't run off.

A shadowy movement had Jilly turning toward the

corner of the room. Thinking the kitten had seen a mouse or a bat—though why he would flee rather than fight, she didn't know—Jilly tensed, ready to flee herself.

There was nothing there—not a rodent, not a person, not an animal. Not even a ghost.

The cold enveloped her an instant before the scent of cinnamon filled the room. It wasn't unpleasant, but the skin on Jilly's arms prickled and she found it hard to breathe.

Her hair fluttered as if there was a breeze. She glanced toward the window, but it was shut tightly, and the panes in her room were still the only solid ones in the entire inn.

CHAPTER TWELVE

"WHAT'S EATIN' YE?"

In the middle of mixing a batch of horehound for a little girl's cough, Jilly glanced at Addie.

"Excuse me?"

"Ye haven't been yerself for nigh onto a week now."

Addie was right. Since Jilly had started smelling cinnamon that wasn't there, feeling breezes that couldn't exist and experiencing temperature changes beyond the realm of possibility, she'd been out of sorts. She was always searching for...something or someone.

In a corner, an empty bedroom, behind her in the night. She was jumpy, spooked—in Addie's words, not herself. But if Jilly told her friend what had occurred, she would only insist they were ghostly manifestations. Despite everything, Jilly still wasn't ready to believe in them.

"I haven't been sleeping well," she hedged.

Not only was she afraid she'd awaken to a strange and new phenomenon, but Henry hissed at odd hours of the night. Zorro had taken it as a matter of pride to release Mario from any lock they could fashion on the dog cage, and Jilly never knew when Evan would be at the inn or out carousing with the Seitz brothers.

The first night he'd driven off in his pickup, he hadn't returned until after she'd left for Addie's the next morning. She'd been worried sick, wondering if he'd had an accident.

She'd gone home at lunch, only to find all four of them working with hangovers. Men. They were nothing but overgrown boys—even when they were blind, deaf and toothless.

"I'll give ye a tonic. You'll sleep like the dead."

"That's what I'm afraid of," Jilly muttered.

"Don't get sassy. You'll take the tonic and be glad of it."

"Yes, ma'am." Jilly hid her smile.

Addie was a wonder. She'd taught Jilly more in a week than she'd learned in a lifetime. Not only about mountain medicine, but about people, animals and friendship. Addie was the first, and best, friend Jilly had ever had.

She'd also taught Jilly how to cook many of the "gifts" they'd been given as payment for their services. Jilly hadn't had to go grocery shopping since she'd come to South Fork, which allowed her to use the stash from selling her rings for repairs alone.

At least her improved culinary skills meant that Naomi and Ruth had stopped bringing Evan dinner, lunch and dessert. They hadn't stopped coming over, but Jilly no longer felt inadequate whenever they did.

In truth, she rarely felt inadequate at all anymore. She could soothe a rash, lance a boil, brew a tonic of bitters and she could cook. That ought to get her a husband. Around here.

Jilly frowned and glanced at her bare and calloused feet. She could run all the way into town and back without a wince. Her fingernails were short and stained with berry juice. Her hair was tangled; her clothes older than her last marriage certificate. And it was only when she tried really hard to care that she did.

Her husband quest seemed less and less important with every passing day.

Not that she'd given up on it, of course. She was taking a break, a little vacation. She was entitled. Sooner or later she'd have to go back to her world. Once there, she didn't have much choice but to marry again. The skills she'd learned in South Fork were far from marketable.

Jilly finished with the child and sent her on her way. The yard was empty of new patients. Not a pig or a dog to be seen.

"So, tell me." Addie tossed a bit of this and a handful of that into a pot on the stove. "How's Evan in the sack?"

Jilly choked. "I didn't— We haven't— What?"

"He's a right handsome fellow. No wonder you can't sleep. Try sex first. Much better for the constitution than a tonic."

"Does everyone in South Fork think we're…intimate?"

"Not intimate."

Jilly breathed easier.

"Just havin' sex."

"Why would everyone think that?" she demanded, unreasonably embarrassed, even though she *had* wanted to sleep with Evan the first time she'd set eyes on him. But she hadn't known the folks in this town then, hadn't healed their ills and listened to their troubles. She didn't want them thinking…that.

"Why?" Addie repeated. "Why not? Two young, single people, alone at the inn. What's the matter with ye?"

"Not me," she muttered.

"Him?" Addie's eyes widened. "Well, that's interestin'."

"He wants love," Jilly found herself explaining. "And love is something I can't give him."

"He seems pretty lovable to me." Addie waggled her eyebrows.

"He is," Jilly blurted before she could stop herself.

"Then what's the problem?"

Why had she said that? Evan was sweet, sexy, adorable. She enjoyed every minute she spent in his company. When she was away she looked forward to seeing him again. But that wasn't love, was it?

"Love isn't real," she said. "It doesn't last."

"Which is it? Not real or not lasting? Can't be both."

Jilly frowned. The woman had a point.

"People *think* they're in love, but they aren't. If love was real, it would last forever."

"What do you think my man is hangin' around the inn for?"

"Got me."

"Because love does last. Forever. He's waitin' on me."

"Why did you sell the place?"

"I couldn't stand to see him and know I couldn't be with him yet."

"You actually *see* him?"

"Of course. He's there, ain't he?"

Jilly kept her opinion on that to herself as Addie set a cover on the kettle, then brushed off her hands. "Where'd you get the idea love isn't real?"

"My mother."

Addie snorted. "I don't like to say nothin' agin folks' mamas, but yours is plumb crazy. Love is the only thing worth livin' for. Doesn't she love you?"

"Family love is different than romantic love."

"You've got an answer for everything, don't ya?"

Genevieve had. Whenever Jilly had brought up the notion of a love for all time, her mother had shot it down with her cool tone and a logical explanation.

"Love isn't necessary," Jilly said. "You can live without it. A marriage works the best when based on friendship and mutual respect."

Addie wrinkled her nose. "I ain't nuzzlin' up to someone I *respect*. And livin' without love ain't no way to live."

The vehemence in her friend's voice made Jilly

pause, then blurt, "There's something you don't know about me, Addie."

The old woman shrugged. "I know all I need to. You're good with sick folks, kids and critters. In my book, that makes you special."

Jilly was struck dumb. She couldn't recall anyone ever calling her special before.

"I've been married four times."

"Aw. I'm sorry."

"On purpose. I marry old men for their money. It's kind of…my job."

Addie raised a shoulder. "Nice work if ye can get it."

"Do you hear what I'm saying? I'm a gold digger. A trophy wife. A…a—" She couldn't think of any of the other terms she'd heard in reference to herself.

"If you don't like what you're doing, quit doing it."

How simple. And impossible. Jilly had no other choice if she wanted to eat. Sadly, she'd become quite fond of the process.

Addie put a hand on her arm. "There is love, Jilly, and it does last forever. Just like there's magic in this world and ghosts from the next. You only have to believe."

"THIS HAS TO STOP," Evan muttered as his head pounded in time with Barry's hammer.

The sun blazed unmercifully. He probably should have spent the day inside, with the windows covered, but there was a leak in the roof, and Barry's bum knee predicted rain.

Evan had taken to going to the Seitz brothers' cabin whenever he couldn't sleep and partaking of their home brew. The liquid tasted like turpentine, scoured his throat and stomach like it, too. But the concoction was strong, and he was able to sleep. Usually on their couch or even the floor.

He could sleep and not dream of Jilly.

"What's gotta stop?"

Barry stood next to Evan on the roof, hammer dangling from his arthritic fingers. Today was the first time Evan had let him touch a tool. So far, Barry hadn't broken anything, not even himself.

"The drinking. The sleeping at your house." Evan climbed down the ladder. "I'm twenty-nine years old."

"Hell, I'm seventy-nine." Barry joined him on the ground. "I think it's fun."

The old man could pack away moonshine like a mule, and he was rarely the worse for it. Neither were Larry or Jerry. According to them, their mama had dosed them with moonshine to cure every ailment under the sun. They had built up an immunity in the cradle.

"Speaking of mules…" Evan began.

"Were we?"

Evan tried to remember, but the alcohol had killed a few too many brain cells. Conversations were becoming muddled in his mind. "Never mind. Where's Lightning?"

"There." Barry pointed behind Evan. Unfortunately, he used the hand holding the hammer. When his decrept fingers reached belly level, they gave out and the hammer fell.

Evan foolishly made a grab for the tool. So did Barry. With a hand holding a carpet knife. Pain sliced through Evan's forearm. The hammer landed squarely on his toe.

While he was jumping around cursing, a soft, wet nose nuzzled the back of his neck.

"Hey!" he shouted, then scooted away.

Lightning neighed and stomped his hoof. The old horse thought it was hysterical to creep up on him and nibble at his neck.

"Everyone's a comedian," Evan muttered. "Stop that!"

Lightning wasn't chastised. He shoved Evan in the shoulder with his head, then clopped away.

"You're bleedin'."

"What?" Evan glanced down.

Blood dripped off his fingertips in a steady stream. There was already a good-size puddle next to his foot.

Dizziness washed over him. He'd never been comfortable with blood. Especially his own.

"Hey, you're as white as Matthew Tolliver's ghost."

Barry grabbed Evan by the shoulders and gave him a little shake. The motion only served to make Evan's headache worse and caused the world to spin faster. Little black spots danced in front of his eyes.

"Larry!" Barry shouted in Evan's face. "Get your butt out here now!"

The spots crashed together, making a black curtain in Evan's mind.

The next thing he knew someone was patting his face and calling his name. The hands were callused, but softer than his own. He caught the scent of jasmine. The voice was familiar, bringing with it delicious thoughts of kissing under the stars and making love at midnight.

"Jilly?"

"Open your eyes."

A circle of faces surrounded him. Behind their heads, the sun shone in a bright blue Arkansas summer sky.

"What happened?"

"You took a nosedive. Luckily, Barry caught you, or that pretty nose would be broken." Jilly smiled and tweaked it.

"I fainted?"

He tried to sit up. She pushed him right back.

"Stay there. You'll just get blood all over everything."

Suddenly he remembered what had happened. Right up to the time the little dots had gone boom and the lights went out.

"Where did you come from?" he asked.

"Jerry ran down to get me."

"Jerry? Ran?"

He glanced at the old man, who didn't seem to know what was going on any more than Evan did.

"I heard you calling for Larry." Evan turned his gaze to Barry.

"I did. Callin' Jerry wouldn't do no good, since he's out of batteries for his hearin' thingee. But then Jerry had to run to Addie's, 'cause Larry'd only run into a tree."

"Well, thanks," he managed to say, his head spinning with the explanation and the blood loss.

"You ever fainted before?" Jilly asked.

"Once."

"Sight of blood bother you?"

"I'll never make a doctor."

Addie appeared with a bucket of water and set it next to Jilly. She squinted at Evan's arm. "That's gonna need stitchin'."

"Hell." Evan tried to sit up.

For the second time, Jilly shoved him back. "You're still too pale."

"All my blood's running into the grass. Pretty soon there'll be zombies walking around with the ghosts."

Jilly made a horrified face. Addie made the sign of the cross, then followed it with the odd finger-twisting motion he'd seen folks make to ward off evil. Or the devil. He wasn't sure which. Maybe both.

"You shut your mouth, Evan Luchetti," Addie admonished. "Sometimes you git what you ask fer."

"I was joking. I read somewhere that blood on a grave will raise the dead."

"What have you been reading?" Jilly asked. "*The Ghoul's Guide to Life and Death?*"

Evan shrugged. He couldn't remember where he'd read that little tidbit, or why he'd brought it up now. He must have lost more blood than he'd thought.

"That's not a matter for funnin'. Blood on a grave *will* raise the dead, if'n you have the right blood and the right person doin' the lettin'," Addie muttered.

Jilly rolled her eyes so only Evan could see.

"I need to get to a hospital." He cursed. "I hope I have enough cash to cover this."

"You don't have insurance?" Jilly asked.

"Do you?"

She frowned. "Not for very much longer."

"I'm a self-employed laborer. I can't afford common luxuries like health insurance." A fact that never ceased to annoy him. "Me and about forty-three million other people in the U.S."

"Never mind that now," Addie snapped. "Wash your hands, girl, then wash him. I've put a pot on to boil the thread and the needle."

"You're going to sew up his arm?"

"No." The old woman headed for the inn. "You are."

Jilly's mouth opened, then closed. "I—uh, don't think that's a good idea."

Addie paused on the porch. "Stitches ain't brain surgery. I've put in a thousand of 'em."

"Then you do it."

"You need the practice. I don't." She disappeared inside.

Jilly bit her lip. "I'd rather not practice on you."

"And I'd rather you didn't."

"That's settled then."

"Uh-huh."

"Here we go." Addie was back.

"Evan and I decided you should stitch him up."

"You don't get to decide."

"Excuse me? It's my arm," Evan protested.

Addie gave an aggrieved sigh and knelt, slowly, next to Jilly in the grass. Her joints popped and she grunted. "Look here."

She held her gnarled hands out in front of her. They shook like maple leaves in a high wind. "Any questions?"

Addie handed over the needle and thread. Jilly glanced from the implements to Evan. "I'll drive you to town if you want me to."

"Nearest hospital is in Little Rock," Addie interjected.

"Doctor?"

"Forty miles."

Evan sighed. He didn't like blood. He wasn't crazy about pain. But he liked paying for medical services, with cash he didn't have, even less.

He peered a brow at Jilly. "Can you do it?"

"Of course she kin," Addie interrupted. "Ye think I'd hand her a needle if she couldn't do the job?"

Jilly's shoulders straightened. Her lips tightened. "I can do this."

"Get to it then." Evan turned his head away so he wouldn't have to watch.

"We're leavin'," Barry said. "Sorry about cuttin' ye, boy."

He and his brothers were gone before Evan could say, "Accidents happen."

The cleaning of the wound wasn't bad. The first prick of the needle wasn't good. Evan caught his breath and Jilly hesitated.

"Just do it, girl. No time for foolishness from either one of ye."

"Yes, ma'am."

Jilly pricked him again. The thread tugged at his skin. Evan didn't like the sensation, but at least he didn't feel as if he was going to pass out or throw up.

"Make a stitch, then a knot t' make sure it don't come loose."

Jilly gave a tiny tug and Evan winced.

"Sorry," she whispered.

"I'm okay." He already felt like the world's biggest sissy for fainting. He wasn't going to cry while he got the stitches.

"What happened the last time you passed out?" Jilly asked.

"I hit the ground hard."

She snorted, then pricked him again with the needle. "I meant why did you faint?"

"Oh." He was having a hard time concentrating while anticipating the next bite of pain. "I was crossing a field and got caught crawling under some barbed wire. There's a scar on my back. Fifteen stitches worth."

Plus a tetanus booster and a lecture from his father. Kids had died running into barbed wire—usually riding a horse or an ATV. Get a strand of barbed wire rammed into your throat going twenty or thirty miles an hour and your life expectancy dropped to zero.

"I didn't see any scar."

She'd noticed his back. The thought made him forget the pain. But he wasn't dumb enough to glance in her direction. Blood he didn't want to see.

"The scar's low, probably below the waistline of my jeans."

She made a noncommittal murmur. He wanted to see if she was blushing. When she blushed her skin took on a rosy hue that made him think of strawberry milkshakes. When she blushed he wanted to lick her freckles and maybe her toes.

"Yer doin' fine, Jilly. I'm gonna make a poultice fer when yer finished."

Evan listened to the slow tread of Addie's feet as she retreated.

"How did you run into barbed wire?" Jilly continued.

"Nighttime."

"You don't know where the wire is on your farm?"

"Wasn't my farm."

"Ah. Girlfriend?"

He shrugged with his good side. He'd only had one girlfriend—Ashley—and she'd considered him nothing more than an amusement. The memory still stung.

"How old were you?"

"Sixteen."

"Sixteen and creeping out at night for…ice cream?"

"I've never heard it called that before."

She cleared her throat. "Where were your parents?"

"At home asleep. Didn't you ever sneak out?"

"Where would I have gone?"

"With your friends. Car ride. Walk in the woods. Beer party. Bonfire. Slap and tickle with the new boy."

She laughed. "My life was nothing like that."

"What was it like?"

Her laughter faded. He turned his head, stared at the sky, then slid his gaze in her direction. "Talk to me so I forget what you're doing."

She glanced at her hands and sighed. "My father left us. We lived on the streets awhile. My mom couldn't get a job. She—" Jilly broke off.

"She what?"

He figured her mother had turned tricks when times got tough. His brother Aaron worked with runaways in Las Vegas. His wife had been one of them, once upon a time, until she'd started stripping—a step up from hooking, but a step nevertheless. Shit happened, as Dean would say. You did what you had to do.

"She got married," Jilly finished.

"Huh?"

"My mother was—is—beautiful. She married for money. Several times. Now she's the Countess... something-ski."

"Ski?"

"Polish count."

"And you?"

"What about me?" Her voice was defensive, a bit shrill, she poked him and this time he felt it.

"Hey!"

"Sorry."

"You were telling me about your childhood. Why was yours so different from mine?"

"Did you ever sleep on the streets? Eat out of a garbage can?"

He turned his gaze on her. No wonder she was so desperate to sell the inn and acquire some cash. He wanted to question her further, but figured he should probably wait until she wasn't sticking him with a needle.

"Can't say that I have," Evan murmured. "The last person to sleep on the street in Gainsville was Freda Lallenheimer. Her husband, Fred, locked her out after she came home from the Daughters of the American Revolution meeting at 3:00 a.m. singing selected offerings from the soundtrack of *Moulin Rouge*."

Jilly smiled. "Go on."

"As I heard it, the daughters had broken out the peppermint schnapps in an attempt to cure the common cold."

Jilly's gaze sharpened. "Does that work?"

"No. But you no longer care that you have a cold."

"Darn. I could have used a cold cure." She shrugged. "Oh, well. Then what happened?"

"The chief of police found Freda stripped down to her slip in the town square, brushing her teeth in the water fountain. He took her home, where his own wife was already sleeping off the effects of the cold medicine."

"And did the chief let Freda live at his house?"

"For about two weeks. Then he couldn't stand one more rendition of "Diamonds Are a Girl's Best Friend" and dropped Freda off at home. She and Fred pretended nothing had ever happened."

"I'll bet no one goes hungry in that town, either."

"Of course not. That's why there's a ladies' auxiliary. Word gets around that a family is having tough times, and food magically appears on their doorstep."

Jilly's fingers hovered over his arm. "Magic?"

"Well, Illinois farmers have their pride. They don't take charity. But if the food just appears, they wouldn't let it go to waste."

"That would be a sin."

"Now you're catching on. So what happened after your mother got married?"

"I was sent to school. Switzerland. Vienna. Paris."

"Really? Cool."

"Not."

"I've never been farther than here."

"Count yourself lucky."

"Why?"

"I was an outsider. The poor stepdaughter."

"You sound like Cinderella."

She flicked a glance from his arm to his face and then back again. "How come a red-blooded American male knows so much about Disney movies for little girls?"

"Zsa Zsa."

"Since when does Miss Gabor give a fig about Walt Disney?"

He laughed. "Zsa Zsa's my niece. Her real name is Glory. She has a thing for hats, purses, matching socks. She's two."

"Precocious."

"And then some." One of the few things he missed about Gainsville was Glory. "Seeing the world sounds like fun."

"It didn't suck." Jilly took a deep breath. "Actually, it did. I was eight when I was sent away. I wanted my mother, but she wasn't there."

"Did you tell her how you felt?"

"Of course."

"And?"

"She didn't care."

Evan couldn't fathom a mother who didn't care that her child was lonely and miserable. His mother, as uncuddly as she was, would have moved heaven and earth to make any one of her children happy.

"I'm sorry," he murmured.

"I shouldn't complain. I didn't starve or freeze for long. And I'll never do either one again."

CHAPTER THIRTEEN

JILLY WAS HIGH on life. Or maybe just high on herself.

She'd stitched up Evan's arm and managed to sew a straight line. The blood hadn't bothered her a bit. The only thing that had was talking about her childhood.

In the middle of straining pasta for the tuna salad she was making for dinner, Jilly paused. She wasn't going to think about the past. She wasn't going back to the way things had been, and there was no reason to fear that she was.

Jilly took a swig of white wine from her cup. "Tastes the same whether it's in plastic or crystal."

Her mother had always said everything tasted better when sipped from expensive glass. Mother was wrong.

What else had she been wrong about?

Zorro chittered and tugged on Jilly's skirt. Absently she leaned down and gave him a quick hug. After the brief show of affection, he began to bat one of Henry's cat toys around the kitchen. Zorro was happiest when playing with someone else's things.

She turned toward her pasta just in time to see Lightning's lips reaching for a taste. "Out!" she shouted.

He jerked his head up so fast he banged it on the window frame.

"Shoo!"

He gave her his usual puppy-dog look and backed away. She had to get Evan to put glass in that window before Lightning ate their dinner out from under them some night.

"Yoo-hoo! Anyone home?"

Naomi, followed by Ruth, ducked into the kitchen. They glanced around the room. Both frowned to see only Jilly and Zorro.

"Evan's resting. He had a little accident."

"We heard."

"From Addie?"

"From Crawdad Gates, our neighbor. Addie told Jose Buntrock and he told Suz Orlon and—"

"She told Crawdad."

"No. I think she told Mavis Melrose. But she told—"

"Never mind," Jilly interrupted. "I get the picture."

"Picture! That's why we came. We wanted to show you one of Miss Dixie. We found it this morning."

Jilly finished tossing the ingredients for the salad into a big bowl, dried her hands and crossed to the kitchen table. Naomi opened a scrapbook and pointed to a photo. "Ain't she pretty?"

Why Jilly had been expecting a plain, older woman wearing a black dress and sensible shoes, she couldn't say. Miss Dixie had operated a bordello. She'd been run out of town on a rail. She was progressive, a maverick, a madam.

Nevertheless, the sight of the beautiful young woman in a minidress, with platform heels on her feet and a headband stretched around her forehead in Native American fashion, surprised Jilly.

"She always wore Jandolet perfume. Mama said the company stopped making it long about 1972, but she always kept a tiny bit in a golden bottle...." Naomi breathed in deeply. "Cinnamon never smelled so good."

"C-c-cinna—" Jilly couldn't get the rest of the word past the sudden blockage in her throat.

"You chokin'?" Ruth whapped her on the back so hard Jilly stumbled into the table. Zorro growled and scooted out the door.

"I—I'm fine."

So she'd smelled cinnamon in her bedroom. So what?

"Do you know which room was Miss Dixie's?" she asked.

"The one you're sleepin' in." Naomi tilted her head, narrowed her eyes. "You seen her?"

"Of course not."

She'd only smelled her.

But wait a minute, Jilly rationalized. If she was sleeping in Miss Dixie's room, that could explain the phenomenon. The scent had permeated the walls, the floor, the ceiling, and was merely being released into the air at a certain temperature.

That explanation made a lot more sense than a ghostly presence wearing perfume that hadn't been manufactured for thirty years. Didn't it?

"So you're sayin' you ain't seen no ghosts."

"None."

"Nothin' strange goin' on?"

Jilly shrugged. "Strange is in the eye of the beholder."

"What's that mean?"

"Never mind. Who else is supposed to haunt this place?"

Naomi stared at her for a long moment. Jilly stared right back. She wasn't going to admit anything, because there wasn't anything to admit. Eventually Naomi gave up and answered the question.

"Well, there's Matthew, of course, and a black man who was hung in yonder tree. One of Miss Dixie's girls." Naomi lowered her voice. "She died tryin' to get rid of a baby. Terrible thing. Who else, Ruth?"

Ruth snapped a salute.

"Oh, him. That's right."

"Who's him?" Jilly asked.

"The soldier. Died in the back bedroom at the base of the stairs."

She shivered as she remembered the door closing behind her, the chill, the breeze when there wasn't any breeze at all.

"Goose on your grave?" Naomi asked.

"What?"

"Yer cold all of a sudden. Goose on your grave. Ain't you ever heard that?"

Jilly shook her head. Graves. Ghosts. Geese. This was all too much for her.

"*What* soldier?" she pressed.

"From the war."

"World War Two?" Jilly guessed.

The girls exchanged a glance. "She *is* a Yankee," Naomi allowed.

The way she said it annoyed Jilly. How would they like it if she called them losers? She eyed the size of Ruth and decided she wasn't going to try it.

"Whenever we say war in these parts we're talkin' about the War of Northern Aggression. The *Civil* War," Naomi clarified for any idiots who didn't know the common Rebel term for it.

"What side was he on?" she asked.

"What other side is there?" Naomi drawled.

"Uh, Confederate?"

Naomi didn't bother to answer such a stupid question.

"What's his story?"

"If I recollect rightly, he'd come home for a visit."

"He lived here?"

"No. Much farther south. This was a stage stop back then."

"Evan mentioned that. But he said it was high-class."

"No lie."

"What would a soldier be doing in a high-class stage stop?"

"He was with Quantrill."

Jilly searched her mind for the name. "Border Wars. Guerillas."

Not regular army, but renegades who'd followed their own rules, and in the chaos, got away with it.

"He was on the run," Naomi continued. "Hiding from the Jayhawkers."

"I thought those skirmishes were in Missouri and Kansas."

"Not always."

"So what happened?"

"Arkansas was right on the border between the North and the South. Missoura folks declared for the North, ye know, but then sent just as many troops fer the South. We don't hold with that kind of behavior in Arkansas."

"Wishy-washy," Jilly commented.

"Exactly. But the problem with bein' in the middle is that ye get overrun by both armies. Captain Bontemps had the misfortune to come through town when the Yankees were about. He hid at the inn."

"And?"

"They shot him."

"Just like that?"

"In his bed. It was a damn disgrace," Naomi declared.

When her sister gasped and put her finger to her lips, she rolled her eyes. "I can say damn if I want to, Ruth Wilder. Especially if I'm talkin' about murderin' Yankee scum."

"You do know that the war's over?" Jilly asked.

"Tell it to Captain Bontemps."

Jilly hoped she wouldn't have the opportunity. She straightened at the thought and gave a self-derisive laugh. She didn't believe in ghosts. She was tired, nervous, out of sorts. Which was the only reason she was experiencing things that couldn't actually be true.

"So…uh…" Naomi craned her neck trying to see into the next room. "Where are the Seitz brothers?"

"Gone home at a run the instant Barry sliced Evan's arm. I don't think they like blood too much. Neither did Evan."

"My ma always says if men had to birth babies the world would have been over long ago."

Jilly laughed and the two women joined in. Laughing felt good after the tension of the day. She'd managed to sew up Evan's arm, but she hadn't been whistling Dixie while she did it.

"Did you want to talk to the Seitzes about something? I can give them a message tomorrow if you like."

"Uh, no." Naomi gave an uneasy shrug. "We were just wonderin' where they'd got to."

Jilly glanced at Ruth and was surprised at the blush staining the woman's cheeks.

Hmm. She'd thought Ruth was after Evan, but maybe she'd been wrong. Was Ruth interested in one of the brothers, despite each of them being born long before her, or even her mother?

Then again, Jilly wasn't one to throw stones anywhere near that glass house.

After the sisters left, silence settled over the inn once more. Until Lightning expressed his annoyance at missing out on the tuna salad, snorting through loose lips just outside the kitchen window.

"Be quiet out there!" she shouted.

He neighed and kicked the side of the house.

Mario's cage rattled. By the time Jilly reached the living room, Zorro had the thing open, and the dog raced after the raccoon, barking as if he were being attacked by evil forces.

Peter, who'd been sitting in the open dining-room window, dived for the safety of the yard and didn't come back.

Mario and Zorro raced upstairs and—

They woke Henry. The pitter-patter of twelve little paws thundered above her head. Jilly discovered herself smiling. Why, she had no idea.

She was in the middle of a *Beverly Hillbillies* nightmare, but she'd never been happier in her life.

EVAN AWOKE TO THE SOUND of scurrying feet, yipping doodle and squalling cat.

Sometimes he felt as if he'd stepped into an alternate universe. One where he was the only sane human in an insane menagerie. But Jilly seemed to enjoy the animals, and they were drawn to her. Several times he'd gotten up before dawn and caught her sleeping with a cat, a dog, an opossum and a raccoon curled around her legs.

A movement in the doorway now made him tense. He'd seen a lot of shadows at the inn, but whenever he gazed directly at them, nothing was there. This time when he looked at the shadow, he saw Jilly hovering in the hall.

"They woke you," she murmured. "Sorry."

He sat up. When her eyes widened and stuck to his chest he remembered he wore nothing but his boxers. Evan reached for his shirt.

"That's okay," he said. "If I sleep now I'll never sleep later."

The sun had faded. Night hovered at the edge of the horizon. Evan could barely see Jilly's face, but he found himself studying everything else about her. She'd changed in the few weeks she'd been here.

He'd thought her beautiful that first day—cool, sexy, sophisticated, completely different from any woman he'd ever known. He'd wanted her. What else was new?

But in sharing a house with her, as well as a common goal, he'd come to know her so much better than any other female he'd ever met—save those with the name of Luchetti.

She wasn't just pretty, she was smart, compassionate and strong. What other woman would spend every day with Addie dosing pigs and chickens, lancing Lord knows what on the asses of strangers, and rocking children until their sore tummies went away?

Seeing her now—barefoot, hair loose, no makeup, the clothes Naomi and Ruth had given her more a part of her than the frothy green suit Lightning had wrecked could ever be—she seemed happy. Evan wondered, not for the first time, if she could be happy with him.

Except she didn't believe in ghosts, love, magic or any of the things that made the world special and interesting.

"I suppose your injured arm will slow down the work around here."

"Nah. The brothers are coming along pretty well. At first I figured they'd be more trouble than they were worth, but they've stopped breaking things. They even fixed the porch this morning, and they didn't make it worse before they made it better."

"High praise," she said, and he heard the smile in her voice. "So we're on schedule?"

"Ahead. Another month and we'll be ready to paint the walls and lay the floors."

"Then?"

"Unless you plan to furnish the place, too, the painting and the carpeting are the end."

"I doubt I can afford furniture. Besides, I like to decorate my own space. Who knows what the new owners will want to do with this one? Antiques, I'd think. Or maybe they'll go modern. Though I wouldn't."

Her voice had turned sad. She leaned against the doorjamb staring past him out the window.

Evan wanted to lighten her mood. The story of his life. Wherever there was a sad woman, or one in need, there was Evan Luchetti with the tools to fix her right up. Just call him the love carpenter. He snorted.

"Something funny?"

"Uh, no. Nothing."

"Dinner's ready. I'll meet you downstairs."

She turned and walked into her room across the hall. Evan stood and reached for his jeans.

Before he could put them on Jilly came back through the door, and they smashed into each other. His pants fell to the floor as he caught her by her shoulders. Her arms went around his waist, beneath his unbuttoned shirt, and her palms slid against his skin. His breath caught as his body tightened.

"Down boy," he muttered. Now was not the time.

Jilly was trembling, her breath catching as if she'd just run miles instead of yards. With every hitch of her breath, her breasts rubbed against his ribs, his belly, and he was having a difficult time taming the beast in his boxers.

"What's the matter?"

She lifted her head, and the light green of her eyes was nearly obliterated by her dilated pupils. The contrast was stark in her overly pale face.

"Remember when I said I didn't believe in ghosts, or magic, or—"

"I remember," he interrupted, not wanting to hear again that his dreams of everlasting love, his hopes of a bright and shiny family future, were foolish. "What happened?"

"I saw…" She glanced over her shoulder and mumbled, "I'm not sure."

"A ghost?"

"Maybe." Her fingers tightened on his arms as she faced him again. "Maybe everything I never believed in is true."

Pressing her cheek to his bare chest, she stroked his back lower and lower until her hands slid beneath the waistband of his boxers.

Jilly had said she didn't believe in ghosts any more than she believed in love. Now she'd admitted the possibility of one then stuck her hand down his pants. Evan wasn't exactly sure, but that sounded like love to him.

He opened his mouth to ask, and her hand closed around his erection.

Huh. That felt a lot like love, too.

JILLY HAD GONE TO HER room, planning to change before dinner. She couldn't quite recall everything that had stained the sky-blue crop top she wore, and she didn't really want to. But she couldn't sit across the dinner table from Evan wearing a shirt that sported more bodily fluids than the floor of an emergency room at rush hour.

She'd just knelt to root through the box of clothes when Henry, who must have been hiding in an attempt to get away from Mario, hissed and shot out from under the covers, disappearing down the steps. The front screen door banged open, then closed. The room suddenly seemed several degrees chillier than it had when she'd walked in, and she could swear she smelled cinnamon again.

"Miss Dixie?" she'd whispered, and crossed herself. Amazing how three years in a Catholic boarding school in France came back when you needed it the most.

Jilly had gotten to her feet and turned around. As usual, nothing was there. The window was closed. The room should be sweltering. There was no reason to feel chilled or smell traces of a long dead perfume, but she did.

At the edge of her vision, in the corner at the far side of the room, she detected a shadow. Jilly focused on the dimness, and when it seemed to darken, solidify, almost become a shape, she ran.

Right now she wanted to chase the memory away, forget the breeze, negate the smell. Maybe if Evan touched her as she'd been wanting him to, the cold that lived deep inside of her would disappear.

Jilly went on tiptoe and pressed her mouth to his. Her tongue swept his lips, plunged inside and did a seductive dance. She tightened her grip, and he leaped in her palm as the friction between her body and his increased.

He cursed and pulled her hand away. "Are you sure about this?"

"More sure than I've ever been about anything."

She drew him toward his sleeping bag, then tugged him with her to the floor. He didn't resist, joining her on the soft, shiny material and returning his mouth to hers.

His hard, rough, skilled hands were everywhere, making her shiver, but not from the cold. If all she'd had to do was panic to get Evan to kiss her so deliciously, she'd have done it the instant she met him.

Why he'd changed his mind about having sex with her, she had no idea, and she wasn't going to ask. She was going to enjoy the moment. Something she'd done far too little of in her life.

The door slammed and they both started. Evan lifted his head and frowned. "Weird."

Jilly yanked his mouth back to hers. His lips were both hard and soft. Warm, sweet, skilled. She'd kissed a dozen men, at least, but she'd never kissed one who kissed like Evan.

Though they'd agreed not to do this, that didn't mean she hadn't thought about it. From the way she'd caught him watching her every now and again, he'd thought about it, too.

"Touch me," he murmured against her mouth. "Any way that you like."

She wanted to do things to him she'd only read about. She wanted him to do things to her she'd only dreamed of.

"Your hair." She ran her fingers through the long strands that seemed to encompass every imaginable shade of brown. "I want to feel it." He tilted his head. "All over me."

His lips lifted. "I can do that."

"I bet you can do anything."

His smile faded. She didn't know what she'd said, but she'd spoiled the moment. Since she didn't want him to think, to examine, to stop, she shoved his loose shirt from his shoulders and tasted his chest with her tongue. The flavor of his skin only made her want to taste more.

She eased him onto his back and skimmed her lips over his ribs, across his belly. His erection leaped against her neck. She wanted to taste that, too. Boldly she freed him and took him into her mouth.

Her hair was a curtain that shaded her from the world. She could do anything behind that curtain, and she did.

His heat warmed the chill inside her. The pulse of him against her tongue brought desire to life. His moans called to a part of her that had never existed until now.

Suddenly he grabbed her forearms and dragged her up his body. Their mouths met, and he eased her onto her back again. His length fitted against her in just the right way. Her eyes widened at the sensations a mere flex of his hips sent throughout her ignorant body.

He was completely naked, she still wore all her clothes, yet she was on the verge of something mind-altering, if she could just…

Well, she wasn't quite sure.

His mouth moved away, and she whimpered.

"Shh, I'll make it better soon. I promise," he murmured.

His hand slipped under her shirt, and his quick, clever fingers unsnapped her bra with one practiced twist. His palm smoothed along her side, her ribs, her belly.

She wanted him to touch all of her without hindrance, so she grabbed the edge of the garment and whipped it over her head. The stained top flew into a corner along with her bra.

Evan raised himself on one elbow. His face reverent, he traced a fingertip over the blue veins in her breasts.

Instead of filling his hands with their weight, and his mouth with their tips, he leaned down and let his hair cascade all over her. She caught her breath at the sensation and went still.

Evan treated her as though she was a precious gift and made her feel like one, too.

While he learned her likes and dislikes, she learned them, as well. Sex had never been about her. But with Evan, that was no longer the truth. With him, sex was about them both.

While he kissed her, touched her and let her do the same to him, the sun left the sky and the moon rose. Silver spilled through the trees and across the floor, bathing them in speckled light. She traced a flickering shadow across his stomach with her lips, and his skin rippled.

She lifted her head, watching the muscles contract beneath her touch. "You're ticklish?"

"Guess so."

"You didn't know?"

"I've never felt like this before."

His words came too close to an imaginary line, so she slid up his body and took him inside. He gasped as she fitted them together, held on tight as she started to move. His blue eyes shone brightly in the moonlight, holding hers and saying things she didn't want to hear.

She closed her own eyes and reached for that mythical something everyone was always talking about. But once again, it was nowhere to be found.

Suddenly she was falling. Her eyes flew open as she landed on her back in the tangle of sleeping bag and blankets. Evan, face intense, muscles bulging beneath skin shaded both bronze and silver, murmured, "Tell me what you like."

She didn't know, had never been asked.

"Teach me." She tangled her fingers in his hair and drew him closer. "Love me."

"I will." He kissed her, mumbling something against her lips that sounded suspiciously like, "I do."

Which was just sex talk. It didn't mean any more than her plea for love. She'd been talking about love in the carnal sense, nothing more.

"Don't think." He kissed her brow, then the corner of her eye. "You think too much."

She'd never been accused of that, but in this case he was probably right. She wanted sex for the sake of sex. She needed to stop worrying about her inadequacies and the future. Sex was about the moment. Something she'd never been able to live in very well.

Sighing, she arched, and he slid against her in amazing and new ways. His hair brushed her neck, and bright lights flashed in her head. She had an instant to wonder if there was a storm on the way, and then she couldn't think anymore as her body tightened, clenched and soared far away from every thought.

When she *could* think again, she started to laugh. No wonder people spent half their lives trying to recreate this feeling.

Evan lifted his head from her shoulder. She bit her lip, but she couldn't stop snickering. She'd just learned a secret. One everyone else had already known.

"You do know that laughing at a time like this is the quickest way to hurt a guy?"

"I—I'm sorry, it's just, I've always wondered, but I never…knew."

"Never?"

She shook her head, and his amusement gave way to concern. He touched her face, pushed her hair from her forehead. "That's not right, Jilly."

She stared into his eyes and murmured, "It is now."

They lay together as the moon moved across the sky and the shadows moved across the floor. He held her hand, played with her fingers, then her hair. The lazy motions, as if they had all the time in the world just to be together, were both relaxing and arousing.

Sometime in the night, he showed her again everything she'd been missing. The second time was even better than the first and when he fell asleep, his legs still entwined with hers, Jilly stared at the ceiling.

This was sex. Great sex, but just sex, and she couldn't

let the soft, mushy sensation just below her heart and above her belly turn into something solid and real.

But as she drifted toward sleep, a sound that had been missing ever since she'd come here, a sound that allowed her to sleep and not to dream, penetrated her drowsy consciousness. In Evan's room she could hear the creek, and the rush of the water over the stones reminded her of the surf on the beach.

She fell asleep for the first time in a long time feeling as if she'd come home.

CHAPTER FOURTEEN

MORNING ARRIVED and with it Evan's sanity. He hadn't used protection. He hadn't even thought about it. He'd been too busy getting Jilly naked and getting inside of her.

He should be panicked, terrified, but he wasn't. He was head over hills crazy for Jilly, and if he'd gotten her pregnant, well, he'd do the right thing, which was what he wanted to do, anyway.

She lay in his bed, such as it was, hair blazing across the pillows. Light filtered through the window. Soon the sun would be up, and the brothers would arrive. If there wasn't coffee and breakfast on the table, they'd come searching for him. Evan didn't want anyone walking in here this morning.

He'd lived in a small town all his life, and he knew what would happen. Gossip. Innuendo. Whispers.

Though Jilly was a grown woman and he was a grown man, he still didn't want anyone talking about the best thing that had ever happened to him as if it were another fling in a long line of them. He'd been there already and done that enough.

Evan woke her with a kiss and a cuddle. She smiled, stretched and opened her eyes. Evan wanted to make love to her all over again, but first he had something to say.

"I'm sorry."

Her face clouded, and he wanted to kick himself. For a man who'd been here dozens of times before he ought to be better at the morning after.

"Not about this," he blurted. "Not about us. But I never asked you about protection and I—"

"I'm on the pill."

He breathed easier. Even though the image of her carrying his child, walking through the pasture barefoot, with her hair cascading down, did funny things to his insides, he wanted to do something right just once in his life.

She stared at him expectantly. There was more to modern sex than the mere fear of pregnancy.

"I've never been with anyone without a condom," he assured her.

"Careful boy," she murmured.

"I'm not a stupid man."

"I never said you were." She patted his face and annoyance surfaced.

"This isn't a reenactment of *The Graduate*. You're much better looking than Mrs. Robinson."

"Flattery will get you everywhere. I was thinking more along the lines of *Summer of '42*."

Evan frowned. "I didn't see that movie."

"Probably before your time."

"You aren't *that* much older than me."

"Funny, I feel ancient."

"And I feel…" He tried to describe the lightness in his chest, that sense of possibility that had been with him from the moment he'd woken all tangled up in her. "Well, almost like a virgin again."

She laughed. "I haven't been a virgin since…well, marriage door number one."

"Number one? How many times have you been married?"

She didn't want to tell him, he saw it in her eyes. If they were ever going to move beyond partnership and friendship, something he very much wanted to do, she needed to trust him.

"Jilly, I don't care about what happened before. I only care about what happens from now on."

She searched his face and her unease faded. "Four," she said.

"You've been married four times?"

"Yes."

"And you've never had an orgasm."

"Is that all you can think about?"

Well, it seemed like a pretty important point from his end. Four marriages and bad sex in every one. Why on earth had she ever opened marriage door number two? Would he be able to convince her to open door number five, with him? He'd better take this slow or he'd spook her back to California.

"All I can think about right now is breakfast," he murmured.

Jilly sat up. He yanked her back. "Where do you think you're going?"

"I can't make breakfast like this."

He let his gaze wander from the top of her tousled head to the covers pooling around her naked waist. She had spectacular breasts. Round, full, real. Not that he'd ever seen any fake ones in Illinois. Those things were expensive.

Jilly tugged the blanket up to her neck. He reached out slowly, and pulled it back down. Then he let his fingers trail over her neck, her collarbone, the swell of perfect pale skin.

"Let me show you what I mean by breakfast."

JILLY'S HEAD WAS STILL spinning as she made her way to the creek to wash up. She liked what Evan meant by breakfast.

Wading into the stream, she relished the cool lapping of water against her skin. One night, one morning in his arms and all she could think about was Evan.

Which wasn't exactly true. She'd been thinking about little else *but* him since she'd gotten here. Except now she knew what she'd been missing—for most of her life.

She'd just rubbed soap all over her body and into her hair when something swam past her hip. Used to the brush of fish in the creek, she didn't care at first. However, when that same something bumped her more solidly than a fish ever could, she opened her eyes.

An alligator floated in the water right in front of her belly.

"Fergus!" she admonished. "You could have given me heart failure."

He opened his toothless mouth, then shut it again. His unblinking eyes remained fixed on hers.

"What are you doing here? You've got your own pond."

Fergus bumped her again. He certainly was acting strange. Even for an alligator.

Uneasy, Jilly washed off the soap and rinsed her hair. She climbed out of the creek, made use of her towel, then got dressed. The alligator followed.

"Is something the matter with Addie?" she guessed.

He blinked once. She wasn't sure if that meant yes or no, but she wasn't taking any chances. Jilly lit out for Addie's at a run.

The weeks spent barefoot, the days spent working with people and animals, had strengthened her. She could run a long way and not become breathless; her feet were as hard as the weathered boards of the inn. She reached the cabin in minutes.

The place appeared deserted. Of course, it was early yet. Folks shouldn't be knocking on Addie's door until at least 7:00 a.m. Since most of her critters—except for Fergus, who was attached to Addie something fierce—had taken up residence with Jilly, the lack of movement wasn't unusual. Nevertheless, Jilly was worried.

She knocked on the door. No one answered. Hesitantly, she turned the knob.

"Addie?" she called into the darkened interior.

Again, she received no answer, so she went inside. The cabin was dark, the windows still shuttered from the night. The sun didn't penetrate the shadowy corners of the room.

Jilly hovered in the doorway, waiting for her eyes to adjust. When they did, she saw a lump on the mattress. An Addie-size lump that wasn't moving.

She let out a muffled cry as she hurried over and dropped to her knees next to the bed. Reaching out, her fingers trembled. What would she do if Addie was dead?

But when she touched the lump, it moved, groaned, then cursed. "What're ye doin' here, girl?"

Relief flooded Jilly. "I thought you were dead."

Addie turned, and Jilly caught her breath. Pale and drawn, the old woman appeared even older. Her eyes burned with fever, her skin was dry and her lips were cracked. Her long hair was unbound, tangled and sweaty.

"What's the matter?"

"I'm dyin'."

"You are not!"

"Just 'cause ye wish it don't make it true."

"You were fine yesterday."

"Not really." Addie took Jilly's hand. Her fingers felt like a bagful of bones; her skin scraped against Jilly's like sandpaper. "I been holdin' on until ye came."

"Th-that's crazy. You can't just die right now."

"No?" Addie smiled softly. "Ye don't know much about dyin' then."

Jilly had never been so panicked in her life. Addie was her best friend, her first friend, her only friend. How could she leave like this?

"You...can't."

"I can. But you're right, I'm not goin' quite yet. I been waitin' years for ye to show up in South Fork."

"I don't understand. Did Henry tell you about me?"

"I never talked to Henry. His lawyer—weaselly fellow, but ain't they all—took care of the sale of the inn."

"How could you have been waiting for me if you didn't know I existed?"

"I knew you were out there somewhere, and the good Lord would see fit to send ye to me when it was my time t' go."

"You're not making any sense." Jilly laid her palm against Addie's forehead. "And no wonder."

Addie knocked away her hand. "I'm not out of my head. Everyone knows that when it's time for a magic woman to leave this earth, another one comes."

"Magic woman? Me?"

"Who else?"

"No, Addie. I don't believe..."

Jilly's voice trailed off. She'd almost said she didn't believe in anything she couldn't sell, but if she could admit to the possibility of ghosts...

Well, wasn't anything conceivable?

Magic. Power. Even love?

Jilly put the last thought out of her head. Love was something she couldn't deal with right now. Not with Addie so sick.

"What should I do?" Jilly asked.

"A little more practice, a few more days, maybe weeks, then you'll be ready to take my place."

"Addie, I can't."

"Of course ye can. Are ye tellin' me ye don't enjoy the work? That ye don't like the people and the animals?"

Jilly looked around the sparse cabin. No heat, no electricity, no plumbing. "I can't stay here."

"Never said ye had to. Ye can work out of the inn. Watcha been fixin' it fer?"

"To sell."

"I figured ye'd have changed yer thinking on that by now."

"Why? I need the money."

"Do ye? Do ye really?"

"Of course. I've got nothing."

"Ye've got a lot more than ye think, Jilly Hart."

Jilly opened her mouth to protest, and someone knocked on the door.

A young girl, who seemed to be no more than seventeen or eighteen, waddled into the room. She appeared about eight years pregnant.

"The Lord works in mysterious ways," Addie murmured.

"How you figure?" Jilly couldn't take her eyes off the young woman's huge belly.

"Ye need t' learn how to deliver a youngun. Here's Belinda all ready to go, and she even came to us."

"You want me to—?" Jilly squeaked.

"Who else? I'm not up t' it."

"A doctor would be an excellent choice."

Addie hoisted herself out of bed. "Women been birthin' babies without the help of a doctor for centuries. Now strip the bed." Addie pointed at a pile of fresh sheets. "Remake it with those. I'll boil the water."

Jilly's eyes met the young woman's. "You want me to drive you to the doctor?"

Belinda shook her head, then sat heavily in a chair next to the door. "Can't afford no doctor. Addie brought me into the world. I trust her."

"But she—"

"If she says you're the new doctor, then ye are. I trust ye, too."

Warmth spread through Jilly's chest. The girl trusted her. She was delusional, but Jilly felt blessed nevertheless.

"You're sure?" She tried one last time.

Belinda caught her breath and water seemed to come from nowhere, cascading over the chair and splashing at her feet.

"She's sure," Addie said briskly. "Now move. Belinda's ma had her in less than an hour."

"Does that mean something?" Jilly asked as she yanked the covers from the mattress.

"Means that even if she took ye up on that offer of a

ride to the hospital, ye'd be deliverin' her baby on the road. Daughters follow their ma's in little else but havin' babies. Better ye help her out here, with me at yer side. I *have* done this a few times before."

"How few?"

"Less than a thousand. More than a hundred."

Jilly frowned, and Addie waved her worries away. "I've seen it all. I know what I'm doin' and soon you will, too."

"Delivering babies is serious business, Addie."

"Darn tootin'. So let's get serious." She tugged a chair nearer to the bed. "Get my ax from the woodpile and be quick about it."

Jilly, in the middle of spreading a plastic sheet over the mattress, paused and turned. "What?"

She struggled with horrific images of what the ax might be used for.

"Get the ax, put it under the bed." When Jilly continued to stare at her blankly she stated, "To cut the pain."

Belinda chose that moment to moan. Jilly glanced at her. The girl was gripping her belly and making a terrible face.

"How about some morphine instead?" Jilly suggested.

"No drugs," Addie insisted. "The ax will help. Do what I tell ye."

Jilly did, bringing the dusty implement inside and shoving it beneath the bed as instructed. When she walked past Addie, the old woman took her arm and whispered, "Mind over matter. If she believes it'll help then…"

"It'll help."

Addie nodded with a satisfied expression as Jilly assisted Belinda into the bed.

Addie was right about more than the ax. Within the hour, Belinda held her brand-new son, and Jilly knew more about childbirth than she had ever wanted to. Birthing babies was sweaty, painful, messy work—even for the mother.

Watching Belinda and the baby, Jilly understood she'd done something special, something real, something—

"Magic," she whispered.

EVAN WOKE A SECOND TIME that morning to find Larry, Jerry and Barry staring at him. He started and reached for Jilly, but she wasn't there.

He vaguely remembered her saying she was going to the creek, then she'd make breakfast. He didn't smell any coffee.

"What's the matter?" he croaked, sitting up and peering around the room for his clothes.

"Lookin' fer this?" Jilly's underwear hung from Barry's finger.

Evan snatched it away and shoved the garment beneath the sheets.

Barry laughed. "No cause to be embarrassed. About time you two went at it."

"We didn't go at it," Evan muttered, crawling out of bed and digging fresh clothes from his bag.

"No? Too bad. If I was a younger man, I sure would."

"You three keep your traps shut. This is between Jilly and me."

"My lips are sealed." Barry snapped his gums together. "Oops." He reached into his pocket and inserted his teeth, then clicked them once for good measure.

Evan glanced at Larry, who covered his eyes. Jerry stared out the window. He hadn't heard the conversation in the first place. Maybe they were safe from loose lips.

"Is Jilly downstairs?"

"No. That's why we came up. We need our coffee. It's purt near seven in the mornin'."

Evan didn't like the sound of that.

He threw on his clothes and ran downstairs. No coffee. No breakfast. No Jilly.

Unease made him head to the living room. Peter was asleep in the corner with Zorro. Mario had piddled on the floor directly in front of the door. He did that a lot. Evan despaired of the animal ever understanding the difference between inside and outside. Sometimes he wondered if Mario had a brain in his head. But he was sweet and funny, and Evan already loved him.

He hunted for the doodle, found him curled up behind his cage fast asleep. Evan frowned. It wasn't like Jilly to leave Mario free and unsupervised. She hated cleaning up piddle even more than she hated...talking about love.

Evan shifted his shoulders. *Hell.* Had she run back to California, after all?

"Jilly?" he called.

The only answer was Henry's meow. Evan glanced onto the porch, where the black kitten had deposited a dead chipmunk.

"Thanks, pal. Not hungry."

Evan walked outside, ignoring the disgusting gift.

"Jilly?" he shouted.

Lightning appeared around the corner of the house. He snorted and shook his head.

"Where is she?"

The ancient horse plodded across the field in the direction of Addie's. He stopped, as he always did, at the property line and neighed, once, twice, three times.

Evan crossed the expanse of grass and wildflowers, then left Lightning behind as he ran down the hill to Addie's house. He burst into the cabin, nearly fainting with relief when he found Jilly there. Addie was asleep in her chair, as was a young woman in Addie's bed.

Jilly glanced up from the bundle in her arms. At first he didn't comprehend what he was seeing. Then the bundle squirmed and started to cry.

Evan couldn't tear his gaze away from Jilly's face. For an instant she resembled the picture of the Madonna his mother kept on her nightstand.

"Wanna take a peek?" she asked.

Evan shook off the odd sensation and joined her. Together they stared at the squalling, red-faced infant.

"I used to think every baby looked like Winston Churchill," she murmured.

"And now?"

"Now I think they look like…themselves."

The baby's cries increased in volume. Jilly glanced at the young mother and Addie. "Shh." She kissed the baby's downy head, but the child wasn't interested.

"Here." Evan held out his arms. "I'm pretty good at this. Really."

She shrugged and handed him the baby. Kim's daughter had been a royal pain in the butt until she was six weeks old. In truth, she still was, but he liked her that way.

He brought the child close to his chest and did the universal motion for quieting babies, the one he'd observed both his mother and his sister perform with Zsa Zsa. The one he'd perfected over many an afternoon with his niece while Kim escaped to anywhere but there. Evan did the mommy sway and, like Zsa Zsa, the baby quieted.

Jilly stared at him openmouthed and he shrugged. "I'm good with women."

"That's a boy."

"Oh." He frowned at the still-red baby face. The child might not resemble Winston Churchill, but he didn't look like a boy. Or a girl, either. "Well, I'm good with babies, too."

"You have amazing talents."

He wiggled his eyebrows. "I thought you'd never mention them."

She blushed and glanced at Addie, but the old woman was still sleeping.

"Delivering babies must tucker her out. She isn't as young as she used to be."

"I delivered the baby."

Evan nearly dropped him. "You?"

She stiffened. "You don't think I could?"

He stared into her determined face, then at the baby's head. "I've told you before, I think you can do anything."

"You know what?"

Lifting his gaze to hers, Evan was captured by the combination of budding strength and fading fragility. Jilly Hart was an amazing woman.

"Right now, so do I."

CHAPTER FIFTEEN

THE WEEKS THAT followed were better than the weeks
that had come before. Jilly spent every night in
Evan's room. She let the critters have hers. She didn't
need it.

Evan taught her things in the darkness that made her
blush in the light. She never grew tired of touching him,
kissing him, of just being with him, and he appeared to
feel the same way about her.

Addie had improved. She still tired easily, still spiked
a fever now and again, but she was able to teach Jilly
more every day.

"You'll do fine," Addie assured her.

"I didn't say I was going to stay."

"What else ye gonna do with yer time?"

Addie had a point. Jilly's life, which had seemed a suc-
cess thus far, now appeared appallingly futile. Who cared
if her hair was highlighted, her nails done, her clothes and
makeup perfect? Certainly not Jilly, and while this should
disturb her, it didn't. She had far too much to do in any
given day to worry about such foolishness.

Folks had taken to pounding on the door at all hours.

Evan and the brothers had fixed up the parlor on the first floor for an office.

Jilly had treated so many diseases—some she recognized and some she did not—that she'd lost track of them. Those people she couldn't help, she sent to the doctor or took there herself.

Amazingly, the natural cures worked more often than not. The mind over matter nature of Addie's medicine could not be denied.

But the most astonishing development was the progress at the inn. In lieu of payment, people pitched in. The place could be ready to go on the market as early as next week.

Jilly sighed as she made supper. Lightning appeared in the window and sniffed the aroma of pork chops and wild rice. She'd gotten so used to him hanging his head over the sink, she didn't know what she'd do if he wasn't there to talk to every night while she cooked.

"I almost wish…" Jilly began.

Lightning snorted, blowing horse snot all over the dishes in the sink.

"Hey! You're lucky those were dirty."

He nickered—half laugh, half apology. Once, what seemed a lifetime ago, she hadn't liked him. Back when she'd been Jillian Duvier. Now she was Jilly Hart, healer of the Ozarks. She felt like a comic book heroine, and she wanted to stay that way.

"I wish the inn wasn't nearly done. What am I going to do then?"

She'd have to make a decision. Would she stay or would she go?

"Hi." Evan's soft greeting made Jilly's stomach flutter. He slipped his arms around her waist and kissed her neck. "What's for supper?"

"Is that a serious question, or is it code, like breakfast?"

"Do you want it to be code?" He slid his hand under her shirt, then beneath the elastic of her bra, holding her breast and teasing her nipple in the same motion.

Lightning eyed them with interest. "Shoo." Jilly flicked the dish towel at his nose and he backed away. "You really need to watch what you're doing in front of the children," she teased.

"That horse is older than I am."

"How long do horses live, anyway?"

"Hell if I know."

He had both hands up her shirt, and she was starting to forget something she really needed to remember. His erection pressed against her back. His mouth latched on to her neck as he rolled her nipples between clever, callused fingers.

"What do you say we christen the kitchen?" he murmured.

They'd christened each room as he'd finished it. They'd even christened the creek. His pickup. The back porch. At first she was nervous about having sex here, there, everywhere. But Evan had a way of making her forget anything but him.

"Yoo-hoo!"

Jilly tore out of Evan's arms an instant before Naomi, then Ruth, walked in the door. Suddenly she remembered what she'd been meaning to tell him.

"Ruth and Naomi are coming for dinner."

"I see that."

She glanced at him, afraid he might be angry, but he was smiling. Evan was the most easygoing man she'd ever met. He winked at her, promising delights for later that she'd better not think about now.

"I'm going to take a shower."

One other change—plumbing. As much as Jilly regretted how quickly the inn was being completed, she didn't regret running water and indoor facilities.

"Weren't the Seitz brothers coming?" Naomi asked.

"Crap." Jilly'd forgotten that, too. She was supposed to ask the brothers Seitz to stay. For some reason, Naomi, or maybe Ruth, liked them.

Her only excuse for being so absentminded was a case of stomachache in a seven-year-old boy. No fever, no tenderness; most likely he'd snuck too much candy, so she'd spent the better part of the afternoon mixing horse-mint tea and gathering wild ginger to ease his discomfort.

"I'll…" Jilly was going to say call them, but she didn't have a phone. Even though the electricity was working, she and Evan had decided they didn't need one yet.

Another example of how things had changed. Jilly Hart, who'd never left home without her cell phone, hadn't had access to wireless service for over a month, and she didn't miss it.

"I'll walk over after I shower," Evan offered.

"Thanks." She gave him a smile.

He wiggled his eyebrows before he headed upstairs.

"Can I help with dinner?" Naomi set a glass bottle on the table.

"No, thanks. Everything's done that can be done for the moment. What's that?"

"Mama sent it over. Her special brew."

"Brew? Like beer?"

Ruth grinned.

"Not hardly," Naomi said. "This'll take rust off an old ax and the edge off any problems you might have."

"Moonshine."

Jilly had heard whispers of stills that had been passed down through the generations. Most moonshine was used for medicinal purposes these days. Addie kept a big jug under her bed. Of course, around here a hangnail required a good dosing on many an occasion.

"We like to call it home brew," Naomi insisted. "Want some?"

Jilly shrugged. "Why not?"

She brought glasses, and Naomi splashed in generous helpings of the clear liquid. The three of them tapped rims. Jilly sipped while Naomi and Ruth gulped.

The moonshine went up her nose and straight to her brain. She coughed. Naomi laughed and urged Jilly's glass toward her mouth again. "Better take another."

She did and the need to cough went away. Jilly could understand why folks drank the brew medicinally. If the moonshine didn't cure whatever ailed you, the stuff would definitely kill it. Barring that, you wouldn't care.

She chuckled, remembering Evan's tale of peppermint schnapps and the Daughters of the American Revolution. Certain cures appeared to cross the boundaries between North and South, young and old.

They sat at the kitchen table. Naomi filled their glasses again. The more Jilly drank, the better the stuff tasted.

"We have a favor to ask."

"Mmm?" Jilly asked midsip.

"Ruth and I…well, really Ruth, but I'm interested, too."

Ruth made an impatient sound. "Git on with it."

Jilly blinked at the low rumble of Ruth's voice. She'd never heard it before. She stared at the woman as if Lightning had suddenly walked in and started singing. For Ruth to speak, the favor must be very important.

"We want to do a spell," Naomi blurted.

Once Jilly would have laughed. Now she merely tilted her head and asked, "What kind of spell, and why tell me?"

"A…well, not a love spell exactly. A—"

"Prediction," Ruth whispered.

"Of what?"

"Who Ruth should marry."

Jilly glanced at Naomi, then back at Ruth. "You want to get married?"

"Don't everyone?"

"Not necessarily."

Ruth shrugged and filled their glasses again. Jilly could have sworn the level of the liquid in the bottle hadn't gone down a bit, even though they'd each had three helpings. The more she imbibed, the more sane the idea became.

"Our daddy," Naomi continued, "says any woman who doesn't want to get married is unnatural."

Ruth ducked her head. Jilly figured unnatural in these parts meant lesbian.

"I never really wanted to get married," Jilly admitted.

Ruth's head came up. "Why not?"

"I didn't *want* to, I had to."

Ruth's gaze fell to Jilly's middle.

"Not *had* to had to. I mean, had to." Jilly took another drink. "I didn't have any money."

"You married a man for his money?" Naomi said.

"Shh." Jilly tried to put her finger to her lips, but missed and nearly poked herself in the eye.

"You're a…a—"

"Yep." Jilly nodded emphatically before Naomi said the hated words.

"Professional wife."

"Huh?" Jilly blinked, but they were smiling, not sneering as so many other women would and had.

"Wonderful," Ruth breathed.

"You can help us." Naomi stood and pulled a small cloth bag from the pocket of her skirt.

"Help how?"

"I want to get married," Naomi said.

"You got someone in mind?"

"Of course." Naomi sniffed, but she didn't elaborate.

Jilly's eyes narrowed. She remembered Naomi eyeing Evan up and down every chance she got. Not that he wasn't pretty to look at, but he was hers.

"Think again," she muttered.

"What?"

"You can't have Evan."

Naomi burst into laughter. "Evan? I don't want to die young. I wanna get married and have babies. Don't you?"

Jilly's mouth fell open. She *had* been thinking about babies a lot lately. Mostly because she'd delivered a few and taken care of even more. That was the only reason bundles of joy danced through her dreams.

"What are you talking about—die young? And what's wrong with Evan?"

"Nothing. But I've seen the way you stare at him. You'll stick my head in a bucket of pig innards if I so much as touch him."

Jilly almost denied the accusation, until she paused and considered. She *would* do something violent if Naomi put her hands on Evan.

"Who do you have in mind?" Jilly asked.

The sisters exchanged glances. Ruth shrugged.

"There's a boy on the other side of our ridge," Naomi explained. "His farm lines up to ours. We been meetin' after moonrise in the cornfield."

From Naomi's blush, Jilly had a pretty good idea what had been going on in that cornfield.

"So get married."

"Can't until Ruth is. Daddy says—"

"Oh, right." Jilly remembered them saying something along these lines before. "Oldest gets married first."

Naomi poured them another shot. "Daddy is fixed in his mind on the matter."

Together they drank, then muttered, "Men."

Jilly set down her glass with a decisive click. "What's your plan?"

"Ruth's perfectly willing to get married. 'Cept none of the men around here are interested."

Ruth sighed.

"She don't know nothin' but this place. She's not good with words. She don't have no schoolin' but what she had to have. Marryin' is the only way for her. You understand that."

Jilly did. However... "I don't see how a spell will help."

"We use the hair and fingernail test to hunt up the man. Once he knows the spell picked him, he won't have no choice in the matter."

"How's that?"

"Daddy, and his shotgun, believe in the hair and fingernail test."

Jilly had often lamented her lack of a father. But talking with Ruth and Naomi, she was suddenly glad she'd only had her mother to contend with. Mother had been difficult enough.

"Why do you need me?" she asked.

"We want to do the spell here. Now." Naomi put her hand on top of the sack. "Is that all right?"

Jilly hesitated, but only for an instant. She was curious to see what, if anything, would happen.

"Okay." She slammed back the rest of her drink. "Let's do it."

THEY STARTED A FIRE in the fireplace. Evan had finished the repairs the day before with the help of a local mason, whose ringworm Jilly had cured with the juice of a green walnut.

"Now what?" she asked, fascinated in spite of herself.

"Open the door," Naomi instructed, and Jilly complied. "Leave it open."

"Are you sure?"

Jilly glanced into the yard, where Lightning snoozed standing up, even though Peter, Zorro, Henry and Mario were chasing each other around his legs as if he were a maze.

"The animals will take that as an open invitation to come in here and play."

"Put this on the doorstep."

Naomi handed her a branch of some tree Jilly couldn't identify. "What is this?"

"Dogpone."

The hill people called many plants and trees by names Jilly had never heard of. This was one of them.

"It'll keep animals from crossing your threshold."

"Could have used this before now," Jilly muttered as she laid the branch across the opening.

Mario saw her and started to yip. He came flying in her direction, and all the others followed him like the Pied Piper. He'd become their leader, which was downright odd, since Mario wasn't the sharpest tool in the shed. Evan insisted he'd grow a brain eventually, but Jilly had her doubts.

He flounced up the steps and skidded across the porch. His ears flopped nearly to his paws. He almost tripped over them in his eagerness to drool on her knee, or maybe piddle on her foot.

Then he saw the branch and paused. Henry ran into his butt, hissed and batted at his tail. Mario sniffed the leaves and yelped. The last Jilly saw of him he was headed for Cleveland at the speed of sound, with Henry, Peter and Zorro right behind him. Lightning didn't bother to wake up.

"Think he'll come back before dark?" Naomi stood at her side.

"Zorro is pretty good about bringing home imbeciles and house pets."

"I thought they were one and the same."

Jilly laughed and put her arm around Naomi. Together they joined Ruth on the floor in front of the fireplace.

Jilly's head was fuzzy from the moonshine. She vaguely wondered what had happened to Evan, then forgot about him when Ruth suddenly cut off a hank of her hair.

"Hey! Watcha do that for?"

"We need fingernail clippings, too." Naomi grabbed Jilly's hand.

Jilly tugged it back. "This is supposed to be for Ruth."

"Can't hurt for all of us to try. Besides, the spell works better with a group."

Ruth finished cutting a lock of her own hair, clipping a few fingernails and binding everything into a green leaf. She did the same with Naomi's hair and nails. Then she looked in Jilly's direction. Jilly put her hand into Ruth's.

When all three leaves sat bound and ready in front of the fire, they scooted in closer.

"Now we put the leaves into the ashes," Naomi said. "The next man you see will be your husband."

A flutter of excitement came to life in Jilly's belly. She knew the proceedings were just foolishness—like the séances and Ouija boards some of the girls had messed around with at school. Jilly was never invited to the parties, but she'd often heard them giggling together. She'd always wanted to join in the fun.

She glanced at Ruth, then Naomi. They were her girlfriends. Her pals. Comrades in silly spells to predict their future. She'd missed this as a child, and she'd never known she'd resented that until right now.

"Thanks," she murmured.

"For what?" Naomi shoved the first leaf into the ashes.

"Including me."

"We needed to do this at the inn."

"Why?"

"The spirits help with the spell."

Jilly's excitement dwindled and her shoulders slumped.

Naomi shoved in the second leaf. "But we'd have asked you anyway, no matter where we had to do it."

"How come?"

Naomi glanced at her. "We like you."

The warm glow returned to Jilly's chest. They liked her; they really, really liked her.

"I like you guys, too." She put her arms around them just as Naomi thrust the final leaf into the ashes.

The lights went out. All three of them froze.

"Uh-oh," Ruth muttered.

A chill wind whipped through the inn, blowing the dogpone across the floor and causing the small flame in the fireplace to flicker.

The thump of shoes sounded on the porch steps, then strolled across the porch. Jilly squinted but saw nothing—not a shadow, not a person. No one.

The sound came closer and closer. The sisters shrank back and so did Jilly. Her ears must be playing tricks with her because she could have sworn the footsteps stopped directly in front of them.

"You see anything?" Jilly whispered.

Naomi and Ruth both shook their heads and stared at the empty air.

"Jeez," Jilly grumbled, "is there anything alive around here?"

"I am." Barry Seitz limped into the room. "Barely."

Jilly glanced at the fireplace, where their leaves had all caught on fire, then back at Barry.

Aw, hell, she thought. *He's just my type.*

CHAPTER SIXTEEN

"I DON'T SUPPOSE YOU HAVE any hidden treasure at your place?" Jilly asked. "Black gold? Texas tea?"

"What ye jabberin' about?" Barry asked.

"Never mind."

She wasn't marrying him, and that was all she had to say about that.

Evan strolled in. "Where are the kids? And Lightning? Place is deserted." He frowned at the fireplace. "What's with the fire? It's gotta be eighty degrees."

Jilly glanced at the Wilder sisters. Ruth stared raptly at Barry. Naomi threw ashes on the flames with the fireplace shovel. No one appeared interested in answering him.

"Jilly?" Evan pressed.

"We just wanted to test it. Works fine," she said brightly.

He gave her an odd glance, then shrugged. "Supper ready?"

"Sure. Can you set the table?"

"Glad to." He went into the kitchen whistling. Barry followed, leaving Jilly alone with the girls.

"What's going on?" she snapped.

"We got our answer. You saw him."

"You are not marrying Evan," Jilly snapped, grabbing Ruth's arm as the bigger woman headed for the kitchen.

Ruth shook her off as if she weighed no more than a mosquito, and kept on walking. Jilly hurried after her, half expecting Ruth to toss Evan over her shoulder and disappear into the hills.

She reached the doorway just in time to see Ruth hold out her hand in front of Barry. In her palm lay the remnants of the green leaf.

Barry blinked at the mess, then squinted at Ruth. "Me?"

She nodded. He sighed. "Guess it'll be good to have a woman around the house at last."

"How did he know?" Jilly whispered.

"Any hill man worth his salt knows what a group of women in front of a fireplace on a hot August night is up to."

Ruth leaned down and kissed the old man's cheek. He smiled and took her hand.

"She doesn't seem upset. Does he have money?"

Naomi gave her a strange look. "What's money got to do with anything? Ruth's been in love with him for years. He never paid her any mind. Wouldn't leave his dim-witted brothers. But now, with the spell and all, he's got no choice."

"But—"

"He doesn't have a pot to piss in. His cabin, the land,

all gets split three ways." Naomi's forehead furrowed. "Though I guess it'll be Ruth's quicker than not."

Well, that made a certain sort of sense. Land out here was like money. Wasn't it?

"I don't understand why Barry is Ruth's intended. We all put our leaves in the ashes."

"You want him?"

"No, thanks."

Naomi grinned. "The spell says the first man you see."

"I saw him. So did you."

"But Ruth's leaf went into the fire first."

"Ah." Jilly's gaze went to Evan. "Whose was second?"

He glanced up and saw her in the doorway. Their eyes met. Jilly's stomach danced as his smile made her remember everything they'd done last night.

"Whose was second?" Naomi laughed. "Whose do you think?"

EVAN WONDERED if the Wilder sisters and Barry would ever leave. After collecting all the animals, the girls had produced a bottle of moonshine. From the giggles of all three women, this wasn't the first time they'd seen it.

He sipped at his glass slowly. Home brew rotted not only the gut but the brain, as well, and he'd heard from more men than one what moonshine did to the libido.

He'd never had a problem getting it up—quite the opposite—but he wasn't taking any chances. Tonight he planned to make love to Jilly, then ask her to marry him, and he didn't want anything to spoil that.

"I'd best get back to the boys."

Barry hoisted himself to his feet. Ruth jumped up, too. As near as Evan could tell, she had done a spell that indicated Barry should be her husband. Barry believed it, and now they were engaged. Life was so simple in the Ozarks.

"I'll go with you," Ruth murmured.

Those were the most words Evan had heard Ruth string together at one time. Maybe Barry would be good for her.

"Thanks for the vittles," Barry said. "Ye think ye can stop by the cabin in the morning, Doc?"

Jilly glanced around the room, then frowned. "Who's Doc?"

"You are."

Her eyes widened. "Am not!"

"It's what they call a woman like you in the hills," Naomi said. "A courtesy."

"I never heard anyone call Addie that."

"Most folks have known her all their lives. You're from away. Just natural they'd be more formal with you."

"I don't want anyone calling me Doc," she protested.

"Fine. Mrs. *Duvier*."

Barry mangled her last name so badly it came out sounding almost obscene. Evan had to purse his lips to keep from laughing.

"Would ye check on my brothers in the morning?"

"Of course. First thing."

The other two Seitzes had declined dinner on account of a stomach ailment. Most likely too much moonshine, if Evan knew them very well at all.

Ruth and Barry left the inn hand in hand. Naomi began to clear the table.

"I can do that." Evan took the dishes. "I'm sure you have other things to do."

"Yeah." She headed for the door, pausing to whisper something to Jilly, which made her smile. Then Naomi waved and disappeared into the night.

"What was that all about?" he asked.

"She had to see a man."

"I didn't think she could date until Ruth did first."

"Seemed to me like Ruth had a date."

Evan glanced at the door through which everyone had disappeared. "I guess she did."

He dumped the dishes into the sink and proceeded to wash them while Jilly finished clearing the table.

"Do you think that's weird?" he asked. "Barry and Ruth?"

"Me?" She snorted. "Hardly."

Evan wasn't sure what that meant, but he didn't want to ask right now. Right now he wanted to kiss her.

When she brushed past him to slip the silverware into the soapy water, he captured her mouth with his.

Her lips opened on a sigh. He loved how she leaned into him, her breasts squishing against his chest, both firm and soft at the same time.

She smelled like the earth and tasted like a winter wind. Wild rice and peppermint candy. He put his arms around her and only succeeded in getting her shirt wet because he'd forgotten to dry his hands.

She squealed and yanked her mouth away. "You're soaking, and now so am I."

"I can fix that." He nuzzled her neck.

"How?"

She let her head fall back. Her hair brushed his wrists. Her hip bumped his thigh.

"Let's get naked."

He swung her into his arms and spun her around. She laughed, a sound so free and childlike he stopped in midspin and stared at her.

"What?" Her laughter died and confusion took its place.

He almost told her right then that he loved her, but he wanted to do this right.

"Nothing," he said. "The word *naked* just makes my brain kind of freeze."

"You and every other man."

"Yeah, we're funny that way."

He headed out of the kitchen still carrying her.

"Put me down, Evan. You'll hurt something I might need later."

"I'm not carrying you with my penis."

She snickered. "That's not the only part of you I'm interested in."

He paused at the bottom stair. "That might be the nicest thing you've ever said."

"Then I haven't been nice enough."

"You can make it up to me."

"I can, can't I?" She wrapped her arms around his neck and kissed him so long and deep he nearly dropped her.

"Put me down," she murmured into his mouth.

He released her, and she slid along his body.

Then suddenly, she was gone, and he was left puckering up all alone. His eyes shot open. She ran up the stairs. "Last one naked is a rotten egg!"

Her shirt came flying back and hit him in the face. His brain was still stuck on "naked."

Evan stripped off his own shirt and tossed it over the banister, then chased her up two flights of stairs and into his room. He stopped dead just inside the door.

"Guess I'm the rotten egg," he murmured.

She stood completely unclothed by the window, the light of the moon turning her skin the shade of marble. Her red hair drifted across her shoulders and she tossed it back, making her magnificent breasts dance.

He shook his head to clear away the lust. He should ask her now. Go down on his knees, beg her to be his wife, then make love to her. But the idea of going down on his knees gave him other ideas. Ideas he couldn't get out of his head.

"Evan?" Confusion clouded her face. He was standing here like an idiot, gaping, probably drooling, while she was nude and waiting for him to join her.

He yanked off his pants, shoes, socks, and crossed the room. "You're so…"

Mesmerized by the scent of her hair, her skin, the

green of her eyes, he couldn't complete a coherent thought. Everything about her made him crazy. He was amazed he'd managed to get this far on the inn without killing himself when he zoned off remembering the taste of her lips or the way her body would clasp around him and make him come.

"I'm so what?" she asked.

He blinked, trying to remember what he'd been going to say.

Beautiful? She was much, much more.

Special? Lame, even for him.

Hot? Please. He wasn't sixteen.

She continued to stare at him expectantly. He had to say something. Evan opened his mouth and let the first word that came to his lips fly free.

"Mine."

She didn't say anything, simply looked at him. For an instant he thought she'd walk away. Evan held his breath. Had he blown it without even trying?

Then she smiled and kissed him lightly. "Okay. I'm yours."

Evan took her in his arms and made the words reality.

JILLY AWOKE AT THE TIME when the moon drops below the horizon and the sun hasn't yet begun to light the sky. The darkest hour. She wasn't sure what had woken her. Evan was pressed to her back, his breath stirring her hair, his heart beating against her shoulder blade. Nothing wrong there.

She listened. Not a bird twittered, not a coyote howled, no animal raced through the woods, the yard, even the house. All was quiet, so why was she as tense as a hound dog faced with the butt end of a polecat?

Something shimmered at the edge of her vision. With no light in the room, how could anything shimmer?

Jilly turned her head but the sparkle was gone. Still, a pervasive sense of unease made her get out of bed and move to the window.

She looked outside. Lightning stared at her from the yard. He pawed at the ground, tossed his head and galloped faster than she'd ever seen him move to the edge of the hill. Then he stared down at Addie's place before lowering his head and pawing at the dirt some more.

Something wasn't right.

Since she wouldn't be able to sleep again until she checked on Addie, Jilly threw on her clothes and ran down the stairs, careful to step over any critters in her path.

The four kids were scattered across the lower level. Only Mario lifted his head and woofed once.

"Shh." She put her finger to her lips and he stopped, then laid his head back down. He was catching on to a few things—although *sit*, *stay* and *go potty outside* seemed to be beyond his comprehension. Sometimes she worried about him.

Jilly hurried across the grass in her bare feet. She'd never bought shoes, never found her green-and-silver tennies. She'd left her high heels and strappy sandals in the suitcase with the silk shells and rayon suits. Her feet were as hard as leather, the idea of toenail polish almost laughable, and she just couldn't work up the energy to care.

She ran full tilt to the edge of the yard, where Lighting was waiting. Pausing, she peered into the darkness, but Addie's place was as dark as the night.

Lightning shoved her hard in the middle of the back, and she stumbled down the hill a few steps. "All right, all right. I'm going."

Jilly half slid, half jogged to the bottom, then glanced back at Lightning, who stood exactly where she'd left him. He was better trained than Mario, which wasn't saying much.

She hurried on to Addie's cabin, hesitating outside. What if the old woman was sound asleep? What if she wasn't?

"Better safe than sorry," Jilly muttered, and went inside.

The lamp was turned so low she could barely see Addie in the bed; Jilly couldn't tell if she was breathing.

Jilly rushed over and knelt on the floor. Her own breath became as shallow as Addie's. She touched the older woman's shoulder, and Addie's eyes opened as she smiled. The expression took twenty years off her face.

"I was dreaming of Matthew." Her gaze went to the corner of the cabin. "He's waiting."

Jilly's neck prickled, and she spun around, but she and Addie were alone in the room.

"My time's come," her friend murmured.

"No!" Jilly flinched at the volume of her voice. "I still need you."

She thought of the talks they'd had, the things she'd learned, the days she'd spent joyfully in Addie's company. Addie was the mother she'd always wanted.

The old woman took her hand, pressed her hot lips to Jilly's fingers. "You don't need me. You've got Evan now. The love of a good man, and yers for him, will give ye the strength to do what needs to be done."

"I don't believe in love."

Addie tried to snort her opinion of that, but she was too weak to emit more than a slight cough. "There are some things that don't need to be believed to be real. They just are. Love's one of 'em."

"And I suppose ghosts are another."

The old woman nodded and winked at the empty corner. "Matthew's in this room now, and just because you don't see him doesn't make him any less there."

"And magic?" Jilly whispered.

"If you believe, more than you can imagine will come true. The mind is a powerful thing. But the heart is even stronger."

Why were Addie's words making sense? Because Jilly wanted to believe in the power of love and the myth of magic?

"You'll be fine now," Addie said. "I believe in you."

"I'm not ready."

"I say ye are."

"I'm not good enough."

"Ye always were. Just needed a little time with someone who cared."

"Please don't go."

"Have to. Should have gone before, but you *weren't* ready then. Matthew was patient, but his patience is purt near out. So's mine. But don't worry. You'll see me agin."

Addie's eyes slid closed, and no amount of begging on Jilly's part could make them open. She held Addie's hand as the old woman's breathing became slower and slower, then stopped altogether.

And then Jilly held her hand some more.

CHAPTER SEVENTEEN

THE POUNDING ON the door didn't wake Evan from the best sleep he'd had in years. The yipping and yowling did. The kids didn't appear to care for whatever, or whoever, was standing on the porch.

The sun had been up for a good long while, judging from the slant of the rays across the floor. Jilly was nowhere to be seen. Where the hell were the brothers?

Unease filtered through Evan as he found a pair of shorts and slipped them on. Something was wrong, and he had a bad feeling he was going to find out what as soon as he opened the front door.

Evan trotted downstairs. The dog and the cat were making all the noise, with no sign of the opossum or the raccoon. Not a door or a window existed that could keep Zorro inside when he wanted to be out, and Peter usually went AWOL with him. They were creatures of the night. Being pets couldn't change that.

Evan shoved Mario into the cage before the doodle ate his way through the wall trying to get at the visitor. Henry was howling as if someone had died. The hair on Evan's neck lifted.

"Aw, hell," he muttered, and yanked open the door.

As soon as he did, Henry scooted into the kitchen and didn't come back.

A woman and a man stood on the other side of the screen. They were dressed as if they'd just come from a wedding, or maybe a tea party—the man in a lightweight suit and shiny shoes, the woman in a wispy summer dress the shade of a lemon drop. A hat of the same color hid her hair and shaded her face. She held a white pocketbook in perfectly manicured hands.

In contrast, Evan felt like a pig—no shirt, no shoes, and he hadn't shaved in a few days. What was the point? His hair had grown longer since he'd come here, reaching past his shoulders. It was no doubt tangled after last night's encounter with Jilly's roving fingertips.

The woman's lip curled as she let her gaze wander over him from head to toe. Evan straightened. This was his place, or near enough. She had no right to knock on his door, wake him up, then sneer.

"Can I help you?" he asked.

"I just bet you can. But right now I'm trying to find Jillian Hart Duvier."

"And you are?"

"Her mother."

Evan cringed. He felt positively underdressed now. But he'd been in situations like this before, and the best way to handle them was to pretend you hadn't been caught with your pants down.

"Nice to meet you, ma'am. I'm Evan Luchetti."

She gave a long, labored sigh. "She's screwing you, isn't she?"

Evan blinked. Such language from a woman who appeared as if she could give Miss Manners a lesson had him floundering for a comeback. He wished Dean were here. His brother would have a million.

Jilly's mother threw up her hands. "I go out of the country for a few months and look what happens. She can't get herself decently remarried. No, she has to disappear into the hills and do the nasty with Jethro."

The man, who was at least fifteen years younger than her, never said a word. Jilly hadn't mentioned a brother, but that didn't mean she didn't have one.

Evan tensed. If he'd come across anyone who looked like he did right now shacked up with his little sister, he'd be honor bound to punch him in the nose. Maybe Evan should just let the guy take a swing and get it over with.

"This is my husband." Jilly's mother waved a careless hand in the young man's direction. "Count Stanislaski."

The count clicked his heels and bowed. Evan's eyes widened. Was he serious?

"He doesn't speak much English."

Lucky for Mrs. Hart. Or was it Countess Stanislaski? She seemed to enjoy doing all the talking.

"I'm sorry." Evan attempted to make amends. "We didn't know you were coming."

"If you had a phone that would have been remedied. Now, where's my daughter?"

"I'm not sure."

"She's not upstairs, sleeping off the wonder of your touch?"

Evan gritted his teeth. Regardless of what her mother thought about him, he hadn't been taking advantage of Jilly. He loved her, and she loved him.

"I can assure you, ma'am, this isn't what it looks like."

She made a very unladylike sound, but she didn't seem to care. "Believe me, it is."

"No, we aren't— I mean we are…"

"Which is it?"

Evan took a deep breath. He'd wanted to say this to Jilly first, but if he had to tell her mother, then so be it.

"I love her."

"I bet you do. Who wouldn't? She's gorgeous, smart. Every man's dream. But you appear penniless. Jilly doesn't waste her time on men with less than a million to their name."

"I don't understand."

"She hasn't told you?" She laughed. "Jillian, Jillian. That really wasn't fair."

"Told me what?"

"Her occupation. Her talent. Her calling."

Evan shrugged.

"She's a gold digger, sweetie. You're much too young and much too broke for Jillian to ever love."

He couldn't speak; he could only shake his head.

"You don't believe me?" She turned toward the limo

behind her and snapped her fingers. The door opened
and a man stepped out. Well dressed, well kept, he had
to be pushing sixty—to the limit. "Meet Jilly's fiancé.
Rupert Murton. They're to be married just as soon as
we can find her."

The man nodded once, then glanced away, as if Evan
were of no more consequence than a servant.

Huh, he thought, she *had* been screwing him.

WHEN JILLY DIDN'T SHOW UP to check on Larry and
Jerry's stomach troubles, the brothers Seitz came to
Addie's. Therefore Jilly was able to send them to town
for the appropriate powers that be. Still, the sun had
been up for hours before Addie's body was removed and
all the people were gone.

In the old days, Barry had informed her, someone
would have sat with the body until the funeral. Death
watch, he called it. Jilly was glad the old days were
gone. Although sometimes, around here, she wondered.

Peter and Zorro wandered in, but there was no sign
of Fergus. Jilly checked the pond and found him
floating there alone. She'd heard of crocodile tears,
but she had no idea if alligators could cry. If they
could, she had no doubt Fergus was weeping right
now. She left him where he was and went up the hill
with Peter and Zorro.

Lightning met her at the top of the ridge. He
shoved her in the chest, nearly toppling her back
down the hill.

She rubbed between his eyes. "I know. It's just not going to be the same without her, is it?"

He lifted his head, lowered it, then plodded behind her as Jilly headed for home.

Still preoccupied with Addie, Jilly didn't see the limo until she nearly ran into it. The sight made her heart skip into her throat. Jilly looked up and met the icy stare of her mother.

Zorro started chittering as if he'd seen a coyote, and ducked behind Jilly's legs. Peter scooted under the porch.

"Hello, Mother."

"Don't 'Hello, Mother' me! I had to call Henry's attorney to find you. Fly commercial to get to…where are we?"

"Arkansas."

Genevieve's gaze caught on something behind Jilly, and her eyes narrowed. "Why is there a horse in the front yard?"

Jilly glanced at Lightning and shrugged. "Where else would he be?"

"The barn?"

"Why would I have a barn?"

Genevieve made an aggravated noise deep in her throat. "Never mind. What is that *thing* hiding behind you?"

"A raccoon."

Her mother's eyes widened. "And *what* are you wearing?"

Jilly glanced down at her faded cotton skirt and white tank top.

"Your feet!" Genevieve put a hand to her forehead. "You need an immediate emergency pedicure."

"I don't need anything except Evan."

"Your Jethro boy-toy?"

Jilly's mouth tightened. "What did you do?"

"Less than you. Honestly, Jillian, a carpenter? If you were going to go slumming, couldn't you at least pick a contractor or an engineer?"

"Where is he?"

"Inside, talking to the count and Rupert."

"Who the hell is Rupert?"

"Don't take that tone with me, young lady. Not when I've gone out of my way to bring you a brand-new husband."

"You told him, didn't you?"

"About your past? Of course. You should have. The poor fool is in love with you."

Jilly's heart gave a single, hard thud against the wall of her chest. "He is?"

"I had to tell him what a stupid idea that was. As if you'd live here with him, scrub the floors and pop out children." She shuddered. "Maybe *he* has a Cinderella fantasy, but I raised you better than that. You're meant to be the princess, not the chambermaid."

Jilly tried to speak but could only shake her head. Losing Addie so suddenly. Having her mother turn up where she wasn't supposed to be. Discovering that Evan not only knew her dirty secret, but that he loved her, or at least he had. This was all too much for her to handle.

"Mom—"

"Mom? Since when do you call me Mom? Next thing I know you'll be addressing me as Ma and picking your teeth with a blade of grass. Get your things, Jillian. We're leaving."

Zorro's chittering was getting on her nerves, so Jilly patted him gently on the head and urged him toward the backyard. He growled at her mother, then scurried away. Peter crawled out from underneath the porch and followed. No one appeared eager to remain in the same zip code as Genevieve Hart. Jilly could hardly blame them.

The screen door opened, and Jilly caught her breath, yearning for the sight of Evan. Instead, two strangers stepped out—one young, one old. She didn't have to guess which man was for her.

"Jillian, meet Rupert."

As she'd suspected, the white-haired gentleman smiled. He took in her wild hair, old clothes, dirty feet, and his smile froze into something akin to a grimace.

"Don't worry," her mother said briskly. "She cleans up very well. She's been having a little fling. You don't mind, do you?"

Rupert cleared his throat. "Of course not. If you'd like, we could take him with us. I have some work to do on my estate."

Jilly's eyes widened. Was he suggesting what she thought he was? That she take Evan along for her amusement, like a pet?

"No, thank you." She tossed her head.

Her mother made a sound of exasperation. "If you gentlemen will wait in the car, I'll have a word with my daughter."

The young man, who must be Count Whatski, led the way, and the two men climbed into the idling limo. Jilly joined her mother on the porch.

"Sit down," her mother ordered.

Jilly did, but only because her legs were too weak to keep her standing. She'd heard the lecture before, and it always followed the same refrain.

"Love is a luxury, Jillian. Not for women like us. Never, ever marry for love."

"Poor men are for play. Rich men are for keeps," Jilly recited. "I've been living by your rules all of my life. I know them by heart."

"Then how could you forget them?"

"You saw him. It was easy."

EVAN STOOD JUST INSIDE the window. He could hear everything Jilly and her mother said.

You saw him. It was easy.

He'd been easy, obviously. A poor man to play with. Why did that hurt so much?

Because he'd never been anything but an amusement to every woman he'd ever known. Most men wouldn't care, but Evan did.

Why he'd thought Jilly was different was a mystery to him now. He'd wanted so much to have his dream that he'd ignored the truth.

Jilly was from another world, and she'd never be able to live in his. She'd been slumming, playing, amusing herself, while he'd been falling in love with a woman who didn't exist.

"I need to talk to Evan," Jilly said.

He tensed. Evan didn't want to talk to her, couldn't face another woman telling him he was nothing more than a one-night stand. Just because they'd been together for more than a night didn't make what they'd shared anything beyond that.

He'd given her something no other man ever had. An orgasm. That just might earn him another gold star toward his gigolo merit badge.

"Wait a minute," Jilly's mother snapped. "We're not through here."

Evan took the reprieve and ran with it. Lucky for him his truck was parked out back. He was able to load all the kids into his pickup, except for Lightning, who was too damn big for the truck bed and had disappeared again anyway. The thought of Fergus made him pause, but he couldn't figure out how to transport an alligator several hundred miles without making him miserable, sick or worse.

He would just have to trust the Seitz brothers to keep an eye on both the alligator and the horse. They ought to be capable of that much.

Leaving his tools, his clothes, his camping gear behind, Evan climbed into the truck. If he drove straight through, he might make it home by supper.

"YOU'RE WRONG." Jilly pulled her arm from her mother's grip. "We *are* through. I love Evan, and I'm going to tell him so."

Her mother laughed. "You're mistaking great sex for true love. Don't be foolish. Don't ruin your life. You can have both Rupert *and* Jethro."

Jilly's lip curled. "That's disgusting, Mother. I wouldn't do that to Evan, or myself."

"Don't you remember what it was like? No food, no house, no clothes? You want to go back to that?"

You want to go back to a life without love, girl? Believe you me, it ain't worth livin'.

Jilly cocked her head. That had sounded just like Addie.

Her mother snapped her fingers in front of Jilly's face. "What's the matter with you?"

She shrugged. "Must be hearing ghosts."

"Ghosts?" Her mother rolled her eyes. "I suppose you'll tell me next that fairies live under the cabbage leaves. You've got magic dust that'll grow all the food you need. And you can live on love."

"I'd rather believe in something than nothing at all."

"You want to starve here, with him?"

Jilly looked around the yard, up at the inn, into the trees and beyond. She listened to the birds, breathed in the musty aroma of the creek, let the sun shine on her face, and she knew.

"I'll starve, freeze, die if I have to. But I'm not leaving Evan. Ever."

Her mother's lips puckered, as if she'd just sucked a lemon. "You choose him, you lose me."

"Aren't you supposed to love me no matter what?"

A crease marred Genevieve's perfect brow. "Why would you think that?"

"Unconditional love?"

"Never heard of it."

"There's a shock," Jilly muttered.

"I'll write you out of my will, Jillian. You'll get nothing."

"Which will be different from what I've been getting from you all my life, how?"

"Sarcasm is unbecoming. I've given you plenty."

"But not one thing I truly needed. Goodbye, Mother."

"Don't come crawling back to me when you're nine months pregnant and you have two toddlers in the back of your Chevy."

Jilly smiled at the image, which was supposed to frighten her, no doubt, but instead made her long for the future. "I won't."

The last she saw of Genevieve, Rupert and the count was the taillights of their limo disappearing down the dusty lane.

"Evan!" She ran into the inn, anxious to tell him everything she'd discovered.

The huge, old building echoed back her call.

She continued to shout his name, on the first floor, the second, the third. Outside, down by the creek, into the woods.

His truck was gone, and that didn't bother her—until she noticed the dog cage was gone, too. As were the dog, the cat, the raccoon and the opossum.

Damn him. *He'd* left *her*.

CHAPTER EIGHTEEN

EVAN ROLLED INTO Gainsville long past the supper hour. He'd stopped in Bloomington and bought everyone cheeseburgers, except for Peter and Zorro, who appeared to prefer chicken.

He was going to have to keep an eye on them. If they raided his mother's chicken coop, she'd shoot them. Literally.

The town appeared the same. No big surprise. Gainsville hadn't changed in all the time he'd lived there. Oh, they'd added a hospital, the television repair store was now a coffee shop, the pharmacy had moved into the grocery store, but for the most part Gainsville was exactly the same now as it had been fifty years ago. One of the things he both loathed and loved about the place.

Evan waved a finger to every car he passed, and the other drivers did the same. In farm country, it was rude not to greet everyone you met on the road.

His father's silos appeared on the horizon, tall and white, an American flag waving on top of each signaled they'd been bought and paid for. Considering the price of a silo, this was saying quite a bit John Luchetti had always been a farmer's farmer and Dean was just like him, which had only made Evan's differences stand out all the more.

He lifted a hand from the wheel and touched the longer length of his hair. His dad was going to have a stroke when he caught sight of him now. Maybe he'd get a haircut, make the old man happy.

The image of Jilly running her fingers through his hair, whispering how much she loved it as he caressed her with the tips of each strand, shot through his head, and he forced it right back out. He'd come home to forget her, and forget her he damn well would.

He wheeled into the long gravel lane that led down to a stone farmhouse and several white outbuildings. Dogs streaked from every direction, barking a welcome.

His father's dalmatians, Bear and Bull, were joined by Bear's offspring, the doodles. The resulting sound was nearly deafening, especially when Mario, thrilled to see his brothers and sisters, joined in.

"Quiet!" Evan shouted as he got out of the truck.

Bear and Bull shut up, though they continued to perform three-foot-high leaps to emphasize their excitement. The doodles stayed on the ground but kept barking.

The slam of the farmhouse door and a snapped, "Zip it!" had every doodle scurrying for cover. Evan lifted his gaze to his mother's.

She hadn't changed, either—sturdy as the stone of

their farmhouse, steady as the breeze from the west. Her long ponytail had once been brown, like his, but he couldn't remember it as anything other than white.

Her hands were hard; her eyes were blue. The lines around them had come from both laughter and the sun.

"'Bout time you showed up."

She walked down the porch steps in bare feet, and he was reminded again of Jilly. The pain surprised him, and he fought the sigh. Forgetting her wasn't going to be as easy as he'd hoped.

"You know I don't like it when you disappear for weeks at a time."

Had it been that long? He'd lost track of the days while living with Jilly. Life at the inn had been charmed, his work there gratifying, the friendships he'd made good ones. He hadn't thought of calling home since he'd asked for a doodle.

His mother opened her arms, and Evan went into them for a hug. She'd never been the cuddly type. Too many children too close together had taken care of that. But in the past few years she'd made a conscious effort to be more hands-on. Which meant he and his brothers now got more than their share of hugs and kisses. The newfound shows of affection took some getting used to.

Suddenly she stiffened and pulled away. "*What* is that?"

He turned. Zorro and Peter peeked over the side of the truck bed.

"Well, I couldn't just leave them there," he said.

His mother put a hand to her forehead. "If I'm not mistaken, that's the same doodle I got rid of."

"Mario?"

"We called him Forest."

"As in 'can't see him through the trees'?"

"No, as in Gump. Notice anything strange about that dog?"

"Well, he is a little…special."

She laughed. "I'll say. He never could catch on to the whole potty-outside thing."

"Why did Dean send him to me then?"

"Why do you think?"

Stupid question. Mario had been Dean's idea of a joke. Well, the joke was on Dean. Because the doodle was back here to stay.

Henry jumped on top of the dog cage, arching and hissing.

"Stop that!" she ordered. Henry did. Animals and small children obeyed Eleanor Luchetti without question.

"A cat?" She glanced at Evan. "Like we don't have twenty too many?"

"One more won't hurt."

"Evan." She shook her head. "Aaron always brought home strays, not you."

"I figured you missed the excitement."

"You figured wrong," she muttered, but she didn't tell him to get rid of them, so Evan guessed the animals were as welcome as he was.

That was what he liked about home. No matter what

you did, where you roamed, who or what you brought back with you, you were welcome.

"Your old room is empty."

"But…" He glanced in the direction of the threshers' cabin, where he'd lived before he'd left the last time.

"Dean and Tim need space of their own. No one's in the big house but me and your dad. Plenty of room for you."

She'd turned away, but from the slope of her shoulders he could tell she was holding back tears. His mother had rarely cried, until recently.

Evan laid a hand on her arm. "Bobby?"

She shook her head. "Since Colin saw him in Pakistan there's been nothing. Not a word from him, not a speck of information worth having from anyone in power."

"What do they say when you call?"

"Same old party line—he's a Special Forces operative, and his status is classified." She threw up her hands. "All I want to know is if his status is dead or alive. I'm his mother. Is that too much to ask?"

"If he was dead, they'd tell us."

"Would they? What if he died somewhere the U.S. Army isn't supposed to be? What if his being alive, or the threat of his being alive, was keeping some moronic terrorist from performing his idiotic terrorist act?"

Evan sighed. "I don't know, Mom."

"Neither do I. Bobby told me there'd be times we

wouldn't hear from him, but I didn't think he was talking about years."

"No one did."

Evan had called asking for information about Bobby on several occasions. They told him even less than they told his mother. Basically, back off.

His brother Colin, a former foreign correspondent, had nearly gotten himself killed searching for Bobby in the Middle East. He'd been kidnapped, tortured, then rescued by Bobby himself.

Bobby had dumped Colin at a hospital and disappeared again, after telling Colin to let him stay lost. Colin was of the opinion that their brother had been recruited for Delta Force, the elite antiterrorist unit. Colin was probably right, but that didn't make Bobby's disappearance any easier for their mother to bear.

"How's Zsa Zsa?" Evan asked, in an attempt to lighten the mood.

Eleanor wiped her eyes, even as she laughed. "That girl was born a high-fashion model. She cracks me up."

Evan smiled. Zsa Zsa cracked him up, too. He wanted a daughter, or two, exactly like her.

His smile faded. The way he was going, he doubted he'd ever have one.

"Two years old and already she frowns and points if I wear white shoes before Memorial Day. Where does she get this stuff?"

"It's a mystery," he said, though he had a pretty good idea. Kim had a shoe fetish and a wicked sense of humor.

"Well, well, one of the prodigals decided to come home." Dean leaned against the porch rail. "Should we kill a calf?"

"Not a calf, Daddy. Ew!"

Tim ran past Dean, threw his arms around Eleanor's waist for the fastest hug in the west, then hurried toward Evan. But he was distracted by the animals in the truck.

"Hey!" He clambered up the tire and hung over the edge. "That's the weirdest lookin' cat I ever seen."

Tentatively he reached out to pet Zorro. The raccoon batted his fingers with gentle paws, and Tim giggled.

"He's never seen a raccoon?" Evan asked.

"Not riding shotgun," Dean said dryly. "Where'd you find him?"

"Whoa!" Tim scrambled into the truck bed and lifted Peter up high. "What's this?"

Dean snickered. "Bringing home roadkill now?"

"Someone has to. You should be thankful I didn't bring the alligator."

"You're shittin' me."

"Twenty-five cents, Dad."

Dean ignored his son. "You have a pet alligator?"

"I wouldn't call him a pet, exactly. And he wasn't mine."

"Seems pretty damn dangerous to me."

"Fifty," Tim muttered.

Dean shot him a glare that was pure Eleanor. Tim glanced at the sky and began to whistle.

"Fergus, the alligator, doesn't have any teeth. He's older than—" Evan shrugged "—Mom."

"Watch it, bub," she said, but she smiled.

"Kitty!" Tim shouted. "And Forest's back. Just like you said, Dad."

"What did *Dad* say?" Evan asked.

"That you'd never be able to stand him and you'd bring him home. I didn't want to lose any more doodles."

Eleanor gritted her teeth and pulled at her hair behind Tim's back.

"Nice, Dean."

His brother shrugged. Tim promptly launched himself at Evan, who caught him in midair. The boy wrapped his legs around Evan's waist like a monkey.

"So, didja nail that lady, Uncle Evan?"

Eleanor's eyes went wide. Dean choked. Evan wanted to.

"That doesn't sound like a good idea to me. Nailin' people. Why'd Dad tell you to do it?"

"Dean?" Their mother's voice was set a notch below eruption.

"Tim, you aren't supposed to listen in on the phone. We've talked about that."

Evan set Tim down. The boy hung his head. His hair, which always seemed overgrown and unruly no matter how often it was cut, fell over his freckled nose and bright blue eyes.

"Sorry."

"Sorry doesn't always help, pal. Apologize to Evan, then Gramma, then get your butt to bed."

"It's still light out!"

"You'll be lucky if you see the sun in the next week. Do what I told you."

"Sorry, Uncle Evan. Sorry, Gramma." Tim lifted his skinny shoulders, then lowered them. "But I still don't understand why you'd nail someone."

"Tim!"

The boy flinched at Dean's bellow. Their mother frowned and shook her head. Dean took a deep breath and appeared to be counting to ten—a parenting trick he'd no doubt learned from the master at his side.

"I'll explain it to you later," Dean said gently. "Now go."

"Yes, sir."

Tim headed in the direction of their cabin, dragging his feet so much they could follow his progress by the dust spurts alone.

"Anyone want to explain to me what he was talking about?"

"No, ma'am," Evan and Dean said at the same time.

"I didn't think so. Evan, I'm glad you're home, but you know the rules."

She went into the house without waiting for his answer. He did know them. They all did.

No women in his room. No staying out all night. Her house, her rules. Which was why he'd moved to the threshers' cottage. He glanced at Dean, who shook his head.

"No room at the inn. Besides, you can't have women at my place with Tim around."

Evan wasn't interested in women. Not now, maybe never again.

He gave a mental roll of the eyes. He wasn't the type of man to remain celibate. But right now the thought of touching anyone but Jilly depressed him. Which was foolish. She'd never loved him. She'd only wanted him. She was no different than any of the others, and he deserved more.

"You okay?" Dean asked.

"No."

Zorro opened the dog cage, and Mario started chasing Henry around the yard. The other doodles joined in and Henry scampered up a tree, hissing at them from a low branch.

"Knock that off out there!" his mother shouted from the kitchen window.

Every living being went still, and Evan smiled. "There's no place like home."

"Man, you've been gone too long."

"I know."

JILLY WANTED TO FOLLOW Evan, but she didn't have a car. Even if she had, there was the funeral to arrange, then attend.

Ruth and Barry got married the day after that, Naomi and her beau the week after that.

There was an epidemic of poison ivy, followed by an

outbreak of chicken pox. Jilly had to close up Addie's house and move all the perishable herbs and cures to the inn, along with Fergus.

The alligator was depressed; she couldn't blame him. She missed Addie, too. Almost as much as she missed Evan.

By the time she gave Naomi instructions on caring for Fergus and Lightning, hitched a ride to Little Rock, then rented a car and drove to Illinois, three weeks had passed. She hoped she hadn't waited too long.

Since that first day when she could have sworn Addie had spoken to her, Jilly hadn't heard another word. She missed the old woman, but Addie had promised they'd meet again. Jilly figured on the other side.

Driving into Gainsville, Jilly stopped at the gas station for directions to the Luchetti farm. The old man behind the counter peered at her suspiciously. "You're too old to be another long lost kid. Unless you're John's. If you are, I'd turn right around and head on home. Ellie isn't anyone you want to mess with."

Since Jilly had no idea what he was talking about she ignored the comment and repeated her request for directions.

"Down that county highway about five miles or so, then turn right and drive another mile. Stone farmhouse. Three silos. White outbuildings. Can't miss it."

"Thank you."

He was right. The farm was the only one for miles, making it a bit hard to miss. She turned into the lane, wincing as the carriage of the Volkswagen Beetle dragged against the gravel.

Before she could turn off the car, she was surrounded by dogs. Mario was one of them. Jilly let out the breath she'd been holding.

Evan was here. Somewhere.

She stepped out of the car, ignoring the yapping and the jumping and the drooling.

"Shoo!" She flapped her skirt at the nearest animal, a full-grown dalmatian, but that only seemed to excite him more.

The screen door banged. "Get!"

All the dogs scattered. Jilly looked up and got her first sight of Evan's mother.

Evan had her eyes, although Mrs. Luchetti's weren't half as warm and welcoming.

"You're another one of Evan's girls."

Jilly frowned. How flattering. For an instant she hesitated, tempted to turn tail and run. But she'd decided to fight for what she wanted, and what she wanted was Evan. She'd do anything to have back what she'd lost.

"No, ma'am. I'm *the* girl. I've come to marry him."

Mrs. Luchetti's eyes narrowed. "And who might you be?"

"Jillian Hart. Jilly."

"She's the one Uncle Evan was supposed to nail."

A little boy peeked around the older woman's skirt. "Did it hurt?" he asked. "Gettin' nailed?"

"Tim, find your father."

"But—"

"Now."

The child ran. Jilly would have, too, if that tone had been aimed at her.

A tug on her skirt made her glance down to discover Zorro climbing upward. She snatched him off her clothes and cuddled him close. He patted her cheeks with his paws.

"Hey. I missed you, too."

He chittered, then wiggled until she set him down so he could run after Tim. Peter waddled out from beneath the porch and followed.

"The animals are yours." Mrs. Luchetti's eyes were no longer so frosty.

"Yes."

The older woman's gaze lowered to Jilly's stomach. "You pregnant?"

"No!"

"That's a first. All my children seem to put that particular cart before the horse."

Annoyance caused Jilly to speak more sharply than she should have. "Mrs. Luchetti—"

"Ellie."

"Fine, Ellie. I've come to talk to Evan. I messed things up pretty badly."

"How?"

"You're awfully nosy, aren't you?"

"Not when we're talking about my son's future, his

happiness. He came home different. No more women, no more one-night stands. Which isn't like him."

"That's not the Evan I know."

"Glad to hear it. If he's changed because of you then I thank you. He had me worried."

"He's a grown man. He can take care of himself."

"True. But I'd rather he was taken care of by someone who loves him. He's always been at loose ends. Aimless. Drives my husband to distraction. I knew once Evan found someone to love, he'd settle down and find his place. Since he came back from Arkansas he might be home, but this *isn't* home for him anymore."

"You think his home's in Arkansas now?"

"No, I think his home's with you."

"Gramma!" The little boy erupted from the cornfield behind the house. "I couldn't find Dad."

"What now, Mom?"

Evan emerged from the field. The first thing Jilly noticed was that he'd cut his hair. Her eyes burned, and she wanted to cry. Had he done that because of her?

Evan saw her and stopped dead.

"Hi," she managed to say, blinking back tears as her throat went tight with longing.

She wanted to throw herself into his arms and beg him to love her, but the stiffness of his manner, the way he wouldn't look at her, made Jilly nervous.

"I, uh…" She glanced at Ellie, then at Tim.

"Come on, sweets. Let's go feed the animals." Ellie shook her head. "Raccoons, opossums and doodles, oh my."

The two joined hands and disappeared behind the barn.

"You...you cut your hair," Jilly blurted, then wanted to rip out her tongue. Of all the stupid things to say when she had so many other important ones.

He shrugged and reached up to tug at the strands, which now brushed his jaw instead of his shoulders. "Only a little. Compromise for my father."

"Your father?"

Evan made an impatient sound. "I cut my hair, he lets me live here without driving me insane about cutting my hair. Was there something you wanted, Jilly?"

"You."

There. It was out in the open. That hadn't been so hard.

"I know you want me. Story of my life. I'm your Jethro boy-toy. The stud who made you come. It's natural you'd want to keep me around. As long as your husband doesn't mind, why not?"

She winced. "You heard my mother."

"It was a little hard not to."

"You should have stuck around to hear the rest."

"I heard enough."

"You missed the part where I told her I loved you. That she could take Rupert back wherever she got him, and she could keep her fortune, too."

His head lifted; his forehead creased with a frown. "What are you saying?"

Jilly walked toward him. She took a deep breath, then took his hand and knelt right there in the dirt. "I love you, Evan Luchetti. Will you marry me?"

"Huh?"

"That wasn't exactly the answer I had in mind."

He reached down and lifted her to her feet. "You want to get married?"

"Please."

"To me?"

"Who else?"

"I'm broke."

"Me, too." She laughed. "Isn't it great?"

"Not really." He turned away. "I can't let you do this. You're used to luxury. You deserve a life I can never give you."

"I've lived that life. Money over love. Companionship instead of lust. It's not worth it. You told me the universe likes to prove us wrong, and you were right. Everything I came to Arkansas not believing in— ghosts, magic, lust, love…I believe in every one of them now."

"I don't know, Jilly—"

"If you want to think about it, fine. You can find me at the inn." She started to leave, then turned around. "But I want my cat, my dog, my raccoon and my damn opossum back."

He faced her. "I thought you were selling the inn."

She shook her head. "I'm going to run it as a bed-and-breakfast."

"Have you ever run a hotel or restaurant before?"

"Nope, but I've been in quite a few."

"That's a little different."

"I never lived on my own, had a pet, delivered a baby or fell in love before, either."

Jilly waited for him to say something. When he didn't, she sighed. "I owe you money."

"I don't want it."

"Seventy-thirty was the agreement. But I'm not going to sell the place so…why don't you send me a bill?"

She headed for her car, but stopped at the sound of his voice.

"How about fifty-fifty?"

Her breath caught as hope filled her heart. Slowly she turned, to discover Evan was close enough to touch.

"When you say fifty-fifty," she began, "you mean—?"

"For the rest of our lives."

Jilly threw herself into his arms and kissed him. Her knees went weak, her insides all fluttery—just like the first time.

Evan lifted his head and touched her cheek. "Deal?" he whispered.

She couldn't think of anything else to say except… "Deal."

EPILOGUE

"HERE SHE COMES," Dean whispered. "Ready?"

"I was born ready."

"So I hear."

Evan gave his brother a dirty look, then shifted so he could watch Jilly walk down the aisle on the arm of his father.

Actually, it wasn't an aisle, because they weren't in a church. They were at the inn, and everyone they loved was there. *Almost*.

Addie was gone. Evan had felt terrible upon hearing that she'd passed away, and he'd left without ever knowing about it. But she'd forgive him. Especially if she was watching today, and he kind of thought she was.

Jilly's mom had kept her word, writing Jilly out of her will and out of her life. Evan hoped she might relent and visit once there were grandchildren involved, but having met Genevieve, he doubted "relent" was in her vocabulary. He planned to love Jilly enough to make up for any sadness the loss of her mother might bring.

The Wilder sisters shared the duties of attendants. They'd worn their best dresses, which soon wouldn't fit them. Both were expecting, within days of each other. Barry appeared to have taken to married life pretty well.

Evan's entire family was in attendance—except for Bobby. Those words were becoming a refrain in the Luchetti family. But as long as he hadn't been reported dead, they continued to believe he was alive.

Aaron had come from Las Vegas with his pregnant wife, Nicole, and their daughter, Rayne. It was the first time Evan had met the new additions, and he was impressed. Nicole obviously adored Aaron. His brother was the happiest Evan had ever seen him, and Rayne was a very mature, well-behaved young lady, although he had heard stories of certain misbehavior in the past.

Colin drove in from Minnesota with his wife, Marlie, and their son, Robbie. Evan's brother now wrote a syndicated newspaper column out of his home office so he could take care of the baby, and Marlie's slightly crazy mother, while Marlie ran her day care. Times sure had changed.

Colin's latest column had detailed haunted hotels in America, listing the Inn at South Fork as one of the finest. Evan was amazed at how many people wanted to stay in a haunted house. Even without the new highway, they would have been booked months in advance.

"She's beautiful, bro." Dean, who'd agreed to be Evan's best man, clapped him on the shoulder.

Tim, who had been given the job of holding the rings, bounced on his toes. "Pretty, pretty, pretty."

Zsa Zsa, the flower girl, ran down the aisle ahead of

Jilly and John, whipping rose petals over her head and chanting, "Me, me, me."

Kim tried to shush her, but Zsa Zsa was too wound up. She reached the front of the room and twirled around in a circle so the skirt of her long white dress belled out. She whirled so fast she fell down.

"Splat on my butt," she announced.

Everyone laughed.

Evan couldn't take his eyes from the bride. Jilly wore Addie's wedding gown, which she'd found preserved in a trunk. She'd solved the problem of the garment ending at her ankles by going barefoot. Instead of a veil she wore a circlet of flowers on her head.

His father paused a few feet away. "Knock, knock," John said.

All the Luchetti siblings groaned. Their father's love of knock-knock jokes was an embarrassment to most of them. Nevertheless he always tested new family members to see if they shared his affection for silly riddles. Thus far, he hadn't tested Jilly. Evan should have known he'd been saving one for the most opportune time.

"Who's there?" Jilly replied.

"Demon."

"Demon who?"

"Demon are a ghoul's best friend."

When Jilly giggled, John kissed her on the cheek, then glanced at Evan. "She's one of us."

"One of you," Evan muttered.

"Someone has to be."

John handed Jilly over to his son and joined his wife in the front row.

"Dearly beloved, we are gathered here today…"

WHEN ALL THE GUESTS were gone and they were alone at last, except for the kids, Jilly went to their room and peered out the window. Lightning stood at the top of the hill, staring down at Addie's deserted cabin. The old horse missed Addie even more than Jilly did.

There were times when she could swear Addie was with her—when she was confused about a patient, or uncertain of a treatment; when she was tired, sad or afraid. Her shoulders would slump and suddenly she'd feel a pat on the back; her hair would stir in a nonexistent breeze and the answer to her problem would become as clear as if Addie had whispered it in her ear.

There were still cold spots, the scent of cinnamon in the front bedroom and shadows where shadows shouldn't be. Some folks swore the inn was haunted, and others swore with equal fervency that it was not.

A figure was reflected in the window, and Jilly caught her breath. She hadn't seen a ghost yet, but she wanted to.

"Took me longer than I thought to corral all the kids." Evan crossed the room and tugged her into his arms. "Have I told you today that I love you?"

"Only five times."

"Make it six."

Jilly leaned against his chest and thought of all that

had happened since she'd come to South Fork. Had everything been leading to this?

"When I set out on the husband quest," she murmured, "you weren't exactly what I had in mind."

"Disappointed?"

"Never. You're everything I could ever dream of, and I love you."

She'd never get tired of saying those words. Which only showed how far she'd come from the woman she'd been.

Evan pressed his lips to her hair. "Maybe we should start a quest of our own."

"Really? What kind?"

"How do you feel about a baby quest?"

Jilly turned and wrapped her arms around Evan's neck. "I think that one just might take all night."

* * * * *

Watch for Bobby Luchetti's story in 2005
wherever Harlequin Books are sold.

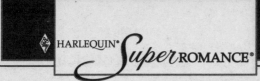

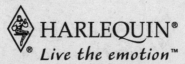

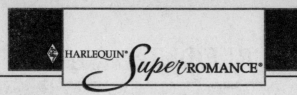

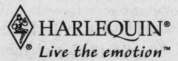

If you enjoyed what you just read,
then we've got an offer you can't resist!

Take 2 bestselling love stories FREE!

Plus get a FREE surprise gift!

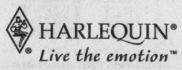

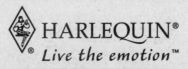

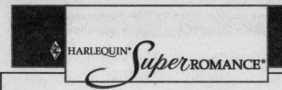

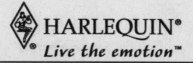